MS DRAUPADI KURU

After the Pandavas

TRISHA DAS is the author of *The Mahabharata Re-imagined* (2009), *The Art of the Television Interview* (2007) and the internationally acclaimed *How to Write a Documentary Script* (2006). Trisha has written and directed over forty documentaries in her film-making career. She's also won an Indian National Film Award (2005) and was UGA's 'International Artist of the Year' (2003). Her films have been broadcast and screened on the Discovery Channel, the STAR Network, NDTV, Doordarshan, in Indian and international film festivals, university campuses and conferences all over the world. Trisha lives in Singapore on the outside and on another planet on the inside.

MS DRAUPADI KURU

After the Pandavas

TRISHA DAS

HarperCollins *Publishers* India

First published in India in 2016 by
HarperCollins *Publishers* India
Building 10, Tower A, 4th Floor, DLF Cyber City, Phase II,
Gurugram Haryana – 122002, India
www.harpercollins.co.in

1 2 3 4 5 6 7 8 9 10

P-ISBN: 978-93-5264-003-4
E-ISBN: 978-93-5264-004-1

Typeset in 11/13.5 Bembo at
Manipal Digital Systems, Manipal

Printed and bound at
MicroPrints India, New Delhi

for b … with thanks

Chapter 1

Draupadi tried again to stifle the yawn. This time she didn't succeed, and her wide mouth flared to reveal the battered remains of a betel leaf on her tongue before she covered it with a dainty hand. Her eyes darted to her husband Bhima, wondering if he had noticed. He hadn't. His eyes were focused, intent on an imaginary figure in front of him. His hands were clenched tightly and his arms were raised, ready to strike at this invisible enemy with an imaginary mace.

He sneered and spoke loudly, 'I will split your thighs like an orange and drink your blood like its juice! Say your last prayers, evil Duryodhana!' He lunged forward and swung his fists in the air wildly with an occasional 'Hah!' for good measure.

Draupadi rolled her eyes and clapped mechanically along with the others in the celestial chamber. For what seemed like the ten-thousandth time since they had got here, Bhima stood with one leg hitched over Duryodhana's imaginary dead body and bowed at the applause, a broad grin on his ageless face.

She sighed. Today was going to be one of those days. A day when nothing pleased, when their afterlife in this heavenly paradise felt like a dream she had to relive endlessly, a conscious sleep from which she could never awaken. She looked over at a nymph who stood next to her with a rapt expression on her face. 'Don't you sometimes wish there was a cliff around here somewhere?' Draupadi whispered, gesturing as though she were preparing to dive.

The nymph gave Draupadi a blank look. Her pert nipples, straining through a sheer toga, showed more surprise than her eyes. Then, eager to please as nymphs usually are, she smiled sensually and purred in the only way she knew, 'Yes, of course. You're right! You say such clever things.' She giggled.

Draupadi stared at the creature for a moment before sighing again. There was no point getting angry at her. After all, nymphs hadn't exactly been created for conversational purposes.

She turned away and began to walk towards her celestial quarters. The clouds beneath her feet felt fluffy and slightly wet, like rabbit fur flecked with early morning dew. Draupadi had quite enjoyed the constant tickling against her soles when she had first arrived in heaven. Now, she often tried to remember what a stone floor or muddy earth had felt like when she was alive.

Alive. What an appropriate word to describe the mortal experience. She remembered a moment a long, long time ago when, as a girl, she had submerged herself under water until she felt faint and then broken through the surface with long gulps of air. Never had she felt more grateful for the invisible sustenance of mere breath. That was mortal life. Where the constancy of pain, want and sorrow made the fleeting moments of pleasure, abundance and joy that much more meaningful. Where all one's senses were forced to engage, to adapt, to conquer, to prevail, to be *useful*. Where the more one's body was punished by injury and age, the more one's mind was rewarded with wisdom and perspective. Where the complexity of relationships was so much vaster than the physical bounds in which they existed or the purposes they served. That had been her life once; when she had been alive. A long, long time ago.

Draupadi sighed yet again. This was becoming a habit, she thought and shook her head in a vain effort to cast off her gloomy mood. As she passed by the gates of heaven, she stopped to look at the two new arrivals who were making their way inside with awed looks on their faces. Very few came in these days, mostly crumpled old men with shaven heads and flowing ochre robes who chanted a lot of gibberish and always had an irritating smile on their faces. For some strange reason, they all seemed to be called 'lama'.

She considered the two men. Draupadi usually never spoke to new arrivals, but perhaps her mood would lighten if she talked about the mortal world with those who had only just arrived from there. She walked up to the men, who huddled together as they saw her approach.

'Be at ease, old men,' she commanded. 'I am Draupadi, queen of the Kurus, wife of the great Pandavas – Yudhishtra, Bhima, Arjuna, Nakula and Sahadeva – who ruled Indraprastha and Hastinapur and brought forth a golden age in the mortal world by vanquishing the evil Kauravas.' She smiled grandly.

The two old men stared back at Draupadi, bewildered. It was apparent from their expressions that they had no idea what she was talking about.

'You know not of me?' Draupadi's eyes widened. 'Do mortals not sing about the valour of my husbands in battle and of my beauty and grace? Do they not still worship us as the children of the gods?'

The men looked at each other and then back at her. They shook their heads with trepidation and said, 'Excuse us, sister. We are monks and we only worship Buddha.'

'Buddha? I've never met him. What is he the god of?' asked Draupadi.

'Sister, Buddha is not a god. He was a simple man,' said a monk.

'A man?' Draupadi was confused. 'Then why do you worship him? Did he have special powers, like the ability to fly or to turn rocks into gold nuggets?'

'No, we worship him because he attained inner bliss,' said the other monk. 'He achieved true happiness.'

Draupadi blinked. 'You worship a man because he was happy?'

'Yes, truly happy. All the time. And so are we. That's why we were allowed into heaven too.' They grinned at her before performing a few jerky bows and then proceeded on their way.

Draupadi was bemused, to say the least, as she watched them leave. Heavenly standards had certainly gone up if one needed to be truly happy all the time to get in. They were probably scared of overcrowding. She couldn't remember the last time she had been even a little truly happy, and her mood plummeted again. So much for talking to former mortals, she thought and stomped towards her chambers.

She sighed yet again as she entered her bedchamber, a white vastness adorned with a cluster of crystals and clouds that made her bed and its elaborate canopy. Around her gathered sparkly butterflies, dragonflies and bees, which affectionately brushed against her face to welcome her back to their midst. She had always loved these creatures when she lived as a mortal woman, and now they were her companions in heaven. Arjuna had dogs in his chambers, he had said. Draupadi liked dogs too but had never been inside Arjuna's part of heaven. That side of their relationship had ended when they left their bodies. Heaven was full of nymphs who gasped and clapped in twirly pleasure at every male antic, and so her five husbands had plenty to keep them occupied and never solicited her company.

That was the best part of being here, thought Draupadi with a smile. She had spent virtually her whole life juggling the five of them so that none felt less of a husband to her than the others. Each had constantly tested her: Yudhishtra with sarcasm, Bhima with fits of jealous rage, Arjuna with self-pity and endless 'what if' conversations and Nakula and Sahadeva with defiance and sulking. She had cajoled, calmed and even coerced them on a daily basis so that they remained fit to function as rulers without killing each other. Exhausting for five women, let alone one.

But then that was me, thought Draupadi with a look of disgust. Ever the tireless one, ever the pillar for all and sundry to lean on, the self-sacrificing little wife who always considered the good of society and her family above her own needs.

'Bah!'

The exclamation slipped out of her mouth just as her friend Amba walked into the chamber.

'Bah?' Amba inquired, with a puzzled look on her youthful face.

'Bah,' replied Draupadi firmly before asking, 'how are you, my lovely?'

Amba looked at her friend Draupadi with a gentle expression. On the outside, they were opposites. Amba was understated and petite, her complexion fair and manner graceful. Her upturned nose, delicate cheekbones and heart-shaped lips perfectly complemented her striking, lotus-shaped eyes. She was every inch a princess.

Draupadi's hourglass curves, on the other hand, oozed a less noble earthiness. She moved like a wild cat, stealthy and strong, trailing her signature scent of lotuses behind her. Her face was catlike as well. Piercing, kohl-black eyes and a wide, arched brow were underscored by full lips and dramatic cheekbones. Her skin, darker than most princesses', could only be described as radiant, and her voice, huskier than most princesses', was widely renowned for being irresistible to men. Her handmaiden had once called it her secret weapon.

'I am miserable. I wallow in self-pity, Amba. It is beneath me,' Draupadi said with a disgusted expression.

'Oh? Why?' asked Amba.

'Because even though I fully appreciate that I am in heaven and have had my youth restored and live among the gods, etc., etc. there is nothing to *do* here! The men are busy recreating their earthly glories for the nymphs half the time and cloistered in pleasure chambers with them the other half; and all the women seem to do is walk around in noisy clusters gossiping about the nymphs and competing with each other to be noticed by the gods!' Draupadi rolled her eyes as she continued, 'It's so frustrating. At least in hell I would have some occupation, like pushing a fiery boulder up a mountain or climbing a slippery cliff for eternity. Anything really, if it meant I had something to do!' She threw up her hands and plonked down on her bed.

Amba shuddered but her eyes twinkled thoughtfully as she sat on the bed. 'Or perhaps swimming for eternity against a strong current or fighting beastly demons who – who bite!'

Draupadi grinned back. 'They do keep them busy down there. In fact, maybe demons even rip off bits of flesh and eat them, and then the flesh grows back and they have to fight to make sure the demons don't rip it off again—'

'Enough, please.' Amba clutched her middle. 'Even I, the only woman of our time to ever experience a battlefield, cannot stomach your imagination, Draupadi.'

Draupadi assessed Amba as she lounged against the puffs of cloud that were her pillows. Indeed, Amba was the only woman of her time to ever partake in battle. She had ridden with Draupadi's husband, Arjuna, standing alongside him in his chariot as the two armies clashed around them. Arjuna had used Amba as a shield while battling his great-uncle Bhishma, who had refused to fire his arrows at a woman and had paid for it with his life.

Quite underhanded of Arjuna, thought Draupadi, for a man who followed dharma, the moral code that had bound them as mortals. But then that had been the only way to defeat Bhishma, a formidable warrior who had always felt more than a little guilty for how he had treated Amba. Many years before Draupadi herself had been born, Bhishma had kidnapped Amba from her swayamwara, a ceremony during which a princess selected her husband from an audience of kings and princes. At the end of many months of misunderstandings, Bhishma had refused to marry Amba; and the princess, with her reputation in tatters, could never marry after that. She had lived out her days as a maiden and sworn revenge on the man who had humiliated her. Many years later, she offered to help Arjuna in his bid to kill Bhishma on the battlefield.

Well, rumour had it that Bhishma chose to be reborn almost immediately after his death, and every time since as well. Probably afraid to run into Amba up here, thought Draupadi with a smile. Not that they ever discussed it.

'Fair enough,' she said. 'Should we stop feeling sorry for ourselves and go find something to pique our interest?'

Amba breathed a sigh of relief. 'By all means!' She got up.

Chapter 2

The two women walked out into the heavenly court, a shimmering crystal amphitheatre that stretched far beyond what the eye could see. As it often was, the amphitheatre was crowded with gods and demi-gods, along with a few former mortals, gathered to discuss the latest goings-on in all the worlds.

Around them rose countless pristine, white marble pillars and large crystal thrones cushioned with clouds. Small groups of immortals gathered at a distance from each other, talking in whispers. Nymphs glided coyly between the groups offering amrith, the nectar of immortality, in golden chalices.

Gods – usually minor ones, since really important ones had their own realms to reside in – were distinguishable because they sat on elevated thrones in the central arena of the chamber instead of mingling with the crowd. They were hazy to look at and changed appearances often. Their human form was an assumed one, and so they looked like different people at different times, usually depending on their moods. Indra, the god of weather and thunderstorms, and the king of the demi-gods, sat on the biggest throne. Today, he was a petite woman of about seventeen summers with feline green eyes and long black hair that fell well past the throne and to the floor of the central arena. That was just like Indra, Draupadi thought, with a penchant for the dramatic as well as young women, in whose likeness he often appeared.

The demi-gods that mingled with each other in the crowd looked a little more like mortals, except for one or two peculiar attributes that gave them away. Some of them were unusually large, while others were as small as birds; some of them were half man–half something else, like a fish or a lion. Others looked perfectly normal but wore elaborate crowns or carried fantastic weapons. A few were the result of a pairing between a god and a demon and looked quite grotesque.

And then, of course, there were the former mortals. Firm bodies dressed in starry togas and faces restored to the prime of post-pubescent youth, they formed the majority of the court. One could easily tell the new heavenly entrants from the old by the cut of their hair and the look on their faces. The old-timers, who wore their hair long, looked a little resigned, while the new ones with shorter hair had a look of wonder on their faces, as if they still couldn't believe their luck.

Draupadi and Amba walked past the others towards a small group in which stood four formerly mortal women. Draupadi recognized her former mother-in-law, Kunti, who had chosen to maintain a middle-aged appearance much to the bafflement of every other woman in heaven – who had all returned to a youthful state as quickly as possible after death. Kunti was short, stout and had a face that could best be described as having clean, disappointingly plain features. Draupadi was one of the very few who knew why she chose not to be youthful again. Kunti had once revealed in a weak moment, when they were both alive, that she had been raped as a maiden, which lead to a lifelong aversion to anything sexual and an utter revulsion for male attention.

So Kunti had chosen to remain in the form that had given her the most satisfaction as a mortal, that of a middle-aged mother. As the former wife of five of Kunti's sons, Draupadi knew what an excellent mother Kunti had been. And grandmother as well. She had practically raised Draupadi's five babies as her own, knowing that her daughter-in-law had neither the skill nor the inclination towards maternal pursuits.

Draupadi had initially resented her offspring being closer to Kunti than to her, but she had eventually admitted that she herself was hopeless with children and bearing her own had been more of a royal duty than pleasure. Having satisfied each of her five husbands with a son of his own, she had gladly handed over their maternal care to Kunti and thought very little of them after that.

Kunti smiled warmly at Draupadi and beckoned her over. As much as they had clashed sometimes as mortals, thought Draupadi wryly as she smiled back, they had managed to form an affectionate relationship in heaven.

Standing next to her was Gandhari, who had been Kunti's sister-in-law by marriage in the mortal world. Draupadi didn't know Gandhari very well, since she tended to be a bit aloof and condescending towards everyone except Kunti. She was one of the most magnificent women Draupadi had ever seen. Standing a head above the others, she was fair, with arresting greenish-grey eyes and a strong, straight nose. Her lips, when they weren't pursed in disdain, were as luscious as the set of her jaw was stately. Her thick, auburn-tinged hair flew in glorious waves over broad shoulders and long, long thighs to reach her knees. She had this way of looking at Draupadi, her eyes travelling from head to toe in a manner one might appraise a mare, that was very disconcerting and a little offensive. Kunti put the habit down to Gandhari having worn a blindfold for most of her mortal life. She was probably so glad she didn't have to be blind any more that she looked at things too hard, Kunti had explained, fiercely loyal to Gandhari as always. Draupadi also recalled Kunti mentioning that she and Gandhari had died hand-in-hand in a forest fire as elderly women.

'Draupadi, Amba, come and join us, my dears.' Kunti smiled, looking upon them as a mother would her young daughters.

Draupadi returned her smile and joined the group, Amba following directly behind her. Gandhari nodded her greeting to both women as Kunti continued, 'I'm so glad you came to court today. We've been having a most interesting discussion about the latest from the mortal world with these two ladies, who have just arrived. Meet Aamaya and Aanya. They're new souls who passed as babies in their first lifetime, so were automatically allowed into heaven as they have no sins under their belt. Isn't that exquisitely lucky? Unfortunately for us, they can tell us nothing of the changes since we were mortal except that their world seemed to be quite noisy and bright with an excess of the colour pink. They were just asking if there had been so much pink in our time.'

'Pink?' Draupadi considered. 'No, as far as I remember. Mostly browns and greens, a little ochre, some red and yellow and, of course, blue as in the sky, but very little pink. Maybe the odd flower or a sari that lost some of its red dye while washing. I always threw those ones away. Nasty colour. Never suited my complexion.'

'It suited mine,' said Amba, 'but I never liked it either. It is such a weak colour. Not suitable for women of a warrior clan like the Kurus.'

'And there you have it, girls,' said Kunti, turning to Aanya and Aamaya, 'we did not have much pink in our time. The Kuru race, to which we belonged, were warriors through and through. Weakness was the lowest, most contemptible of attributes, despised more than any other. We lived and died by the arrow and sword, and the best life was considered one which had its healthy share of battles. We women were taught that although we couldn't fight alongside the men, we could exercise the same courage and strength in governing our households. And in our case, that meant governing our husbands' kingdoms, for they were away a lot and needed wealth to fund their conquests. We were queens, you know.' She smiled nostalgically at Gandhari and Draupadi but then stalled in embarrassment as her gaze reached Amba. She had forgotten that Amba had never been a queen despite being a princess.

Amba smiled kindly at the mortified Kunti and changed the subject gracefully. 'It seems that the world has changed in many ways since we occupied it. Narad Muni, the demi-god who travels between all the worlds and brings us news every century or so,' she explained to the newcomers, 'has not visited us for a long time now, and even when he does, he talks mostly of wars and politics, which interest only the men. I long to know how other things have changed. Like what do people wear nowadays? Or what kind of weapons do they carry?' She smiled at Draupadi wistfully. 'Wouldn't it be interesting to be able to see those kinds of things?'

Draupadi's eyes lit up but Gandhari spoke first, somewhat unexpectedly. 'You could, if you liked,' she said. 'You could choose to be reborn.'

Amba shook her head. 'Rebirth is such an uncertain process. We were lucky in our time to have been granted admittance into heaven just on account of our being dharmic. The requirements are completely different these days. They are far more selective about whom they allow in and rumour has it that they're going to become even stricter. They say that soon only the truly enlightened, in every sense of the word, will be allowed in. Apparently, only one mortal has ever achieved that state without divine involvement. The chances of my being let back in here, if I choose to live another life, are almost non-existent.'

'I know, but wouldn't it be exciting?' said Draupadi. 'To have another chance! To live again, to love again?' She looked at Amba for support but her friend looked away.

'Are you thinking of rebirth, Draupadi?' asked Kunti with surprise.

'No,' said Draupadi. And then, 'Maybe. I don't know.'

'Amba is right,' stated Gandhari firmly. 'Only a fool would give up a place in heaven. I didn't take you for a fool.'

Draupadi bristled, but before she could come back with a scathing retort, there was a deafening crash behind her. She swivelled around to see a billowing cloud of smoke in the middle of the court and, within it, a short, skinny old man in a sage's habit coughing and trying to disperse the smoke around him by waving one arm furiously. His other arm was cradling and playing a tanpura, creating the signature rhythmic melody that always announced the presence of Narad Muni.

'Finally!' exclaimed Draupadi, forgetting Gandhari's comment for the moment and walking towards the celestial messenger along with the rest of the court.

Narad Muni, now rid of the smoke, looked around him and took in the room full of beings all looking his way. His wrinkled eyes immediately lit up and his chest swelled with pleasure. Nothing made him happier than a large audience of eager faces. He took a deep breath and proclaimed loudly in a high-pitched voice, 'Hear me, one and all, for I bring news of all the worlds, god, demon and mortal alike. I, Narad Muni, a humble priest in eternal service to the gods' – he bowed dramatically to Indra on the throne – 'and to all heavenly beings' – his bow swept with a flourish across the court and Draupadi rolled her eyes – 'have much to tell. Tales of war and of ravaged lands. Tales of conquest and revenge, of chaos and of tragedy,' he said, looking suitably distressed at his own words while his eyes not-so-secretly scanned the crowd for reactions.

'Here we go again,' whispered Amba to Draupadi.

'The world of gods thrives in peace. Wise Brahma and Shiva the Formidable send their greetings, and the Supremely Merciful Vishnu mentioned he will soon visit your realm as his avatar Krishna, who is much beloved in all realms and worlds. As you can imagine, the gods are keeping a close eye on the events in the mortal world and shall soon deem, in conference with each other, the right time for Shiva the Powerful to intervene and destroy it. The ever Ingenious Vishnu is, however, of the opinion that the mortals will annihilate their own race in the due course of time and that Shiva the Magnificent needn't go to the trouble himself.'

'Oh no,' whispered either Aanya or Aamaya to Draupadi. 'That's terrible news!'

'Don't worry, they've been threatening that since we first arrived here. I don't think they have the heart for it,' she whispered back. 'Next he'll say that the demons are going to invade us.'

Aamaya/Aanya looked shocked.

Draupadi shook her head. 'They've been threatening that since our arrival too.'

Narad Muni now looked fearful as he continued, 'The world of demons celebrates the events in the mortal world, as you all can imagine. The spread of sin and evil among mortals has lifted their spirits, and they soon plan to enlist the mortals in their plans to conquer the world of the gods for their own. I myself met with the lord of the demon world, Mara, who' – he assumed a grimace and his voice took on a growl – 'bared his bloody teeth and snarled these words to me: *Warn your kin, Narad Muni. Tell the gods to be frightened. Very frightened!*'

'Down with Mara!' shouted a few of the men, reaching for imaginary swords at their waists.

Draupadi whispered sarcastically, 'As you can see, nothing new really happens in either god or demon worlds. They have a different sense of time. The only interesting news is usually from the mortal world.'

Narad Muni now looked around him, poised to deliver the most anticipated bit of his speech. He took a deep breath. 'The mortal world sinks further into the Kalyug – the age of chaos – as expected by the gods. Mortals have been allowed *far* too much freedom for their own good and now imagine themselves as powerful as the gods, which is laughable!' He sniggered. 'They invent new medicines and machines every day and laud their victory over every natural means of mortality even as they create unnatural ones to supersede them. Consumption and leprosy have been replaced by new diseases, earthquakes and volcanic eruptions by toxic substances and fiery explosions. Wars now kill millions instead of thousands. Mortals have always been prone to vice but whereas earlier they at least attempted to be dharmic, now they celebrate their sins. They gather material possessions lavishly and load their bodies with unnatural food and excessive meat like the demons. Avarice, ambition and carnal pursuits rule their lives. Ah' – Narad Muni looked up, clutched his brow with three fingers and shook his head tragically – 'they are but shells of their former selves these days. Such potential unrealized, such a waste of perfectly good intellect. And mind you, it was no small effort of the gods to create them.' He scowled disapprovingly on behalf of the gods.

Silent nods and shrugs across the room returned his gaze, and he dropped it and sighed with much resignation. 'But I suppose it is for the best. The sooner they destroy themselves, the sooner the gods can create a more manageable species. Perhaps crustaceans will do better—'

'But what *more* can you tell us of the mortal world, O Narad Muni, for we know you speak personally to the mortals,' said Draupadi loudly, with an air of restrained impatience on her face. 'Can you give us details? What is society like these days?'

Narad Muni was irritated at the interruption and threw her a look of condescension. 'Society! Degenerate and inconsequential. What are the frivolities of society to the enlightened mind? Nothing, I say! Improve yourself, lady, for you should be above such considerations,' he said scathingly as he looked around to gauge and garner support for his sentiments. He then took a deep breath to apparently calm himself enough to continue: 'Wars ravage the land, as I mentioned ...'

Draupadi looked away in a huff. Amba whispered, 'You should know better by now.'

'I know, I know,' she whispered back. 'I suppose if I want details, I'll just have to—' Suddenly, she stilled as if struck by something. Then, a slow smile began to part her lips and a twinkle entered her eye.

Amba shook her head in mild panic. 'No, Draupadi, rebirth is—'

'Not rebirth. No, not rebirth,' Draupadi said absently as she scanned the room with a sudden urgency. Then she turned to Amba. 'Come with me. He'll go on about war for a while.' She turned and walked away.

Amba looked after her friend suspiciously, but followed, if for no other reason than to keep her out of trouble. Once they had left the court she began, 'Draupadi, you know I love you dearly, but these schemes of yours – if, in fact, you've got another one on your mind – always end badly. The last time, when you wanted to create a heavenly female tribunal, Indra warned us—'

Draupadi turned, emphatically shaking her head. 'This is different.' Amba raised her eyebrows and Draupadi smiled. 'No, I mean it, I promise. All we need is a little help.'

'From whom?' her weary friend questioned.

'From Krishna,' replied Draupadi.

'Krishna? Vishnu's avatar?'

'Yes, it's been around a century since he visited last so he's due for another visit. Narad Muni mentioned he was coming soon. And when he does, we'll ask him to help us!' Draupadi almost squealed with excitement.

Amba lifted one dubious eyebrow. 'Help us do what?'

Draupadi whispered, 'Visit the mortal world!'

'Visit?' Amba was confused. 'What do you mean?'

'Well,' said Draupadi, 'we don't want to be reborn again for obvious reasons. But I'm sure he'll agree that it is more than a little tedious to be stuck up here for the rest of eternity and we do deserve to have some entertainment beyond nymphs which, let's face it, are a bit outdated. Heaven might be able to keep the men happy with eternal sexual pursuits with beautiful virgins but what are women supposed to do with them? They need something for us too so, in that spirit, I'm sure Krishna will support a short, unobtrusive, completely harmless visit to the mortal world. We could remain in spirit if he likes and no one would ever know we were there!'

'That's ridiculous, Draupadi. Krishna will never support such a scheme.' Amba looked relieved at the impossibility of the idea.

'But *if* he did' – Draupadi looked at her friend closely – 'would you come with me?'

Amba smiled. 'He won't.'

Draupadi smiled back. 'We'll see.'

Chapter 3

Narad Muni's visit ended, and the excitement it had caused grew thinner until it disappeared into the usual hum of heavenly existence.

After that, the years passed far too slowly for Draupadi's patience. She spent most of her time plotting – hatching endless strategies to get Krishna to agree to her scheme. Amba was her only confidante and they spent enormous amounts of time together, with Draupadi chattering away and Amba nodding with a small smile on her face.

Amba was generally happy to agree with whatever her friend said because, as unrealistic and outlandish as Draupadi's plans were, she was in better spirits than she had been in centuries. She smiled more readily, talked animatedly to the new heavenly entrants in court and even managed to laugh at a few of Bhima's antics. Amba secretly prayed that Krishna would delay his visit for as long as possible. Only he knew how Draupadi would react when he refused her.

Her prayers, however, went unregarded.

One day, Kunti walked into Draupadi's chamber while they were lounging about and announced that Krishna had arrived in court.

Draupadi jumped up and started pacing the room nervously. 'This is it. This is our chance. I need to be calm. Be calm,' she scolded herself.

Amba groaned as Kunti looked at them, a perplexed frown on her face.

'What's the matter?' she asked.

'Nothing!' Draupadi almost squealed in agitation. 'No, nothing at all is the matter. We're just excited. Thank you for the news, Kunti dear. We'll be out shortly.'

But Kunti, who had seen no such signs of extreme excitement from Draupadi the last ten times that Krishna had visited, stayed where she was. Her expression was guarded and her voice both gentle and stern in the way only a mother's can be. 'What's going on?' she asked, narrowing her gaze at Draupadi, who stared back defiantly, and then at Amba.

Amba was instantly reduced to a sullen teenager and, after a moment, blurted out, 'Draupadi wants to ask Krishna if we can visit the mortal world in spirit.'

Kunti and Draupadi both exclaimed together:

'*What?*'

'*Amba!*'

Amba frowned defensively at Draupadi. 'It's true, and she would have found out anyway. It'll be out of the bag the moment you tell Krishna.'

Draupadi glared at her but then swivelled around to face Kunti. 'Kunti, come with us!'

'What?' repeated Kunti, still shocked. 'No!' Then she shook her head to regain her composure and smiled. 'This is ludicrous. He'll never agree, my dear. Don't set yourself up for disappointment like this.'

'What if he does? Wouldn't you like to see what is going on down there?' Draupadi's voice softened as she continued, 'Wouldn't you want to see how Karan is doing?'

Kunti's face went red. No one in her family had mentioned Karan to her since she had told them about him. Her illegitimate son, born of a rape when she was a maiden princess, had been a secret for most of her mortal life. She had set him adrift in a basket on the banks of the river Ganga immediately after his birth. She never got over that – the guilt of abandoning him to his fate even though there was little else she could have done at the time.

Karan had eventually been rescued and raised by a charioteer and his wife. He had risen to fame in his mortal life, even been adopted into royalty. Unfortunately for Kunti, he had been adopted by the enemies of her five legitimate sons and had eventually been killed in battle by one of them, Arjuna, who had no idea at the time that Karan was his eldest brother.

Kunti could still remember telling Karan the truth, just hours before he was to battle against her sons and their army. Naively, she had hoped that this would make him forsake his loyalties to their enemy and join his birth family. Naively, she had hoped that Karan would be a child to her after all those years.

She had been wrong, naturally. Karan had been bitter and categorically refused to switch sides, swearing his loyalty to those who had nurtured, not abandoned him. After his death, Kunti had told her family who Karan really was, and how desperately she had failed as a mother to her eldest child. When she entered heaven, she had searched for him eagerly. But Karan, who had also been allowed entry upon his death, chose to return to the cycle of rebirth in the mortal world rather than face his natural family.

Draupadi, who knew this, looked deeply into Kunti's distraught eyes. She knew how much it hurt her former mother-in-law then and how much it still hurt her now. Even though she felt a little guilty for bringing it up, this was, Draupadi was sure, the only thing that would influence Kunti – that desire to make up to Karan. She kept silent and hoped.

Kunti was struggling with her emotions, her face set in stone but her eyes unearthing aeons of utter sorrow and remorse that had lain entrenched in her soul. As impossible as she knew Draupadi's idea was, this might be her only chance. She said in a shaky voice, 'Ask him. Then we'll see.' And she turned and left.

Draupadi let out the breath she hadn't realized she had been holding and turned to Amba, who was glaring at her with an uncharacteristic ferocity.

'That was underhanded and downright mean,' said Amba angrily. 'Will you stop at nothing to get your way? Even if it means hurting people like that?'

Draupadi's eyes widened a little in surprise at Amba's tone, but then her own ire was stirred. Perhaps hers wasn't the most sympathetic approach and yes, perhaps she had been a tad underhanded in trying to convince Kunti, but nobody could accuse her of not wanting the best for the people she loved. She replied with equal anger, 'I didn't hurt her. Karan hurt her, if you remember. I'm giving her the opportunity to fix that hurt. We were all hurt in some way as mortals, Amba. I didn't exactly dream of being married to five men but it happened. You were forced to stay unmarried your whole life by Bhishma, who ruined your reputation. All of us women were hurt and used by men who were too busy chasing their own ambitions to give any thought to us. So, I wonder sometimes, when will it be our chance to find some happiness? Don't we have the right to try and do things for ourselves after spending the whole of our mortal lives sacrificing for others? Yes, I reminded Kunti of Karan, but I assure you that she thinks of him quite enough when she's alone anyway. Wouldn't it be wonderful for her to see Karan doing well and also have some fun while she's at it? This will be a good change for her. It'll be a good change for all three of us.'

Amba stared back at Draupadi with a studied expression on her face. To be reminded of her own mortal life: of how she had been captured, humiliated and then refused by Bhishma, of how she had then wandered from palace to palace, a ruined woman who had decided that revenge would be the only purpose worth living for. How she had waited when no one would avenge her or even help her – either because they were too afraid of Bhishma or because they didn't think she was worth the undertaking. She had ended up waiting for a lifetime, until finally Arjuna had presented her with the opportunity to face Bhishma in battle and take part in his killing. She remembered even now the moment that Bhishma had fallen to the ground, mortally wounded. A fleeting flash of elation, and then utter regret as she watched her mortal enemy die. A lifetime spent in anger had been a lifetime wasted, she realized. By then she had become an old woman, and it was too late.

As ridiculous as the idea was, thought Amba, maybe Draupadi had a point. She bit her lip and said to her friend, 'As Kunti said, ask him and then we'll see.'

Draupadi's eyes lit up in triumph. There were very few people she couldn't bend to her will. Krishna would be next and definitely the most difficult of the lot. She stood to her full height, nodded to her friend and walked out determinedly.

The heavenly court was in full swing when she entered. Excitement and anticipation filled the air, and people crowded around the centre, trying to get as close to Krishna, a god – no, a *principal* god – in their midst. Draupadi pushed past them all, not caring whom she elbowed and pinched along the way. In the centre she could see Krishna, talking softly to Indra.

He was quite magnificent, she thought to herself. One never, no matter how many times one saw him, got over how he radiated light despite being as black as a starless night. His eyes, cobalt blue like a dancing peacock's breast, shone with turquoise sparks of mischief, as if secretly plotting against those he beheld. He smiled constantly.

He turned to Draupadi now and his smile broadened into a grin. It was a grin that took her back to her own life, when Krishna had also lived as a mortal, and they had been the best of friends. It had been he who had comforted and coached her when she became the unwilling bride of five demanding men. It had been he who had been her constant rescuer, protecting her from starvation, rape, attempted murder and, worst of all, loneliness. Yes, they had a special connection, thought Draupadi to herself. He wouldn't deny her. She hoped.

He beckoned her over with a nod and she went, returning his smile. 'Dear Draupadi' – his gentle voice was soft and yet held everyone's rapt attention – 'heaven suits your beauty.'

'My god Krishna,' Draupadi said lovingly, 'no one can match your beauty, man or woman, mortal or divine. We await your visits eagerly, you know, just to behold you and your presence.'

'Prettily put, my dear.' His eyes became impish and Draupadi felt his soft voice, inaudible to anyone but her, magically whisper in her ear even though he stood many steps away, 'Now what is it you want?'

She smiled guiltily. She thought loudly, willing him to read her mind, 'I am miserable here.'

He continued to smile at her as his whisper returned, 'You are bored?'

'I am,' she thought towards him desperately. 'Terribly bored, terribly lonely. My mortal life was a waste and now I feel my heavenly one is equally wasteful.'

He turned away and began to talk to someone who approached him, but his whisper still continued in her ear, 'Your mortal life was anything but wasteful, my child. You served a higher purpose with your life. Perhaps you feel anger because your own purposes went unfulfilled. I understand your heart. What is it you desire now?'

She watched him carefully, deep in conversation with someone else, and willed his assent as she thought, 'I wish to return to the mortal world in spirit. To visit, not be reborn. For a short while, just to see how things are, what people and places are like now. It will provide a welcome break for us and make heavenly existence more bearable in the future.'

'Us?' he whispered back.

Draupadi became uneasy but pressed on, 'Amba, Kunti and myself.'

'I see,' he whispered and she saw his smile broaden. 'And these women agreed to your scheme willingly or have you held them at sword point?'

Draupadi was sheepish but thought determinedly, 'They want to come whether they know it or not. I am sure of that.'

For a while, no whisper graced her ear and her throat squeezed tighter in dread and disappointment with each passing moment. Krishna continued to speak to the crowds that swarmed around him, eager for his attention. Draupadi thought again, pleading, 'Please, my god. Allow me even a small glimpse of life again. There is so much I was never allowed in my own life. So many regrets, so much unhappiness. Give me a small respite from my thoughts, from this fortunate but meaningless heavenly existence. You know me, you know my mind. I need more than this. Please, O Krishna. We were friends once. Do this for me.'

Krishna seemed oblivious to her pleas and her fallen face. A lump of dismay sprung up, quick and wretched, in her throat. She turned to walk away.

'Stay,' said the welcome whisper. 'We are friends still. Your mind is like a river, careening forcefully through rapid after rapid. It needs to slow down so as to be deep and allow life to thrive within it. You think too much and too fast, my dear.'

Draupadi hung her head and steeled herself for the refusal that was about to come, tasting the bile of bitter disappointment on her tongue.

'Having said that,' he whispered, 'your spirit is strong and full of courage and deserves to run free, even if only for a short while. I do not usually allow spirits to visit unless there is a pressing matter at hand, so I can only allow you a brief spell as a mortal. You will return after a stay of thirty days and thirty nights. Narad Muni will be your guide.'

Draupadi looked up at him and let out a gasp of relief. He had agreed! She smiled and sputtered, overcome with joy and gratitude.

'I am not finished, my dear. The mortal world has changed much since you knew it. It is a far more dangerous place now. Tread with caution and trust your fear. Stay out of the way of mortals and try not to interfere in their affairs. During your time there, try not to make any commitments, and since you will probably be the leader in this expedition, lead your companions with wisdom and patience.' She saw him smile to himself as his whisper continued, 'Of course, I fully expect my advice to go completely unheeded and shall watch with interest to see what kinds of trouble you get yourself into. But remember, my child, this time, even though I will always be present in spirit, I will not be there to rescue you at every pass. You shall, like the rest of the mortals, be responsible for your own choices.'

'I understand. Thank you, thank you, my Krishna,' whispered an overcome Draupadi, barely even comprehending what he said.

Krishna looked at her from across the crowd and smiled. 'This is your second chance, Draupadi. Make the most of it.'

Draupadi nodded and he turned away. She skipped out of the court quickly, in case he changed his mind. She had to find Amba and Kunti.

Chapter 4

'You said I wouldn't be able to pull it off!' Draupadi barged into Amba's lemon-coloured chambers in triumph. 'You said Krishna would refuse. *Impossible,* I believe, was the word you used. *You*' – she bounced on to Amba's bed, her cat eyes gleaming at her friend lounging next to her – 'were wrong. Hah!'

Amba stared back, shaking her head almost imperceptibly.

And then Draupadi noticed Kunti and Gandhari sitting on chaises near the bed. Her heart sank.

Right on cue, Gandhari's imposing voice flew across the room. 'What's this about?' She was looking at Kunti, who had reacted to Draupadi's statement with shock and now sat dazed, her lips trembling slightly. Gandhari then looked over at Amba, who was avoiding her gaze and focusing, perhaps a little too intently, on Draupadi.

It was left to Draupadi, after a quick moment of consideration, to half-heartedly relate their intentions and Krishna's approval of them to Gandhari, who listened with an incredulous face. After it was done, all four women sat in silence, no one really knowing what should be said next.

Gandhari broke the silent impasse with, 'Well, then take me with you.'

They all looked at her in amazement.

Gandhari shrugged with some disdain. 'I know I haven't exactly given the impression that I would be interested in something like this, but having spent most of my own mortal life in a blindfold, well, I wouldn't mind. No, the truth is, I would actually *like* to see some of the mortal world again.' Her eyes softened as she spoke. 'I was young when I put on that blasted blindfold. They had told me I was marrying a heroic, strong warrior king and what I ended up with was a weak, blind man with little intelligence or wit. In my maiden culture, we despised infirmity or any kind of weakness, you know. I was bitterly disappointed and so very, very angry. Sometimes I don't know whether I blindfolded myself as a sacrifice, to join my husband in blindness, or just because I was so angry I wanted to punish us both.' She chuckled bitterly to herself. 'I died blind, you know. After being shut up and denied for so long, the old eyes just gave up. You knew that, sister, when we died together in the forest fire.' She looked absently at Kunti and smiled, still far away in her own mind. 'I can barely remember the sight of a blue sky behind snow-capped mountains or fields of harvest ...' She looked over at the others and seemed to remember herself. Suddenly, she snapped back to her usual, stern self and cleared her throat. 'Anyway, I wouldn't mind coming with you. That's all.'

Draupadi could almost feel sorry for Gandhari. Almost. 'Your mortal state was nobody else's doing but your own, and if you had half as much intelligence as you give yourself credit for, you wouldn't have done such a stupid thing as putting on a blindfold for your entire life. Anyway, that's not my problem. You're not coming with us,' she said firmly.

'Why not?' asked Gandhari.

'Because this group is my responsibility while we're down there and so I get to decide for whom I will be responsible. Moreover, I hardly think that after calling me a fool for talking about going back to the mortal world that you deserve to come,' replied Draupadi with an obstinate look. She had still not forgotten that slight.

Gandhari's eyes became hard and she stared at Draupadi for a moment before replying, with a perfectly straight face, 'I think you'll take me along. You wouldn't want me to tell the others around here about your little adventure, would you? Many of them might get it into their heads to follow you, and may ask Krishna about it, who may even regret his decision to allow—'

'Stop.' Draupadi shivered with barely contained rage. The woman had the gall to blackmail her! How dare she? She took a step towards Gandhari, fully intent on scratching her eyes out, when Kunti intervened.

'Gandhari, I'm surprised at you,' she said. 'Such language and manner is beneath your station. I must insist that you apologize to Draupadi. None of us want to embark upon this journey with that kind of spirit between us. Draupadi is right; this was her idea and she has taken both the risk and the initiative so far. For that, we must acknowledge her leadership. Your wish must come as a request, not a threat.' She looked sternly at her friend.

Gandhari blinked, her expression the tiniest bit sheepish, but then she turned to Draupadi and said in a clipped tone, 'My words were of anger. I would never have done such a thing, obviously. I apologize. Please consider taking me along.'

Before Draupadi could retort, Kunti continued quickly, 'Draupadi, I still consider you my daughter, even though that part of our journey is over. I hope you still consider me enough of a mother to defer to my judgement a little. Gandhari and you may not have always seen eye to eye but she will be an asset to us if she comes along. I know few people with her perceptiveness, rational thought and judgement. She will keep us above fault while dealing with the mortals.' Kunti's face softened as she continued, 'I also know how much she has regretted the decisions she made in her youth and how much it would mean to her to be able to behold the mortal world once again. To grant that wish is in your power, Draupadi, and I am sure you will consider it with the compassion and generosity that I know lies within you.'

Draupadi struggled with the emotions raging through her. Gandhari behaved like a rude know-it-all who thought herself better than the rest of them, but inside, Draupadi knew that Gandhari had as much lost time and suffering to make up for as she did. How much difference would it make, really, to add one more person to the expedition? She was sure Krishna wouldn't mind. But there was one condition she needed to make perfectly clear first.

She stepped up to Gandhari and bent forward so that their faces were only inches apart, their eyes locked on each other. 'Fine. But remember one thing. I am the leader of this expedition. You will listen to me, without argument, without smart back talk, for the entire length of our visit or—'

'Oh, for goodness' sake, ladies, I don't have all eternity to escort you between worlds, you know.' Narad Muni's peeved voice boomed into the chamber from the outside. 'Come along, come along. Let us make haste!'

Amba and Kunti started and stood up, fidgeting with their robes and mumbling, 'Oh heavens, oh god!' in trembling excitement. The air was suddenly crisp with anticipation and promise.

Draupadi felt breathless and a little heady, but she paused for a moment to give Gandhari a fierce look over her shoulder. 'Is that understood?'

Gandhari's generous lips thinned into a white line and she nodded. Once.

'Good.' Draupadi turned and grinned at the others. 'Our adventure begins!'

They whooped and skipped out the chamber door, where Narad Muni was waiting with a scowl of utter irritation. His eye twitched as he exclaimed, 'There you are. Do you think I have all year to stand around outside chambers like a doorman?' He shook his head and grumbled to himself as he strode. 'Really, of all the ridiculous ... Come *on*, walk! The gods have lost their minds. No, no, *this* way ... would live to see the day when Narad Muni would be reduced to ... Faster, I haven't got forever. Shuttling between worlds to *visit*, if you please! Here, through the gate. Sacrilegious! Unthinkable! Abominable! Now wait here. No, not *there*, look where I'm pointing, woman. I have to get you clothes unless you want mortals to see you in what you're wearing right now. You'd be taken for freaks!' He limped off into a foggy cloud with loud *tsks* and exaggerated sighs.

The women exchanged glances as they stood *exactly* where he had pointed. Not much could dampen their spirits at this point. Draupadi could see that Amba had a slightly stupid grin on her face, a complete departure from her usual serene, controlled expression. Even Gandhari, whom she was going to try and ignore as much as possible, had a bit of fire in her usually deadpan eyes.

Narad Muni returned, staggering under the weight of a large pile of clothing, all of which seemed to be either black, white, grey or beige.

'Are we supposed to be in mourning?' whispered Amba.

'I hope not,' said Kunti under her breath.

'Maybe we're pretending to be widows?' wondered Draupadi.

But no one had a chance to reply as Narad Muni was upon them, mumbling loudly, 'No, please *don't* help me. Why should you? I'm only a few hundred thousand years old ...'

He dumped the pile in front of them and started sifting through the clothes. Soon, Draupadi found a small pile of beige material being dispatched in her direction. She unfolded what seemed like the loose upper garment that warriors wore under their armour. It went right up to the neck on top, falling below the hips at the bottom and had sleeves up to the elbows. Draupadi made a disgusted face. In her other hand was a skirt. A plain, beige, straight skirt with a strange, crinkly waistband that snapped right back into place when you stretched it. To go along with that were undergarments, Draupadi supposed. A wisp of cotton that looked like the underwear women wore during their menses, with holes for the legs, and finally, a very strange-looking garment with two cloth cups held together with bands of that same stretchy fabric and a complicated fastening mechanism. Was this for ... ? Her eyes widened and she glanced over at the others, all of whom seemed equally bewildered with the clothing handed to them.

Narad Muni rolled his eyes. 'It's called a bra, for binding your breasts. You put your arms through these straps and fasten it at the back with this hook. And these' – he handed her a box – 'are for your feet.'

With that he stomped off, leaving them to change behind a cloudy screen.

Inside their boxes were pairs of ugly, black pieces of leather which, when Draupadi tried hers on, wound up covering the entire foot. Her feet felt hot and restricted. No pretty toenails peeping out of embroidered sandals, no hint of the sensual arch. No, just a block of blackness covering one of the most alluring parts of a woman's body.

The rest of the garments seemed to be designed for exactly the same purpose. The skirt hung around her rounded hips shapelessly, making her look fat, she was sure. The bra, which she fastened with Amba's help, felt like she was wearing armour, for heaven's sake. She could barely breathe in its tight and restrictive grip and her breasts felt as hard as rocks through the cups. Why? Why were mortal women doing this to themselves?

Finally she slipped on the upper garment and looked around. Kunti, Amba and Gandhari looked as comical as she was sure she did in their boxy, colourless garb. It was a far cry from the light, colourful saris, wispy breast-cloths and single-strap sandals they had worn as mortals.

Draupadi found Amba looking at her arms, half-hidden under her grey, loose garment, and her waist, completely covered under layers of cloth. No jewelled armband to bring attention to the soft plumpness of her upper arms, no gold chain to draw the eye to the curve of her slim waist. No peeking belly button to tease the onlooker with the promise of what lay so close by. Nothing.

'We look like cows!' she exclaimed and they all laughed. None of them had ever worn so much clothing before.

Narad Muni came shuffling back holding a small sack, his face finally showing a hint of pleasure when he beheld them in their embarrassed ridiculousness. Draupadi spoke disdainfully, '*This* is what mortal women wear nowadays? And men still, er, *engage* with them?' She had difficulty believing any man would look at a female wearing such ugly, oversized, excessive clothing. Unless he was a hermit, of course, but that was really beside the point. Hermits were known to find even animals attractive on occasion.

'Do you want to go down there or not, woman?' Narad Muni's irritation returned. 'Which brings me to my next question. Where do you want to go?'

'Where?'

'Yes, *where*, woman.' He twitched. 'Where in the mortal world? Or do you want me to just drop you off in the middle of a desert or a jungle or the ocean?' The idea seemed to appeal to him, for he hummed slightly after he said it.

Draupadi looked at the others. She hadn't thought about that and obviously neither had anyone else.

Then, Kunti suggested softly: 'Indraprastha?'

Indraprastha. The kingdom Draupadi and her husbands had founded and ruled over as mortals. It had been a barren, dusty land before they had gotten there. Over the course of a few years, they had transformed it into a lush township with plentiful harvests and a thriving economy and culture. Indraprastha, albeit small, had been the richest and most prosperous kingdom of its time, its wide roadways lined with gardens and parks that were bursting with colourful foliage and wildlife. Its marketplace was thronged by the wealthy and enterprising, and as for the royal palace, the palace of illusions ... Draupadi's eyes closed as she pictured its arching, undulating white stone walls that were studded extravagantly with enormous frescos of precious and semi-precious gems in every size and hue. Its court had been resplendent with gold doors and crystal arches and carved beams that shimmered and radiated with dancing sunlight, its lavish floors inlaid with murals of the most precious of gemstones. She sighed. Even heaven and its infinite whiteness paled in comparison to the riot of colour and majesty that had been their palace of illusions. It had been home for the happiest period of her life.

'Indraprastha,' she almost whispered to Narad Muni. 'We'll go there.' She blinked gratefully at Kunti, who smiled back knowingly.

'Indraprastha it is.' Narad Muni's shrieky voice broke the moment. 'Now, I don't have all day to explain this, so listen carefully. This ...' He took a pot out of the sack he carried and held it up. Draupadi immediately recognized it as the magical pot of food that Krishna had given her when she and her husbands had been exiled into the forest without any sustenance.

'... is Akshaya-patra, Krishna's magical pot of food, which he is lending to you for this *outing*. It will fill itself up with food every morning and will give unlimited amounts of food until it is washed at night. *You* should know this.' He looked scornfully at Draupadi.

'I do,' she mumbled, but the pot was already back in the sack and now Narad Muni was holding up a handful of what looked like miniature paintings on parchment. 'This,' he continued, 'is money. It is the currency used in the mortal world today. You cannot purchase anything without it. There is enough here for your stay, I should imagine. Hide it carefully, for mortals will gladly slit your throats for it, given the chance.'

Draupadi shuddered. The mortal world was looking like a bleaker place with every passing instant. Especially if she had to wear clothes like these for thirty days.

'Now, as you will see, there are more clothes for all of you in here. And finally, this is a mobile phone.' He held up a small object and sighed loudly at the confused looks on the women's faces. 'Mortals use them to speak to each other when they are not in one another's presence. Each mortal has a sequence of numbers, and when you press those numbers *here*' – he pointed to the keypad – 'the mobile phone of that mortal will ring. As will this one when someone wants to speak to you. Like this.'

A clang, like a temple bell, boomed out of the small object, and all four women jumped in fright. Narad Muni smiled a small smile of superiority and continued, 'That's my ringtone. Quite appropriate, even if I do say so myself. Anyway, I will, of course, pick you up when the duration of your stay is over, but should you want to leave early, then you can use this to call me. My number is 9812 ...' Narad Muni rattled off a series of numbers before ending with, 'but of course I can't expect you to remember that, being women, and so I have entered it into the phone. You only need to press 1 to call me. Is that understood?'

From the blank, apprehensive expressions on all four faces, it was clear his little lesson had been anything but understood, but Narad Muni continued anyway, putting the phone back into the sack and tying it up. 'The number for this phone is written on the back, so you can give that number to anyone whom you wish to call you.' He took a breath, handed over the sack to Kunti and clapped his hands with a sadistic smile. 'All right, I think you're set up and ready to go.'

Draupadi sputtered in confusion with a, 'Wait, what about ... how are we ...' But it was too late. Narad Muni came right up to her and, with a grin that revealed an orange mouth full of pulped betel leaves and rotting teeth, put his hands on her shoulders and pushed her.

Chapter 5

She was going to die!

Oh wait, she was already dead.

Were the two thoughts that chased each other through Draupadi's mind as she fell past cloud after cloud with the speed of a large boulder thrown off a cliff. She was terrified and fascinated all at once. She could feel her mouth ballooning grotesquely as frigid air slammed into it. Her hair slapped her face as it whipped furiously around her and her clothes – well, frankly, she would be more than glad if they were blown off her.

Above Draupadi was a blackness that appeared to be turning bluer as she continued to fall. Below was layer after layer of white clouds. She knew she was going to hit land, or water, at some point. Would there be an impact and if so, would it hurt? She was sure, if Narad Muni had his way, it would hurt like hell.

Then she saw it. The mortal world. A vast expanse of startling colour – vivid blues and greens with specks of amber and light dustings of yellow. It moved ever so slightly, its surface rippling and undulating like a giant creature shivering very slowly. Never had she seen it like this before. It was so beautiful, so vibrant, so ... alive, she thought, as tears welled in her eyes only to be dried up instantly by the wind against her face.

This would be her second chance, and she would make it worth spending the rest of eternity bored out of her wits. She would squeeze every last—

'Aahhh!' Kunti sped past her, snapping Draupadi out of her reverie and back to the realization that she might, very soon, be hitting something. Hard.

'Naarab Moonee, thish hah be'er no bee painfool,' she yelled, with her distorted mouth, into the nothingness with some difficulty.

'It won't be painful,' the air around her rang.

Relieved, she braced herself as land came closer and closer until she could only see a whirl of brown and green and a looming stone structure directly under her and then—

Splat!

As promised, it hadn't hurt. She kept her eyes closed tightly for a moment anyway. Then, as the pungent stink of dung assaulted her nostrils and a distinct wetness spread across her backside, she opened them with a shriek.

'But I didn't say anything about dignified.' Narad Muni's voice cackled with laughter.

Draupadi found herself sprawled in a pile of fresh horse manure with Narad Muni standing nearby, doubled up and shaking with mirth. For a moment, Draupadi glared murderously at him, as though she would like to pounce on his tiny frame and tear him apart. Then, just as he began to look apprehensive, she grinned, throwing back her head and allowing a gleeful laugh to burst out of her. The dung was soaking into everything: her clothes, her hair, it was even splattered on to her face. Her eyes felt dry and gritty from the dust, she felt hot and sweaty, and her neck hurt. But after thousands of years of smelling nothing but the delicate scent of lotus blossoms, with never a moment of awkwardness or discomfort, this just felt ... wonderful.

'You go ahead and try all your tricks, old man,' she said, deliriously cheerful, 'for today I would forgive even Mara himself.'

Draupadi looked around her. Amba, Gandhari and Kunti had all landed a few paces away from her and seemed to be too dazed to do anything but just sit gratefully on firm land. They were in a clearing surrounded by thorny bushes and a few dirty and weak-looking trees. The ground was dusty and orange, not quite as red as she remembered, and it was littered with little fragments and scraps of things she couldn't recognize. Next to them was a small structure about the size of a potter's hut, but painted a shade of grotesque blue and covered in filth and stains, as if people had spat and smeared excrement all over it. It had a metal roof that looked like it could cave in at any moment. From this structure trickled small streams of dirty water that ran into the bushes, coagulating in the mud around it to form a mushy, mouldy mini-swamp. It looked revolting.

'So here we are at Indraprastha, recently renamed New Delhi. On this very spot where we stand were the palace women's quarters where you lived,' Narad Muni said with some drama, fully anticipating the subsequent looks of utter shock on their faces. 'It is now what the mortals call a zoo; a place where they house animals of all description for the viewing pleasure of anyone who can pay the entry price. There are beasts from all over the mortal world here. Sad-looking things, for the most part.'

He waited while he let his words sink in and watched as the women looked around with shock and bewilderment written all over their faces. Then, he smiled and continued, 'This' – he pointed to the vile blue structure dramatically – 'is where mortals go to relieve themselves. It is called a toilet. This will be your home for the next thirty days.'

'*What*?' exclaimed Draupadi and Gandhari, sharing the same disgusted expression.

Narad Muni was clearly enjoying himself. 'From the outside, it is designed to repel mortals, for even before they see it, they will smell it.' He snapped his fingers and the foulest, most retch-worthy stench of urine, excrement and decay began to fill the air around them. Draupadi gagged violently, but Narad Muni snapped his fingers once more and the stench was gone. He continued, 'I've never had anyone attempt to enter here yet, but I've put a magical fence around it, just in case, which will instantly kill any mortal that does try. From the inside, it is quite different. I myself use it during my visits. Follow me.' He hopped over the muddy puddles and opened the rickety wooden door with a slow creak.

Draupadi exchanged apprehensive glances with Amba and Kunti but followed him anyway. She tentatively skipped over the muddy march and entered, trying not to touch anything on the way.

Inside was a palatial sitting chamber; the kind she had become used to when she lived as a queen. It had marble floors and inlaid walls, and stately pillars with gold carvings on them. The room was enormous – completely out of proportion to the tiny, decrepit hut in which it appeared to be housed – and furnished with cushioned divans dressed in ornate brocades. From the ceiling hung a massive crystal sculpture that was breathtakingly intricate. Beyond, behind two large, gilded doors seemed to be an equally ornate sleeping chamber as well. The air inside the chambers was also comfortably cool, in contrast to the dusty heat outside.

Draupadi could hear the relieved intake of breaths as the others followed her inside. This was familiar territory, finally something they could work with.

'The sleeping chamber is behind those doors,' said Narad Muni with a wave towards it. 'I've arranged for four beds, but you will all have to sleep in the same room since this really was designed just for my visits.' He looked at them defensively, seeming to expect some argument at the inconvenience.

'Thank you. It is lovely and we will be very comfortable here,' said Kunti quickly. Then she faltered a little before continuing, 'Now a quick question, if you don't mind, O great Narad Muni.'

Narad Muni's eyes narrowed with suspicion the instant 'O great' left her lips.

Kunti soldiered on, 'I was wondering if you could let me know where I might find my former son, Karan, king of Anga. I was told he chose to be reincarnated and' – she faltered a little – 'I'd like to see him in his present incarnation,' she finished weakly.

The old sage looked at her sceptically with beady eyes. 'Have you got Krishna's permission to contact him?'

Kunti blinked but Draupadi rushed into the conversation. 'But of course,' she declared, confidently meeting his eye with a 'how-can-you-even-think-otherwise' expression. Kunti shifted a little on her feet at the blatant lie but looked directly at Narad Muni, giving nothing away. This was too important.

Narad Muni, already appalled that they were allowed this visit in the first place and seriously doubting Krishna's judgement anyway, accepted her answer. 'Very well. You may find him in the Bal Raksha home for orphans in the Connaught Place area.'

Kunti looked a little stunned. She asked, with a hopeful expression, 'He is ... employed at the home?'

Narad Muni shook his head and said casually, 'He is one of the orphans. His birth mother was a prostitute and his father was one of her ... patrons. She left him there when he was three and died soon after from an overdose of poppy seed extract. The warden named him Karan; it's a popular name for abandoned children these days. He is eleven now, I think.' He shrugged his shoulders.

Kunti, who had borne a lifetime, not to mention several thousand years of sorrow and regret without shedding a tear, broke down at his words. She had hoped, prayed for the last millennia spent in heaven that wherever Karan was, he would be safe and cherished by someone. That he would know a mother's love so great that it would make up for all her maternal misdeeds. This reality was too much to bear.

Gandhari took a sobbing Kunti into her arms and led her to a corner, while Amba and Draupadi looked on uncomfortably. This was an unexpected blow. Draupadi had never really liked Karan herself but she felt Kunti's pain.

Narad Muni, who had instantly become shifty at the advent of tears, muttered hurriedly, 'The last thing is language. The mortals in New Delhi speak Devanagari, now called Hindi, and a new language called English. I've arranged for you all to be proficient in both. Also, there is a hole in the boundary wall about thirty paces to the right of this hut, in case you want to enter and leave the zoo. They won't allow you through the main gate without payment. All right' – he inhaled and rubbed his hands – 'if that is all, I will be on my way. You may call me on the phone in case you wish to return early, otherwise I will return for you thirty days from now. Farewell.' And before any of them could utter a word, he had disappeared into a burst of smoke.

'Typical,' grumbled Draupadi. 'Shed one tear, show one trace of emotion, and a man is out of the door.' She looked at Amba and then at Kunti. 'Now what do we do?'

'I think it might be best to go to the orphans' home,' replied Gandhari from the corner, still holding the sniffing and shaking Kunti. 'Her mind will not be at peace until she sees him.'

Kunti shook her head vigorously. 'No, no. I'm so sorry. I will compose myself.' She looked up at Draupadi and said kindly, 'You've looked forward to coming down here for so long. There must be things you wish to see. You carry on, and I will find the orphanage—'

Draupadi interrupted her. 'That's out of the question. We'll stay together. If you wish to go to the orphanage now—'

It was Kunti's turn to interrupt. 'No. I mean, yes, I would like to go but ...' She furrowed her brow and gazed at Draupadi earnestly. 'If you had a choice, where would you go first? I mean, if this conversation about Karan had not taken place, then what would have been the first thing on your agenda?' She managed a shaky, somewhat pathetic smile.

Draupadi, never known for her patience, began to look a little irritated but Kunti persisted, 'No, tell me. Please. It's important to me.'

Draupadi shrugged. 'I don't know. I suppose I would be interested in seeing the new palace of Indraprastha, or whatever it's called these days ... New Delhi. If they still have palaces in this day and age.'

Kunti's eyes brightened up a bit. 'Good. Then let's go see the palace first. I'm sure they still have them' – she brushed aside the brimming objections with a firm shake of her head – 'and then, after that, yes, I'd like to go to the orphanage and find Karan. Does that sound fair? Please say yes.' She smiled imploringly at Draupadi.

Draupadi was too respectful to roll her eyes directly at Kunti, so she nodded edgily. While not being particularly thrilled to be spending any part of her first day in this world looking at dirty little children, she knew it was the right thing to do.

'Let me get cleaned up and then we'll go for a walk outside.'

Chapter 6

It was a clanging unlike anything she had ever heard. Unnatural, shrill and piercing, a continuous ding-ding-ding-ding like a temple bell gone mad. And it convulsed too, in tiny, quick waves on her hand until Draupadi dropped it with a shriek of her own.

The 'phone' that Narad Muni had given them clattered on to the path they had been walking on. All four women stared as it writhed on the ground, loudly calling out to them at regular intervals. This was not what they had heard in Narad Muni's presence. Kunti shrank back as it inched towards her and squeaked, 'Is it in pain? Do something please, I can't bear to see it suffer like this!'

'Don't be ridiculous. It can't be in pain.' Gandhari stared at it intently. 'It's not a living thing.'

'He said the temple bell will call if someone wants to speak to us. This is different,' said Amba, looking worried.

Draupadi's brow creased. 'If I know that wily old man—'

'Pick it *up*, for God's sake,' a bush next to them muttered.

'*Shhhh*, shut up!'

'*Arre*, you shut up!'

The four women turned towards the bush, which had stopped talking and was now giggling. Draupadi could make out the outlines of a man and a woman locked in what could only be described as a compromising position.

Draupadi grinned to herself. Stinking toilets, horse manure, sack-like clothing, screeching phones and mortals copulating out in the open ... this world was nothing if not interesting.

She bent down and gingerly picked up the phone. 'As I was saying, if I know that wily old man, this is probably his twisted way' – she pressed the protrusion as she had seen Narad Muni do – 'of amusing himself.' The phone went silent.

'What took you so long to answer? So, do you like my new ringtone?' Narad Muni's distorted voice tittered out of the device.

Draupadi glanced one last time at the bush and began to walk away from it. 'Very funny. We were engaged in, er ... studying mortal behaviour. Now, do you have something to say, old man, or were you just trying to trouble us?'

'Yes, one last thing. Don't tell mortals who you really are. They don't believe in things like heaven. They barely even believe in God any more ... tragic, really. Anyway, just make up something to tell them. That's all.' The phone went silent again.

The four women looked at each other as they walked. Kunti said, 'So, what should we pretend to be? Visiting royalty from a foreign kingdom?'

'No, that would be too conspicuous,' replied Gandhari. 'People would ask why the reigning monarch hasn't invited us to his palace.'

'Besides, we're not exactly dressed like royalty,' said Draupadi with some irony. 'In fact, this, uh, bra makes me feel more like I'm dressed for war.' She wiggled uncomfortably.

Amba smiled. 'We could just be common village women who trade in the market. Or gypsies! I'd rather be a gypsy. Then maybe we could' – she nodded over her shoulder at the bush with the cheekiest look on her face – 'do that too.'

Draupadi burst out laughing, and even Kunti, who had been extremely forlorn until now, showed a hint of a smile. Gandhari pursed her lips and strode ahead of them, which made them laugh even harder. She glared at them over her shoulder.

Draupadi said between hiccups of mirth, 'Come now, I never knew you were such a prude, Gandhari. Maybe I should have guessed it, being stuck with Dhritarashtra your whole life. With that nasal voice and the way he used to constantly wring his hands and open and close his lips like a fish' – she shuddered – 'he would have turned any woman off the act.'

'I'll thank you to not say such things about him. He was a good husband,' replied Gandhari half-heartedly, looking ahead. She didn't fool anyone.

Draupadi smiled and looked around. Indraprastha seemed to be much hotter and dustier than she remembered, and when she looked upwards, she was surprised to see a light grey sky instead of the striking blue that had always greeted her in her past life. As she breathed in the heavy air and wiped the sweat from her brow with the back of her hand, she could hear the faint shrieking of monkeys and a myriad of clanging and growling noises, as if a battle between beasts was taking place somewhere in the distance.

They came upon a paved path and began following it. Further along, on one side of this path were animals of every description in large metal cages and enclosures. Most of them were thin, covered in faeces and paced up and down in their cages restlessly, desperately looking for a way out. Some she recognized, some she didn't, but all were, as Narad Muni had said, sad-looking creatures, destined to spend the rest of their days trapped in tiny prisons while people gawked at them. Draupadi knew exactly how they felt. Princesses in her day weren't all that different.

Just then, they arrived at a large, paved clearing. A massive gate of pinkish stone with large domes and arches and carved with unfamiliar symbols greeted them. Surrounding it were the ruins of what had once been a palace garden. Gigantic arches undulated curvaceously around trees, topped with domes of every size and with smaller arches within them. It was a style she had never seen before … simple, yet awe-inspiring.

Close by, towering over their heads, were the ruins of a palace that had obviously been abandoned a long time ago. It was a tall, broken, stone fortress that featured the same style as the gate in front of them, with large domes and arches of different sizes that had been constructed in geometric patterns. It looked rather forlorn against the smooth, paved boxiness of the modern structures in the clearing.

A few people were milling about the clearing. Hawkers walked around selling brightly coloured trinkets and food. A family – a mother, grandmother and two young children – stood excitedly to one side, obviously waiting for someone to take them around. Two men strolled off to another side, walking alongside each other, their hands brushing as they swung their arms. A group of children – all dressed identically in white and blue clothing – walked in a single line surrounded by tense, middle-aged women.

Draupadi looked around eagerly, trying to take in as much as possible. All the people she saw, apart from the identically dressed children, were dressed very differently from each other. In her day, everyone, men and women, had worn different versions of the sari: a cloth draped over the shoulders with a belted cloth draped and tied over the groin and legs, with a small breast-cloth for women. But, as Draupadi observed, there seemed to be no prescribed dress code in these times. Some people wore long tunics, while others wore shorter ones that had various appendages sown on to them or were tucked into lower garments; yet others wore clothes similar to the ones they themselves were wearing. Some women wore the same, tight garment over their hips and legs as the men.

There was one thing though, thought Draupadi, that all the clothes she could see had in common. They all covered the most interesting and attractive parts of the body. Whether they were tight and restrictive or loose and flowy, very little of the skin underneath was visible except for the face and forearms.

Draupadi wasn't the only one who thought as much. Amba said with a puzzled look, 'Why do they wear so many clothes in such hot weather? They must be uncomfortable.'

Kunti replied, 'Perhaps it is out of modesty.'

Gandhari piped in, 'Maybe they're afraid of getting sunburned. My skin already feels like paper.' Her fair-skinned face and arms looked flushed and irritated.

Draupadi had an idea. 'Let's talk to them and find out.'

Gandhari looked apprehensive. 'I don't think ...'

But Draupadi had already walked away and was striding towards two women, a middle-aged one with a younger woman. Obviously a mother with her daughter, the two were standing to one side of the clearing, trying to keep two very excited children in check. Draupadi strode up to them, smiling benevolently with just the tiniest hint of condescension. The women acknowledged her unsmilingly, distracted by the antics of their charges.

Unfazed, if a little surprised, Draupadi ventured some small talk. 'It is a hot day, isn't it?'

The middle-aged woman looked Draupadi up and down disapprovingly, pursed her lips and looked away. The younger woman made a half-hearted effort to be polite and nodded, while keeping her gaze fixed on a young girl of about two summers and an older boy of about five, who was climbing a metal railing next to them.

Draupadi, disconcerted by their rudeness, decided to try another approach. 'What beautiful children you have. A little prince and princess,' she cooed. There was usually nothing mothers liked better than for others to validate their deluded opinions of their children.

The younger woman half-smiled in response and murmured, 'Thank you.' Then, as the boy almost fell off the railing, she barked, 'Abhimanyu, get off right now, before you break your head.'

Abhimanyu. So they remember us! Draupadi smiled as she glanced back at the others to see if they had heard. They obviously had, for Kunti's eyes had lit up despite her previous grief and Amba and Gandhari both had smiles on their faces as they walked towards them.

Draupadi turned back to the young mother. 'What a lovely name your son has. Abhimanyu, a great warrior and prince. May he be as brave and noble as his namesake. And what is your daughter called?'

'Why do you want to know? Are you trying to sell something or ask for donation?' the older woman shot back harshly.

The younger woman looked sheepish, but made no effort to answer. Instead, she busied herself in trying to pull her son off the top of the railing.

Draupadi spoke to the older woman, trying her best to sound polite even though she felt like giving this rude, unkempt hag a piece of her mind, 'No, I don't want anything. I am just chatting. We are new to Indr ... to New Delhi, and we are just looking around and learning as much as we can.'

'Well, go chat with someone else. We are busy.' The older woman turned her back on Draupadi pointedly.

The little boy, Abhimanyu, then came running up to them, made a face and said in a sing-song, mocking voice, 'I am just chaaating. Go chaaat with someone else. You're stupid!' He roared loudly and pounced closer to Draupadi. 'I'm a tiger and I'm going to eat you!'

'Why, you nasty little pest!' Draupadi stepped forward and slapped the boy soundly on his cheek.

There was a collective gasp from all the surrounding women, and Abhimanyu's mother and grandmother wore twin expressions of shock. Abhimanyu gave a loud wail, burst into tears and ran into his mother's arms. His wails grew louder as he saw his grandmother and mother's expressions turn from shock into anger, touched with a hint of fear.

The women began to shout at Draupadi while maintaining a safe distance.

'How dare you slap my son?!'

'Who do you think you are?! This is no way to behave!'

Draupadi was done playing nice. She glared at them and spoke with contempt. 'Your son is a rude little brat, and judging by the way you've behaved with me, I can see where he gets his manners.'

The women might have pursued the matter further, but Draupadi's height and the intensity of her glare, not to mention the presence of her three companions, were enough to scare them off. The women retreated, clutching their brood and walking away hurriedly while glancing over their shoulders to make sure they weren't being followed.

Amba shook her head and ventured, 'Draupadi—'

'No, don't say it. I know. I shouldn't have slapped him. But' – Draupadi smiled wryly at Kunti – 'his name was Abhimanyu after all ...'

Abhimanyu, the son of her husband Arjuna and his younger wife Subhadra, had been a precocious child. And as much as Draupadi had loved his intelligence and inquisitive mind, she had resented the love that his parents had shared and sometimes unfairly taken it out on him. None of her other husbands had dared to introduce her to their other wives or children. Arjuna himself had not dared to do so until he met Subhadra. Only then had he been willing to bear the force of Draupadi's legendary temper; so that he could be with the woman he loved.

Draupadi smiled as she thought about all the pointless misery they had put each other through as mortals. Arjuna and she had shared extremely pleasurable, passionate sex, and for a while, she had even mistaken that for love. She had resented his brothers for taking her away from him, resented having to submit to their grunting, groping affections. They had none of the finesse or charm that he did. When Subhadra came along, she had been viciously jealous. But when she had seen the love that Arjuna shared with Subhadra – a love that encompassed the mind, the heart, the soul and the body – Draupadi had realized that she had never felt that way about anyone. Not Arjuna, not her children; not anyone. Maybe with Krishna; but then which woman *wasn't* in love with Krishna? That didn't count. No, she had loved learning and governance, adventure and animals, loved revenge, or at least the idea of it, for a while but she had never loved other people in that all-encompassing way.

Draupadi shook her head and banished her little reverie to find the other women looking at her tentatively. Ah yes, she had slapped the boy. Bad idea, but he deserved it. She gazed ahead into the clearing determinedly and said, 'Moving on!'

Chapter 7

It was the size of three fully-grown elephants, had the face of a giant housefly and was the colour of green moss. It charged towards them with growling, bellowing and screeching sounds that made their ears swell with pain and hearts pound with fear. All four women screamed as they turned and ran back towards the gate of the zoo, but they were no match for its speed.

The monster, with its massive single eye that was so glassy they could see reflections of the surrounding trees in it, snarled and screeched again as it quickly caught up with them. But then, just as they thought it about to pounce and attack, it turned its gigantic body and sped past them to continue noisily down a large, paved road.

Draupadi breathed a sigh of intense relief when Amba shouted, 'Look! Look what lies under it.'

They all looked in the direction Amba was pointing, at the flanks of the giant beast that had narrowly missed them. Underneath it were ... *wheels*?

They looked at each other in shock. Gandhari shook her head in confusion.

'What is it?'

Before anyone could answer, another beast, much the same only smaller in size, with the same large eye in front and the same roaring, screeching scream, came charging down the road. And then another. And another, and another. Growling, bellowing one-eyed beasts of different sizes, shapes and colours sped, one by one, past them ... on wheels.

'Chariots,' shouted Amba over the din, 'they're chariots. Look, there are people inside.' She pointed at the eyes of the ones that passed closer to them as they stood on the side, atop a slightly elevated path beside the road. There were, indeed, people sitting inside.

'Amazing! Look at how fast they move,' Gandhari said with wide eyes.

'No horses, no bulls, nothing. It's like magic!' Kunti looked equally amazed.

Draupadi laughed out loud in excitement. The mortals rode in fantastical, noisy, horseless chariots that sped around on smooth roads with unnatural speed, their wheels spinning furiously and turning this way and that. It was beyond anything she could have ever dreamed of, and this was *exactly* the reason she had wanted to visit the mortal world. She couldn't wait to ride in one!

'Come,' she said excitedly, 'let's follow the direction in which they are going. Maybe they're riding towards the palace!'

The women started walking in the direction that all the chariots had sped towards, carefully staying on the elevated sides of the road.

They walked until the road they were following abruptly merged into another, growing suddenly into an impossibly large path on which hundreds of chariots seemed to be desperately trying to overtake or overrun each other in a noisy charge towards an invisible enemy. The road was divided into two by an elevated fence that ran along the length of it, separating the chariots that were moving in opposite directions. The cacophony of growls, bellows and screeches was feverishly loud, although the few mortals that walked along the road around them seemed completely oblivious to the noise.

The four women instinctively huddled closer together, worried expressions on their faces. Draupadi looked around, trying to decide which way to proceed. Just then, on the other side of the road, she saw the ruins of a building complex with a large dome on top of it and a large arched doorway, much like the ruins around the zoo. Behind it, Draupadi could see clumps of tree cover.

'Let's go that way.' She pointed at the dilapidated structure across the road. 'It looks quieter and greener. I'm sure the palace won't be in such a ridiculously noisy area.'

Amba looked dubiously in the direction Draupadi was pointing and then at the busy road. 'Fine, but I don't think these chariots are going to stop and let us cross the road. They're going too fast.'

Draupadi looked around to see what the mortals were doing. They were either walking along the side of the road or looking across to the other side but standing in a small group near a break in the fence where the road was painted with large white stripes. Above them, a green ball of light glowed in a yellow box mounted on top of a tall pole. The mortals stood under the light, seemingly wanting to cross the road but not actually doing it. They looked like they were waiting for something.

Never one to wait for anything, Draupadi turned to the other three women and said, 'We can wait for a gap between the chariots and dash across. Then, we can climb over the fence and make another dash.'

Kunti looked worried. 'I don't think that's safe.'

Gandhari shook her head. 'The mortals over there look like they want to cross over. Let's go and stand among them. Then, we can do whatever they do.'

'They're not doing anything,' Draupadi said impatiently. 'I'm crossing the road. Who's coming with me? Amba?'

Amba looked torn.

'Kunti?'

Kunti sighed. 'I think we should follow the mortals, Draupadi, as Gandhari suggested. There must be a reason they are standing together like that.'

Well, she'd be damned if she was going to let Gandhari tell her what to do, thought Draupadi. Tossing her hair back, she jerked her chin towards the side of the road. 'Fine. You three go stand with the mortals and wait. I'll go alone.'

'Draupadi,' began Amba, but Draupadi had already leapt off the side of the path.

This is going to be easy, Draupadi told herself as she felt a rush of blood and her heart began to beat faster than it had in many ages. Her senses, so unused and lethargic just a day earlier, suddenly sprung to life. Her breaths came in short gasps, and her eyes focused on the oncoming chariots, trying to gauge their speed and the gaps between them. Her ears quickly attuned themselves to the growls the chariots made as they whizzed by, and her body felt like a coiled spring, ready for action. She felt the sweat on her brow and the nervous flutter in her stomach and chuckled. She was alive again.

Then, as a tiny gap opened in the stream of chariots, Draupadi leapt in and tried to run across. Behind her, a bellow, one that almost blew her ears out, sounded in the air as a massive, three-elephant-sized chariot whirred past her, sending a strong gust of wind that almost blew her a few steps forward. Luckily, she stood strong, for in front of her sped another bellowing, smaller chariot. She had a brief glimpse of the mortals inside glaring at her with half-angry, half-worried expressions. They obviously thought she was mad. She ignored them as she quickly dashed into another gap, setting off another round of bawling by the chariots.

Just another few paces to go, she thought; but now, coming towards her at full pelt behind a couple of smaller ones was another one of the massive chariots. There was almost no gap in the road for her to make a dash forward and not enough space for the chariot to pass without running her over. Taking a frantic look behind to see if she could take a step back,

Draupadi could see that there was no gap in the flow of chariots behind her either.

In that split second, Draupadi realized that if she stayed where she was, she would be trampled by the massive chariot, and if she stepped back to get out of its way, she would be trampled by a smaller one. She had no choice.

With only a moment left before both chariots were upon her, she took off towards the fence. A few running steps and one bold leap when all at once, behind her, she smelled the burning, metallic stench of the chariot as it screeched past, furiously slapping the back of her skirt and hair. Even as Draupadi's hands reached the fence, she could feel a few hairs being yanked from her head and a sharp pain in her neck as it was whipped sideways by the near miss. She could hear screams – real ones – from the side of the road as the chariot passed; but she was left clutching the fence, unharmed, save for a few hairs.

She climbed and sat on top of the fence quickly and let out her breath in a loud gasp. She was shaking. She looked across the road and saw Amba, Kunti and Gandhari standing rooted to the spot, all wearing terrified expressions. The mortals standing in the huddle to cross the road looked shaken up too. A few of them were shouting angrily at her, gesticulating wildly all the while. Draupadi couldn't hear what they were saying but could guess the gist of it. They thought she was mad too.

Maybe I am, thought Draupadi with a shaky laugh. After all, she had been alive for barely an hour or two, and already she had almost killed herself. She looked in front of her. She was only halfway across the road and the flow of chariots going in the opposite direction on the other side was no less than the previous one. She might succeed in the killing herself department after all, she thought, as she gingerly hopped on to the other side.

But before she could dive into another death-defying dash, something strange happened. All the chariots slowed and came to a complete halt. Draupadi looked behind her. The previously green glow from the box on top of the pole had turned red, and all the mortals who had been waiting to cross the road scurried in a straight line to the other side. With them walked Amba, Kunti and Gandhari.

So there was a system after all, thought Draupadi with an ironic laugh. That stubborn hag, Gandhari, had been right. She quickly weaved her way between the now-stationary chariots and reached the other side of the road, where the others were waiting for her. Amba and Kunti looked furious and Gandhari looked a little smug as she said, 'You should be thankful that chariot didn't run you over. Next time—'

'Save your breath,' said Draupadi firmly. She looked at Amba and Kunti, and her expression became a little sheepish. 'Well, if I had been run over, at least we would have had a good laugh over it back in heaven—'

'That's not funny,' snapped Amba, while Kunti's lips tightened into a thin line.

Draupadi nodded and looked suitably sorry for a moment before smiling and saying cheerfully, 'Come, let's not spoil our adventure by being angry at one another. I will be good, I promise. Let's go find the palace!'

Far from mollified, the three women still followed her as she turned once again towards the ruins and began to walk. They strolled aimlessly for a while, meandering off the large road and on to a smaller, weaving path, walking past large metal gates, signposts and the odd mortal or two. For the most part, they walked alongside tall fences lined with endless hedges.

All the buildings had only a single metal gate that allowed entry. They didn't look large or grand enough to be palaces, thought Draupadi as she peered past one of the hedges to see a large, boxy structure with a small garden in front of it. A few empty chariots were parked in and around the fences, and the women looked curiously inside at the seats and the strange contraptions that filled them.

Draupadi wondered out loud, 'Fences seem to be a common feature in the houses. The windows and doors too are covered. Perhaps these are the homes of noblemen. Narad Muni said that the mortal world is now a dangerous place. Maybe that is the reason they enclose themselves like this.'

Kunti peered into a gate as they walked past. 'Tiny gardens, with barely a tree or two in them. I wonder where the children of a house like this would play if they had to stay inside the fence all the time.'

Down the road, the four women came across a gate with an elderly guard posted in front of it. The man was dressed in a bright blue outfit with a hat. Slung over his shoulder was what looked like a black sword sheath with handles protruding out of the sides. He glanced over at the four women with a bored expression.

Amba, throwing a quick look at Draupadi, quickly murmured, 'Let me try and talk to him.'

She walked up to him and bowed, hands folded in front of her with respect. The guard narrowed his eyes suspiciously at her and said, 'What do you want? Sir is not at home.'

Amba smiled and said, 'Rest easy, loyal servant. We don't want to see your master. We are visiting New Delhi and wish to be directed towards the palace.'

The guard, none too happy at being referred to as a 'loyal servant', frowned irritably. 'Which palace?'

Amba smiled, happy to have at least engaged him in conversation. She replied, 'The palace where the king lives, of course.'

The guard looked at her as if she'd suddenly sprouted a pair of deer horns on her head. He took a step backwards, mumbling, 'I don't know about kings, lady, but if you want a palace with someone living in it, then I suppose the closest thing is Rashtrapati Bhavan. It's that way.' He pointed in the general direction they had been walking in to begin with. 'When you reach the end of this road, turn right on Zakir Hussain Marg. Walk till the end and cross the roundabout road into the India Gate park. Rajpath is on the other side of India Gate. Rashtrapati Bhavan is at the end of Rajpath.'

Then, putting a firm end to further conversation by spitting an orange stream into the drain next to him, the guard moved away, muttering to himself about 'crazy women wasting his time'. Coupling the sentiment with a few unrecognizable words that were sure to be expletives, he turned his back on them and walked back inside the gate.

Amba turned around with a frown. 'Well, we have directions. Although I don't understand why everyone is so rude.'

Gandhari replied as they continued to walk, 'It is as Narad Muni said, I suppose. It's not surprising that along with every other virtue, they've lost their manners as well. They are, quite obviously, a hopeless species.'

Draupadi smiled wryly. 'You do realize that you belong to the same species?'

Gandhari replied firmly, '*Used* to belong. Not any more, thank god.'

Draupadi sighed and continued to look around. She wasn't going to let Gandhari spoil her mood.

After that, there was much walking through busy, clamouring roads with bored mortals dressed in nondescript and over-modest clothing, past large buildings guarded by long, unfriendly fences, dusty hedges and large metal gates. Then, finally, having stopped to ask for directions several times, where they got more of the same incredulous looks, the four women found themselves a single road crossing away from what looked like a large park.

'That must be India Gate park,' said Draupadi enthusiastically. Though she couldn't wait to cross over the road and into the park, this time she heeded the angry glares from the others and patiently walked along the road for what seemed like ages, until they found, in her words, a damned, godforsaken, hell-bound road crossing. Gandhari calmly pointed out that all three curses meant the same thing, and Draupadi glared at Amba for giggling.

The park was a pleasant surprise. There were many trees – finally – and wide, open gardens too. It wasn't much compared to the lush foliage and fauna that they had been used to, but they were grateful to see any kind of greenery at all. After the non-stop roads, none of the women commented on the absence of flowers, streams and wildlife, or minded the gigantic brown patches in the green grass.

Another surprise was visible past the trees. A monument – a colossal arch made out of red stone – appeared to have sprouted from the ground and stood towering over large groups of mortals that scurried this way and that below it. They looked like ants at the feet of a child who had dropped a crumb of sweetmeat. A smaller monument made of the same kind of stone stood at a distance; this one shaped like a canopy to provide shade from the sun.

'Well, this is grand. We must be getting close,' said Draupadi as they walked by the monument.

'Everything is so big,' remarked Kunti, looking around her. 'I'm trying to see how big the city has grown, but it seems to be endless in every direction.'

Draupadi nodded. 'You're right. I can't be sure but we would have already walked well beyond the city gates of our time. This would have been the forest, I imagine, but then it was such a long time ago ...' She squinted into the distance.

Beyond the arching monument, a wider-than-wide, treeless road cut through a bigger park in gentle slopes. On a clear day, Draupadi thought, one would have been able to stand on an incline and see where the road led, for it certainly seemed to be a ceremonial one. But there was a sluggish white haze that hung over everything; and so all she could see was the immediate park on either side. Mortals of every age and type filled the park, some playing sports and others walking or sitting around and eating.

The four women walked along the side of the road for some time, watching the mortal families and the groups of young children running around, playing with newfangled toys. Amba exclaimed as she saw a child blow on a yellow stick, out of which celestial-looking, transparent balls floated into the air. Another child pushed around a toy that looked like a tiny colourful version of one of the chariots from the road.

Gandhari pointed at a painted cart that had oddly-shaped balls of different colours tied to it with string. The balls were somehow floating in the air. Gandhari's expression was incredulous as she urged her companions closer to them. The hawker standing alongside the cart smiled brightly and handed Gandhari a string with a bright red ball attached to it. It floated magically over her head, and if she let go of the string, it floated upwards of its own accord, bobbing towards the sky. She caught the string quickly with a little gasp.

'Incredible,' she said and laughed a girlish, tinkling laugh. Draupadi realized it was the first time she had ever heard Gandhari express amusement. She thought that more incredible than the red ball.

'What is this?' Gandhari asked the hawker.

His smile faltered a little before he replied, 'A balloon, sisterji. For ten rupees only.'

'Rupees? Oh, money, you mean.' Gandhari smiled wistfully, shook her head and gave the string back to him firmly. 'We cannot buy it.'

The hawker did what all merchants throughout the history of time have done. He began to bargain, wheedle and even refuse to take back the balloon, insisting that she should buy it in a whiny voice. Even Kunti ventured to suggest that they should buy the balloon, but Gandhari was resolute, saying, 'There is no need to waste what precious little Narad ... what we have been given. We may need it for food.'

'We have the rice pot,' said Draupadi.

'All the same. Better not to take chances,' replied Gandhari as she returned the balloon to the now sour-faced hawker before marching on.

The road seemed to stretch on endlessly straight for quite a while. Then, the dull haze in front of them lifted and they saw it. At the very end of the road, like a giant, sprawling redstone beast was the palace. The beast's head – a powerful, gigantic dome – jutted out beyond the horizon, seemingly touching the sky. It stood on a hill, like a crown of stone. Two giant arms – filled with palatial buildings, smaller domes, canopies and towering columns – emerged from the beast's head and flowed all the way down the hill, on either side of the massive road. It was larger and more imposing than anything they could have imagined.

For a while, all four women just stood there, staring disbelievingly. Finally, Draupadi said, without taking her eyes off it, 'The style is different, of course. I personally would have put a few murals on it, just to brighten it up. Looks a bit ... bare-faced, but very masculine and grand. You know, as much as I had loved the idea of crystal at the time, our palace didn't really fit into the landscape. This one does. It fits in, yet stands out. Of course, you can't compare the two ... ours was tiny compared to this. I wonder how many people it takes to run this thing.'

Gandhari replied, also still staring at it, 'Probably more people than there had lived in our two cities combined. Our palace was even smaller than yours.'

Draupadi gave her a sidelong glance. Gandhari had lived in the palace of Hastinapur until the Great War, in which Draupadi's husbands, the Pandavas, had fought their cousins, Gandhari's sons, and killed them. The palace of Indraprastha had been built bigger and grander than the one in Hastinapur intentionally. Ever in competition with their cousins, the Pandavas had wanted to get back at everyone in Hastinapur for kicking them out. Personally, Draupadi thought the palace in Hastinapur had been ugly and dingy, its old, crowded corridors a hotbed for gossip and political power-broking. Her own palace in Indraprastha had been light and airy, and if there was a distinct lack of activity in its corridors, it was only because the city itself had been rather small: a collection of only five villages.

Well, it certainly isn't small any more, thought Draupadi with a smile as she looked at the magnificent red palace before her. Her husbands would have been astounded. She certainly was. Kunti seemed to have the same thought as she turned to the others with a tear in her eye and said, 'If only my boys could see this. They'd be so proud of what they began.'

With a tiny glint in her eye, Draupadi smiled at her. 'Each of us had a part to play. Anyway, we must tell them when we get back.'

Amba thought aloud, 'I wonder what the king is like these days.'

Gandhari replied, 'If he is anything like the mortals Narad Muni describes, I wouldn't want to meet him.'

Amba smiled wryly. 'Much as I respect Narad Muni's opinion, I do think he exaggerates a bit. Don't you agree, Draupadi?'

But Draupadi wasn't paying attention any more. A nearby cart had caught her interest. People, especially children, stood around it eating – or more accurately, licking – something out of a cone-shaped bowl. Food had always been one of Draupadi's interests. Even though she had never indulged much as a mortal – it had been imperative that she maintain her figure – she had loved to taste different foods. Just then, she felt a tiny, confusing rumble in her belly at the sight of all the people eating and realized, with utter delight, that she was feeling hungry!

She grinned at the other women. 'I know we're supposed to go to the orphanage now but ... well, I don't know about you, but I haven't eaten anything but betel leaves and amrith in thousands of years and I'm absolutely starving!' She nodded at the cart and said, 'Should we try some food?'

Amba grinned back. 'Yes, let's!'

Kunti smiled indulgently at their enthusiasm, and even though she wanted to move things along for obvious reasons, she said, 'I think that is a wonderful idea. I wouldn't mind some too.'

Gandhari looked suspiciously at the vendor and his cart, clearly trying to figure out how much money it would involve spending. She ventured to suggest in a slightly hopeless tone, 'Should we buy one first and share it?'

Draupadi made a face. 'I'm not licking something you've licked. Let's get one each please.' She discreetly felt the money inside a flap sown into her skirt with her fingers and, remembering Narad Muni's advice to keep her money hidden, walked towards the cart.

The vendor, an old man with the look of someone who had seen it all, followed her with his eyes until she was standing before him. He didn't smile or try and act friendly. Instead, he asked mildly, 'Ice cream for you, beta?'

Draupadi nodded. 'I need four. How much does one cost?'

Sensing that she probably didn't want to spend too much, the old man said, 'Depends on which one you want. I suggest you try a vanilla flavour in a cone. That way, it only costs twenty rupees each.' He glanced over at Amba, Kunti and Gandhari, who had come to stand beside Draupadi. 'Should I give you four vanilla, beta?'

Draupadi nodded again, and he scooped ice cream into four long, conical-shaped cups and gave it to them. Following the lead of the mortals around them, the four women licked it.

Gandhari gave a small squeal when it touched her tongue. 'Snow!' she exclaimed and licked it again. 'I remember this from my maiden days when travellers used to carry it down from the mountains in the winter.' She ate some more with a broad smile on her face.

Amba examined hers as she ate. 'It's really very sweet, isn't it? Everyone else seems to be eating the cup too.'

Draupadi licked her ice cream enthusiastically at first, enjoying the novelty of its coldness. But it was cloyingly sweet and had no depth of flavour, and so she quickly moved on to biting into the cone-shaped cup. It was crunchy, but was also too sweet and flavourless. She was disappointed.

She looked at the vendor and said, disgust filling her voice: 'This is terrible.'

Far from looking offended or worried that she might not pay him, he nodded. 'It is. The kids these days like this sort of stuff. If you don't want it, I'll give it away. Don't waste it.' He held out his hand. She handed the ice cream back to him, and suddenly, out of nowhere appeared an eager-looking boy in tattered clothing. Draupadi watched the boy snatch away the cone-shaped cup with a grin and run quickly back to where a few more equally ragged-looking children sat waiting hungrily. She frowned and turned to the vendor. 'Are there many children like that these days?'

He looked at her searchingly, as if trying to decide whether to take her question seriously. Then he shrugged sadly and replied, 'In Delhi, yes, too many.'

Draupadi asked, 'Is the king a bad ruler?'

Again, that searching look. 'King?'

She nodded at the palace in the distance. 'Who lives there?'

The old man let out a sharp bark of laughter. 'Hyenas. Blood suckers. The scum of the earth. The people in there don't care about us on the street. All they care about is lining their own pockets.' He shook his head and continued, 'Inside there, they sit on their fat backsides, sipping their tea, eating their samosas and fight for power. Outside here, the rest of us fight to survive. The worst is, we chose them. But then, when everyone in the running wears a different face of the same devil, what choice do we really have?'

So it actually was as Narad Muni said. The mortal world had sunk into the worst kind of decay, where children ran wild on the street and ate scraps like stray dogs.

Thinking about stray children reminded Draupadi that they needed to go to the orphanage, and so she asked the vendor if he knew where it was. He shook his head, reminding her instead that she owed him eighty rupees. With some difficulty, Draupadi paid the man and then looked around, wondering who else she could ask for directions.

A little distance away she saw a man sitting on the grass with a black box in front of him. Thin and dark with neatly oiled hair, uncrumpled clothes and a straight back, he had the air of a learned man in unhappy circumstances. In the front of his box was a sign that read, 'Numerologist/Astrologer/Palm Reader. Donations accepted.' It was written in a strange, alien script that she was surprised she could actually read. Not that she had any idea what a numerologist/astrologer/palm reader was, but he might know the orphanage, so she told Amba, Kunti and Gandhari – who were still eating – that she would be back in a moment and walked towards him.

'You,' she said to him authoritatively, 'may help me, if you can. I am looking for the Bal Raksha home for orphans in the Connaught Place area. Do you know it?'

The man looked Draupadi over, his eyes intent and interested. Slowly, he beckoned her to sit in front of him. 'I know many, many things, sisterji. Spare me only a moment and I will tell you all.'

'I don't have time,' Draupadi dismissed him. 'Do you know it or not?'

'I know that you have been hurt by your man,' he replied softly, assessing her every expression. 'I know that you feel you are not living the life you want.'

Draupadi was stunned for a moment but then recovered her wits and even smiled as she realized the familiar hoax. 'Ah, a soothsayer, are you? I have met enough of you to know you will say the same thing to everybody.'

'I am very different. What is your name?' he asked.

'Draupadi,' she replied, lifting her chin.

He quickly wrote it down on a piece of parchment. 'Hmm. Unusual. And your good family name?'

'Why is it unusual?'

He looked up at her. 'Most parents do not name their daughters Draupadi, sisterji. It is bad luck.'

Draupadi could feel her anger rising, but ploughed ahead determinedly. 'Why?'

'You see, Draupadi from the Mahabharata was married to the Pandavas, the five brothers. Great woman, of course, but who will want to name their daughter after a woman who, er, was shared between five men? You know what I mean, no? It is like tempting fate. Now, what is your good family name, sisterji?'

Draupadi stared at him for one long, agonizing moment. So that is my legacy, she thought sadly. Remembered as a woman who serviced five men; a woman whom no one would name their daughters after for fear they might share her destiny. Her life, her strength, her courage in the face of constant challenges ... her *sacrifices* ... they all meant nothing.

'Sisterji?'

She looked up at the man. No point being upset with him. As hurtful as it was, he had just spoken the truth. 'Yes?' she whispered.

'Your family name?' he asked with a touch of impatience.

She thought about it for a while. Then she said with resignation, 'Kuru.'

'Draupadi Kuru,' he mumbled, scribbling furiously on the parchment. 'And your title – Miss or Mrs?'

Draupadi had no idea what he was talking about. 'What?'

He exhaled in patient irritation and then wrote MISS on the parchment and turned it to her. 'Every woman has a title before her name. Miss, like single' – and then wrote MRS next to it – 'Or Mrs, like married. Are you single or married?'

Draupadi looked at the bold MISS and MRS on the parchment. Obviously nothing had changed in the last millennia if women were still titled according to their marital status. 'Is there any other way to be?' she asked doubtfully.

He looked a bit disapproving and replied, 'Some women are using just Ms.' He wrote down MS on the parchment. 'It means only that you are a woman, but no marital status. But it is mostly used by those modern women who think men and women should be equal. It is not used by good, traditional ladies.' He smiled politely as if to imply that she seemed like a good, traditional lady.

A breakthrough. 'Then I shall be Ms,' replied Draupadi almost eagerly.

The fortune teller was not entirely happy with that but he wrote it down anyway before appearing to do some furious calculations on his parchment. After that, he absently asked for her palm, which he peered at with great concentration and a lot of 'hmmms' and 'ahhs'. Finally, he sat back and pondered his parchment for a few moments, his brow firmly furrowed in thought.

Draupadi stared at him for a moment, her palm still outstretched. Only then did she remember that she was here for directions. She made to get up and said, 'Look, if you don't know the way then I'll—'

'Sit, sisterji, please. Your name is not good for your luck. It is too strong and impulsive. The letters in your good family name are influencing your life too much. They are making you dissatisfied and over-emotional. Too much thinking, too fast. I can help you fix everything.' He looked at her hopefully.

Your mind is like a river careening forcefully through rapid after rapid, Draupadi remembered Krishna's words.

The man, seeing that she had not walked away, carried on, 'If you change your name to Draupadii Kuru, with a double i, then that will be better. The old name will be finished and lose its power. You will become calm and peaceful and will accept your life the way it is, without trying to change it. Not thinking, thinking, thinking all the time. It is better you change, sisterji. Then you will be a proper lady.'

Draupadi bristled. Change her name and she would become a 'proper lady', would she? The kind that everyone wanted her to be since she was an infant; who smiled, simpered and sacrificed and accepted whatever nonsense men threw her way because she thought they knew what was best for her. The kind that went through life without an original thought, without asking any questions, without the slightest endeavour to seek something beyond the four walls she was encased within.

Draupadi smiled a bitter smile. Her life would have been easier had she been that woman. The kind of woman that beamed every time one of her husbands said something idiotic that he thought was a stroke of genius, or became ecstatic every time one of her babies had a bowel movement, or argued stupidly with other women over whether almonds or pistachios made a better dressing for a sweet dish. But she wasn't that woman. And she was proud of that. She might have been a failure in everyone else's eyes but she would be damned if their opinions made her think any less of herself. She had qualities that were admired, even worshipped in men;

courage, initiative, rational thought, vision. If more women in her time had been like her, then perhaps her life would have been different. Perhaps the lives of Amba, Kunti, Gandhari and every other woman she knew would have been different.

'I thank you for your suggestion but I'm quite happy just the way I am and I think a name with a … a double 'i' is stupid. Draupadi Kuru; *Ms* Draupadi Kuru is my name, and so it shall stay.' She stood up. 'Now, do you or do you not know the way to the Bal Raksha home for orphans?'

'No.' The man looked peeved and a little desperate as he pointed to the box. 'But donation please, sister.'

'What?'

'Money.' His voice took on a hard edge. 'I tell you your fortune so now you have to give me money. Fifty rupees is okay.'

Draupadi blinked. 'I'm not going to give you money.'

The man erupted. He waved his arms at her and shouted, 'Then why are you wasting my time, you stupid woman? You think I am doing this for charity? You think I am trying to be funny? Get out, get out of my face!'

Shocked, Draupadi was about to launch into an equally loud tirade about imposters and greedy little villains when she heard Amba scream.

Chapter 8

They were surrounded by a group of five young men. Like vultures, they were circling around, leering at Gandhari and Amba. Despite being next to the ice-cream vendor in a crowded park full of other men and women, not one single person stepped forward to help them. Everyone, including the vendor, suddenly seemed fearful and distracted and looked away from the scene. Draupadi looked on in horror as one of the men brushed Amba's back with his hand and then tried to grab at her long, open hair. She screamed again and Draupadi broke into a run towards them.

As she ran, she realized she couldn't take all five men on her own. She needed a different strategy. Draupadi cleared her throat and let out a screech that could be heard on the other side of the park. Shouting like a battle cry again and again, pitching her voice both high and low until she sounded like a complete lunatic, Draupadi charged at the group of men. That was what you did with lions; startled them with loud noises until they weren't sure they wanted to risk taking you on despite being larger than you. She had learned that from her husband, Arjuna.

The men stopped in their tracks, glancing dubiously at her. This was her chance. Draupadi slammed into the man who had touched Amba, throwing the full force of her tall, lithe body against him. He stumbled and fell. Then she screamed at the top of her lungs and waved her hands around her crazily at the other men, slapping her chest one moment and then crouching and jumping at them the next. She roared and cackled, squawked and yowled and shook her head and her long hair wildly.

As she had expected, the men backed off with unsure looks on their faces. They had chanced upon two young beauties in the park and gotten carried away, but now they weren't sure they wanted to take on what was clearly an insane woman and risk hurting themselves. They laughed shakily, made a few rude expletive-filled comments about her and moved away as quickly as possible.

Draupadi continued her lunatic display until they were out of earshot and then turned on the ice-cream vendor, shaking with rage. 'You coward! Why didn't you help them?' She looked at the crowd picnicking around his cart and yelled, 'Is there no man with testicles in this park? How can you all watch innocent women being groped and not do anything? Has this world lost all sense of valour or gallantry? Has no one the nerve to stand up for someone in distress?'

Silence greeted her tirade, and once again the onlookers pretended to be distracted as though she were addressing someone else. Draupadi glared at them all and spat on the ground in front of her. If this was how the mortal world was these days then she was glad she wasn't a part of it. In her day, those men would have received a good thrashing from the crowd and a hearing in front of the kingdom's ruler.

'You've hit upon a big issue in society, actually. Everyone is scared of getting hurt. That's why they won't help a woman who is being eve-teased. One's own skin is more important than valour these days.'

The words were gasped by an out-of-breath man who had just run up to them. He seemed to be of about thirty summers and carried a big bag on his shoulder. A few steps behind ran a middle-aged man, wheezing under the weight of a large black contraption in his arms.

The speaker, panting slightly, folded his hands in greeting. 'I'm sorry it took us so long to get here. We were shooting on the other side of the park and heard you screaming. We rushed over but you' – he nodded at Draupadi – 'had already dealt with the situation. I saw what you did. Very well-handled! You know, that's how you scare lions and bears away as well.'

'Yes, I know that.' Draupadi was peeved. Heroes who came too late to save the day didn't deserve any favour in her book. Still, he seemed harmless enough, with his black-brown hair, pleasant, if not handsome, face and medium build. He looked as if he might belong to one of the upper classes, judging by his demeanour and soft hands. Maybe a merchant or a scholar? His clothes gave no indication of his profession, but they were well made, clean and crease-free. Certainly better than the dishevelled rags they were wearing, she thought as she peered down at herself with a scowl.

'Anyway, I'm Zafar. Zafar Kapoor. I'm a journalist with NPTV. And you all are?' He smiled at the four women.

Just then, Draupadi realized that they hadn't agreed upon a story yet and mentally kicked herself for not being prepared for his question. She saw that Amba, still being comforted by Kunti, was shaking slightly, but her expression suggested she was determined to shrug off what had just happened. Gandhari just seemed stumped. Draupadi racked her mind furiously. Should they just tell the truth and run with it? No, that's ridiculous. He wouldn't believe them and everyone would think they were all insane. Especially after her little performance. They needed a plausible story. Amba had suggested gypsies. No, what if they were arrested? Kunti had suggested royalty. No, they may get taken to the authorities or worse, kidnapped. Village women? Maybe, although their complexions and soft hands didn't exactly suggest a hard day's work in the fields.

Suddenly, Kunti spoke up. 'Nice to meet you, Zafar Kapoor. I am Kunti and these are my daughters – Amba, Draupadi and Gandhari.'

Draupadi, Amba and Gandhari looked over each other. All right, that made sense so far, since Kunti was the only middle-aged-looking one out of them. But now what?

Zafar nodded at the 'daughters' with a respectful smile and said to Kunti, 'Interesting theme with the Mahabharata names. Are you from Delhi?'

Kunti shook her head. 'No. We come from out of the city. We're ... landowners, visiting here for thirty days. The weather' – she waved an unconvincing hand towards the sweltering, dusty road beeping and bawling with the anger of a thousand machines – 'suits my health.' She smiled weakly to try and make it more plausible.

Zafar raised an eyebrow and laughed. 'Okay, you obviously haven't been to Delhi before. Where are you visiting from?'

Relieved, Kunti smiled. 'Indrap—'

'—*pur*!' Draupadi exclaimed loudly, startling everyone around her. Zafar gave her an uncertain glance. 'I meant Indrapur,' she said, giving Kunti the eye.

'Indrapur. I've never heard of it.' He frowned and with an unsure look asked, 'Is it near Ayodhya?'

Draupadi had no idea but said eagerly, 'Yes, yes. It is. Very small place. Almost a village.'

'Must be very different from Delhi. You've had a very rude introduction to it, I'm afraid. Please let me make it up by buying you lunch. Yusuf-bhai,' he said and turned to the man behind him, who had been sweatily fiddling with his black contraption and glaring at them during the whole conversation. He stopped and stared at Zafar with a now-what look on his face.

Zafar said with a placating expression, 'Sorry for this, Yusuf-bhai. Dinner is my treat. Let's wrap up for now and finish the story tomorrow. You take the van back to the office and I'll drive them in my car. If anyone asks, I'm on a recce. Cool?'

'Not cool but fine,' replied a still-peeved Yusuf-bhai in a deep voice. 'You do what you want, hero. Dinner better be kebabs.' He then heaved the contraption on to his shoulder and stomped off.

'Keep the tape with you,' Zafar shouted behind him and then turned to the women with an explanatory smile. 'Tape's still in the camera. We're doing a story on kids beating the heat by swimming in the India Gate fountains. We do it every year but it never gets old, somehow. Children who have nothing but the clothes on their backs, getting them soaking wet with disease-infested water – but they're happy, you know? Most people have a lot more and still can't figure it out.' He chuckled at the irony.

Draupadi, now tired, irritable and uncomfortably sweaty from the whole episode, could barely muster up her patience enough to say, 'Yes, yes. Happy children. How wonderful. In fact, we're looking for children too. We need to go to the Bal Raksha home for orphans in the Connaught Place area. Is it nearby? Maybe instead of giving us lunch, you could help us reach it.' He might as well be of some use, she thought.

'Of course, I know the place.' Zafar smiled. 'My friend did a story on it a few years ago. Rough crowd. Lots of kids from street gangs,' he said gravely. 'Why don't we have lunch first, and then I'll drive you there?' He then began to walk towards the road, gesturing for them to follow.

Draupadi met Amba, Kunti and Gandhari's eyes and nodded slightly. He seemed like a decent man. How bad could it be?

Chapter 9

This is what happens when you tempt fate, thought Draupadi as she hung on to her seat for dear life. She was sitting in the back of the chariot – what Zafar called his 'car' – and it weaved left and right on the road, darting between other cars so precariously that she was sure they would crash into one any minute. Zafar would swerve away from an oncoming car at the very last second, just barely avoiding a collision, and the other car would bellow at him with an ear-splitting shriek.

'Sort of like a chariot,' said Kunti in an attempt to make conversation. Her polite smile, however, was wiped off her face as she was thrown to one side when the car rounded a corner.

'Yes. Being driven by mad horses,' Draupadi politely replied as she tried not to lean too far on top of Gandhari.

Amba, who sat in the front seat next to Zafar, turned her head back slightly and glared at her with an if-you-can't-say-anything-nice-be-quiet look. Then she glanced at Zafar and said tentatively, 'You man this vehicle very well. I can imagine this is much like driving a chariot in the middle of an ongoing battle.'

Zafar frowned, a bit stumped, but recovered quickly and replied in a polite tone, 'Yes, well, not that I've ever driven a chariot, or been in a battle, for that matter, but I can imagine this might be similar. The noise, the dust – it is definitely similar in terms of how many people get killed every minute, for sure.'

'A lot of people die on these roads?' Amba asked.

'Oh yes. Accidents are so much a part of life here that newspapers don't even bother reporting them unless the people who died were famous, important or rich. Or the people who killed them are famous, important or rich,' replied Zafar with a small smirk. 'Crazy world. How about in Indrapur? Not too many cars there, from the sound of it.'

'No,' said Amba quickly, 'not many. It's very quiet. Most people just walk.'

'Sounds like paradise. I should check it out. Maybe take a few days off and go there to unwind. Does it have a hotel? Or maybe one of those old palaces that they usually convert into hotels?'

Draupadi glanced at Amba, who looked around desperately for help. Hotel? Gandhari and Kunti were equally clueless. She thought quickly. Old palace converted into something called a 'hotel'. What use could an old palace have? In her day, old palaces were gifted to deserving courtiers, or really old ones were converted into army barracks or temples. Maybe a hotel was like a temple.

She said, 'Er, yes, but nobody goes there any more because the resident god was said to have links with the demon world. Only an old priest lives there now, but he's gone mad, so ...' She laughed half-heartedly, as if that would help wipe out the look on Zafar's face, which suggested he thought she might be a little mad herself. It didn't.

Obviously, a hotel was not like a temple.

Ever the day-saver, Kunti chimed in with, 'Thank you for helping us. We are most grateful. How long is the journey to the orphanage?'

'Not long,' answered Zafar, with one last dubious glance at Draupadi. 'We're almost there now. Although an orphanage seems an unlikely place to spend a vacation. Any particular reason why you want to go there?'

Questions, questions, non-stop *questions*. If every mortal was going to be like this, their cover would be blown in no time. Draupadi was about to put this impudent interrogator firmly in his place when Amba said, 'Our relative in Indrapur told us about this orphanage. We want to help those poor children, make their burden a little lighter. Even the most unfortunate of destinies can be changed with a little love and support.'

Zafar's face softened into a smile, and he looked at Amba and said with some feeling, 'That's a beautiful thought.' And then, after a moment, 'Just like its thinker.'

Amba blushed and looked everywhere except towards Zafar. Draupadi's irritation vanished and she smiled a little, thankful that even though they dressed to look like cattle, were cowardly and disrespectful, travelled in cramped, noisy, murderous vehicles and questioned everything incessantly, at least mortals still knew how to flirt.

Then suddenly Gandhari, as if awoken from a deep sleep, piped in disapprovingly, 'That is what our *mother*' – she jerked her head towards Kunti – 'taught us. She also taught us not to talk too much and reflect in silence. I think this is a good time to do just that.'

Suitably chastened, Zafar drove in silence until the car reached a small building on the side of the road in the middle of a large marketplace with lots of large, dirty-white pillars and arches. A bright red sign hung above the door of the building and there were many people milling about outside, eating out of colourful parcels. Zafar stopped and began to get out, saying, 'Lunchtime! You all must be starving. I know I am. I could eat a horse!' He chuckled and slammed the door shut behind him.

'They eat *horses*?' Gandhari looked flabbergasted.

'Surely not,' whispered Kunti as Zafar walked around the car to open their doors on the other side.

'I'm not eating a horse,' whispered Gandhari urgently, 'or a cow. Or a monkey.'

'Maybe he can find you a mortal to eat,' whispered Draupadi sarcastically.

Amba giggled just as Zafar opened the door for her. He looked at her laughing face and his eyes softened. He stared, smiling, standing in her way as if forgetting that he needed to step away for her to alight.

Draupadi, Kunti and Gandhari looked on as Amba peered up at him, a little shy. She smiled back and they heard him take in a quick breath. Then, as if his own breath had snapped him out of a trance, he caught himself, stepped back and moved on to open the other doors briskly.

Draupadi caught Amba's eye just as they were getting out and raised an eyebrow, her face questioning. Amba shrugged slightly. Nothing to worry about, her face said. Draupadi wasn't so sure but was so looking forward to eating real food that she didn't give it another thought.

Chapter 10

Well, real food is relative, supposed Draupadi. The contents of her brightly coloured parchment parcel certainly didn't look like food. But judging from the crowds around her, noisily sitting on tables and eating with gusto from the same parcels, she concluded that it had to be edible.

Back when she was alive, Draupadi thought, food inspired the eater and was treated with respect. The way it looked, felt and tasted, and the effect it had on the body were all equally important. Palace food was served on gold platters, each delicate creation topped with a dash of cardamom-scented clarified butter or slivered nuts, and was encased in its own gilded bowl. There were tender leafy vegetables tossed in mustard, fried root vegetables in buttery, creamy curries;

there was goat, deer, boar or bird meat marinated in spices and cooked for hours over slow fires and then baked with fragrant rice or engulfed in unapologetically spicy gravy. The juiciest, sweetest of fruit was made into sweetmeats with velvety cow's milk, raw honey, butter and nuts, and sour or raw fruit was made into fresh, tangy pickles that made tongues dance.

Even villagers in her day enjoyed good food, Draupadi thought as she remembered eating hearty, cooked lentils and onions fried in mustard oil with chillies along with large, thick *rotis* roasted over an open fire until their outsides blackened and became crusty but the insides remained soft and raw. Every morsel, even a plain grain of rice or a humble berry, had flavour and personality.

This was ... she made a face as she looked down at what seemed like a flat cow dung patty in between two pieces of soft dough. She looked over at Zafar and saw him gingerly dip the side of the dough into a tiny tub of red paste and tuck into it. He seemed to be enjoying it. She bit a little tentatively and chewed. And chewed. The dough dissolved tastelessly in her mouth, while the meat – at least that was what she hoped it was – remained obstinately behind, fighting a valiant battle against being masticated.

'This is very good,' Amba coughed politely as she chewed. 'What is it?'

Zafar avoided looking at her, obviously embarrassed by his earlier gawping. 'It's a burger. Have you all never had one?' he asked Kunti.

Kunti, struggling with her own mouthful of belligerent burger, shook her head irritably. Draupadi could sense that she was getting overwhelmed by the noise and impatient to get to the orphanage. She didn't blame her. The noise and commotion inside the eating house was like being inside a birdhouse, its relentless cacophony enveloping them like a blanket. It frazzled the nerves and saturated the senses. What was it with the noise level everywhere, she wondered. One didn't even get a break from it indoors.

Gandhari hadn't touched her burger. She sat stoically staring at it before she spoke. 'What is it made from?'

Zafar smiled at her. 'Well, my guess is cardboard mostly, but they say its bread and meat. In the rest of the world they use beef, but that would never sell in India so they say its mutton. You can never be too sure though. Are you vegetarian? Sorry, I didn't ask. I can get you something else, if you like.'

'Yes. Get me something else,' said Gandhari haughtily, looking at her burger as if it was going to bite her instead.

Zafar looked a bit surprised at her impolite tone but immediately got up with a cheerful, 'Sure. Be right back.'

They waited till he was out of earshot before starting to speak. Draupadi said to Gandhari, 'It was rude to refuse to eat. He has been helpful, or at least he's trying.' She gave her burger a disgusted look. 'Just eat the next thing he brings you.'

Gandhari looked distressed. 'Believe me, I would never refuse food as someone's guest. It goes against everything I have been taught. But' – she gestured to her parcel in disgust – '*how* can they eat this?'

Kunti looked up, a weary look in her eyes. 'I don't know. I don't recognize this world. It screams constantly.' She held her head in her hands. 'My mind hurts and I feel like weeping. The only thing that keeps me going is that I will see my son soon. We must go.'

'Stay strong,' said Amba softly, putting an arm around Kunti's shoulders. 'We must remember that the mortal world is in Kalyug, and chaos is bound to be the norm. Before I went into battle, I was told to meditate, focus my mind on my goal and shut out all the noise. We must all try to do that now.'

Kunti nodded resolutely just as Zafar returned with a parcel containing almost exactly the same thing as the one in front of Gandhari, only the flat dung-like thing in between the dough was a bright yellow colour.

He gestured at it before handing it to Gandhari and said, 'This one is vegetarian. Aloo tikki.'

Gandhari nodded as if she knew what that meant, taking the parcel with a pained smile. 'Thank you. This is much better.'

Draupadi couldn't help but smile at the thought of Gandhari's imminent distress. But as pleasurable as it would be to watch her put away each bite, the sooner they ate, the sooner they could get out of here. So she picked up what was left of her burger, took a deep breath and a big bite.

Chapter 11

Buildings merged one by one into each other as the car sped past them. They all seemed to be conjoined in a hideous canvas of colours and shapes. And yet, some of them were awe-inspiring, reaching high into the sky like the towering trunks of giant trees. Draupadi wondered what it must be like to live in the realm of birds.

The car came to a halt in front of a small, dilapidated grey building of two floors that wore a big sign above the door which read: 'Bal Raksha Home for Children. Opened by His Honourable Minister of State for Welfare 1980–1981, Shree Bridul Ram Chandra Mathare Kapilapuri BBA.'

Zafar stopped the car outside, next to a broken iron gate, and gestured to the building. 'This is it. You should be prepared to see the worst though. I've heard some nasty things about this place. It caters to the red-light area close by. Lots of street cartels and gangs operate in this area too, so it can get pretty dangerous, especially at night. I'll come in with you.'

'Thank you,' said Amba, as they all got out and looked around.

There was a small, muddy yard area in front of the building where clothes had been hung out to dry on strings tied between the gate and a window grill. Under the dripping clothes a few very young children toddled around, looking perfectly at ease, if a little resigned, with their hollow eyes, distended bellies and ragged clothing. They played listlessly, aiming small rocks at bigger ones, kicking at bits of rubbish in the mud and generally looking around disinterestedly. There were no adults with them, nor was there any barrier between them and the busy street a few paces away, with its speeding, smoke-spouting vehicles, foul-mouthed hawkers swearing at each other and weary pedestrians hurriedly weaving through rubbish-strewn, broken paths. The children seemed to be instinctively aware that they needed to stay inside the yard and not one of them ventured near the street.

Such wisdom at such a young age must have come at a terrible price, thought Kunti. She shuddered.

Her heart squeezed painfully as she saw how malnourished the children were. Somewhere in there was her own child; and now she began to dread what she was going to find as they walked towards the front door of the orphanage.

Inside, the windowless hallway was shrouded in darkness and the musty smell of dirty linen, sweat and stale frying oil. They could hear the echoing sounds of a baby crying somewhere inside, of children talking and also of two girls shouting at each other in the distance.

Kunti turned to the others and spoke firmly: 'Why don't you all go play with the children outside and I'll go look around in here.' She smiled tremulously.

Zafar was about to object, but Gandhari replied before he had a chance to say anything, 'Yes, mother. Call us when you need us.' She began to herd everyone out.

Draupadi watched Kunti venture further inside for a moment. It was probably better that Kunti didn't have an audience for her reunion with Karan. She said a quick, silent prayer for it to go well before turning around and following the others outside.

Meanwhile, Kunti had walked into another darkened hallway leading off the first one. She had only passed a few closed doors when a woman's voice, old and gnarled from decades of chewing tobacco, stopped her in her tracks.

'Well, well, well, I'll be damned. You're from up there, aren't you? Hold on,' it drawled, seemingly out of nowhere. Then, out of a rotting, dirty door that Kunti had passed a moment before emerged a tiny, stooping old woman dressed in a faded brown sari. She looked to be of about eighty to eighty-five winters, with a ratty tail of grey hair over one shoulder and no teeth to speak of in a stinking, black mouth that grinned widely. She waddled towards Kunti, looking dangerously close to tipping over with every step, but her eyes – her eyes were breathtaking. As she moved closer, Kunti saw them gleaming like emeralds in bright, parrot-green glory at her own face. They were luminous, hypnotic, almost unworldly.

'You,' the old woman croaked again when she stopped next to her. 'You're from up there, aren't you? I can smell it. It's been so long since I've smelled heaven. Too long.'

Kunti was at a loss for words. Where did one go from here? Should she confess? Or pretend that she didn't know what the woman was talking about? More importantly, how did she know?

The old woman seemed to read her thoughts with those eyes and saved her the trouble of answering by lifting one wrinkled, trembling hand to brush at Kunti's hair and saying wistfully, 'It hangs on you like a blanket, its dust. Heaven, such a place. Who are you? You are not a god or a demon or anything in between. You must be a former mortal. But then why aren't you reincarnated?'

Kunti gulped and said, 'I'm Kunti, queen of the Kurus, mother to the Pandava brothers. Wife of ...' She faltered and shook her head ever so slightly. No, those things were not important any more. She wasn't anyone's queen, mother or wife any more. She was just Kunti, a heavenly being. She took a deep breath and tried again. 'I am Kunti. I've been allowed to visit the mortal world. By Krishna.'

The old woman laughed, twisting her murky mouth. 'Krishna. Such a romantic, ever the little boy. He liked that particular mortal stint. Had so much fun that he kept it. The others were much more tedious. That Ram avatar was a positive bore. Anyway, still having fun, I see.' She expelled something between a cackle and a snort. A black blob of spittle hung precariously from her open lips.

'Who are you?' whispered Kunti.

The old woman raised the wrinkled skin where there would have formerly been an eyebrow and said with a chuckle, 'You don't recognize me? Why, I thought it would be obvious with my dazzling beauty.' Another cackle, followed by, 'I am the Goddess Saraswati, of course. In my mortal avatar as Shashiben, the long-suffering warden of this dump.'

Kunti was stunned. This decrepit old woman was a goddess? How could that be? Gods and goddesses didn't look like this, even as avatars. They were born beautiful and stayed beautiful and miraculous until they left their bodies. They were enlightened, all-knowing and had powerful magic at their disposal. Mortals flocked to them worshipped them, and called upon them to save or destroy kingdoms, slay evil in all its forms and to spread peace and prosperity.

'That was then, this is now,' said Saraswati, reading Kunti's thoughts again with her goddess eyes. 'They discontinued that formula. Mortals were getting too used to us solving their problems for them, apparently. Made them lazy and fatalistic. They started using our names to justify their tyranny and wars. Made it political. They're smart buggers.' She tapped her forehead with one forefinger. 'They'll use anything you give them to their own advantage. But then, that's how they got this far, I guess.'

She sighed. 'Anyway, this' – Saraswati waved a gnarly hand over her body – 'is the new formula. We still have to be do-gooders but now we look like them, function like them and' – another sigh – 'we don't get to keep our powers. Don't have control over when it ends either. If I did, I would have opted out a while back. Instead, I have to wait, let disgusting mortal diseases humiliate this rotting body and die, like any other common criminal on the street.' She spat that black blob on the floor in disgust.

She looked up at Kunti and said, 'So you're visiting. Kurus, ah, yes, I know you. You're the one that let your baby go in the river. I was watching when you did that. Despicable. You should have been reincarnated for that one. But the rules were different then, I suppose. A lot was different then.'

Kunti burned with shame at the mention of Karan. There was no excuse for what she did. She knew that, but still she said, 'I didn't think I had a choice.'

Saraswati let out another cackle-snort. 'That's what you mortals don't understand. You *always* have a choice. It's all about the choices you make. The problem is that you, all of you, want it the easy way. Who says it has to be easy? This ridiculous sense of entitlement is what gets you all into trouble.'

She rolled her eyes. 'Day after day, these whores come here to leave their children, each one weeping louder than the last. They don't think they have a choice either. They do have a choice, just like you did. It's the harder one, but it's there. Instead, I get stuck with their brats. Their snotty, sad little brats who will grow up to be just like their parents. Not because they want to, but because they don't think they have a choice either.'

She laughed a brittle laugh. 'Mortals! So brave in some ways and so cowardly in others. So willing to die for a cause, yet so unwilling to live and suffer for it. As if death is such a big sacrifice. I have tried to teach them, to show them the way. I have lived in hell holes, sacrificed my last grain of food, suffered and toiled to change the way they think. For nothing. Nothing has changed. A complete and utter *waste* of my time.' She spat again and looked at Kunti, her eyes still as intense, but her smile utterly gone.

Kunti was shaking as she replied, 'How can you be a goddess and be so unforgiving? Gods made mortals—'

'Ah, yes, gods made mortals.' Saraswati was on a roll now, waving her arm about, eyes flashing. 'Another excuse! Pass the blame to *us*! You know, the big guns up there have been talking about annihilating the mortal world for a while and I was against it. "Give them another chance," I said. "Let me go down there," I said. Well, I'm going to go straight back up there, once they release me from this damned, mortal straightjacket, and tell them to blow this place to smithereens. Now, enough with this little debate.' She glared at Kunti. 'Why are you here, of all places? I would have thought you'd have more enjoyable things to do and see on your little vacation.'

Kunti battled within herself. Saraswati, the wise and learned goddess she had always heard about, was nothing like this bitter old hag. On the one hand, she felt obliged to argue on behalf of the mortals. But on the other hand, she had her own situation to think about. And that, right now, to her, was far, far more important.

'I'm looking for the orphan Karan. I've been told he lives here,' she said softly.

Saraswati's eyes narrowed. 'And what business might you have with the orphan Karan?'

Kunti was silent for a long moment as her brimming eyes held Saraswati's. Then she whispered, 'He is the baby I left in the river.'

Chapter 12

'I see,' said Saraswati darkly. Her eyes softened for a half-moment before returning to their burning glare. 'That's why you came down, is it? And what do you hope to accomplish by meeting him? Are you going to apologize? He doesn't remember you or his previous lives; but I'm sure you already knew that.' She cocked her head, studying Kunti intently.

'I just want to see him,' said Kunti firmly. Her reasons, however illogical or impractical they might be, were none of Saraswati's business.

Saraswati considered Kunti one last time before she sighed softly and turned and said, 'If he's here, he'll be in the common room. That way.' She pointed down another hall. Then she looked over her shoulder at Kunti. 'That's if he's here. Otherwise, he'll probably be on the street, gambling or begging so he can buy a peg or worse. Or he may be with those loafers he calls friends, stealing purses from coffee shops or buses. I would not get my hopes up, my dear. It is the Kalyug, after all.' With a last, weary glance at Kunti, she turned and hobbled away.

Kunti fought not to burst into tears again at those words. What had her son done to deserve this? How many lifetimes would he have to suffer before his dues were paid? She clutched her head in her hands and balled her fists in her hair, her anger and sorrow threatening to break her again. Then she shook her head furiously. 'Enough!' she whispered to herself fiercely. This moaning and weeping was weak and indulgent. She steeled herself, straightening her back and looking ahead. She had to be strong if she wanted to help him. Pushing aside her sorrow, she walked determinedly in the direction that Saraswati had pointed.

Her heart raced as she rounded a corner and heard whoops of laughter and teasing coming out of one of the doors. Voices, obviously young boys, traded insults beyond:

'Oy, BC, I'll get you!'

'Hah! Try, you MC. I won it, I get to keep it.'

'Come on, bastard, give me some back, na? I'll owe you later.'

'Fuck off. I'm not giving you shit.'

Startled, Kunti peeped into the room. Inside, was ... Karan. She knew him the instant she laid eyes on him.

He was a thin, gangly boy with a medium complexion. A perfect row of even teeth shone through a wide, sneering grin as he held a small wad of money up in the air, out of the reach of the shorter boy in front of him. He face would be craggy when he became a man, much as it had been when Kunti last saw him. He still had brown eyes, much like hers, even in this lifetime. The look in them, however, was very unlike her own. His were hard eyes. The kind that people earned by surviving hell and by becoming the essence of it. An old scar, running from the outer corner of Karan's right eye down to the top of his cheekbone, seemed to fit in perfectly with the persona his eyes reflected.

Karan looked down at the boy in front of him menacingly. 'Get it straight, *chutiya*. Mine. Besides, you fucking cheated anyway.' He smiled knowingly.

The shorter boy's dark, thin face was puffed and angry as he stretched up and grabbed at the money in vain. His eyes spit hatred at Karan as he wailed, 'I didn't cheat!'

'Y-you did,' stammered a small, sallow-skinned boy who stood back behind a table strewn with playing cards and watched the other two bigger boys. 'I saw you cheat, Raja,' he said simply to the shorter boy.

Raja turned his spitting eyes on him. 'Shut up, Goalie, nobody asked you, You want me to call up that freak who wanted to fuck you? I swear I'll sell you to him for a fucking joint and watch you scream like a girl when he sticks it into you.'

Kunti watched in horror as Karan laughed and then suddenly grabbed Raja by his t-shirt, slammed him against the wall and said, 'The only one who will be screaming is you, bastard, in one minute. While I pound your fucked-up face.'

Raja's bravado quickly dissipated upon the threat of physical assault and he starting whining, 'Come on, Karan. I need it, yaar. Ustaad's men will come looking for me tonight.'

His eyes dilated in fear and tears rose quickly to the surface. 'I haven't made my quota for a month now. They won't give me another chance. They'll kill me, Karan.'

Kunti watched a storm of indecision rage on Karan's face as he stared at Raja. Then, after what seemed like a long time, he brought the money forward and peeled off a few notes. 'This' – he held the money up in front of Raja's face – 'is a loan. Only because I need you tomorrow for our job at the park. I'll take it out of your share. Got it?'

Raja quickly took the money, relief flooding his teary face. He stashed it away deftly into his underwear, looking around furtively once before he replied, 'Got it.' Then he stalked off out the door, past Kunti without even noticing her.

She peered into the room again and saw Karan and the younger boy start to pick up the cards. The rest of the money had obviously been hidden away.

Goalie looked at Karan and said, 'Don't trust him.'

Karan shrugged as he looked down at the cards. 'I don't. Not him, not anyone. Let's go. I told Ustaad's guy I'd be staking out the dairy tonight.'

This was her chance. Kunti took a deep breath and entered the room, looking expectantly at Karan.

Karan and Goalie jumped at her entry, instantly hiding the cards behind them. They frowned at her suspiciously.

Kunti cleared her throat and said softly, 'Karan?'

His eyes darted around the room, as if plotting a quick escape. Seeing none, he lifted his chin as his eyes assessed her. He said with forced nonchalance, 'He's left. You just missed him.' He turned to leave quickly.

Kunti stepped forward hurriedly. 'I know who you are. It's all right. I'm not going to hurt you.' She reached towards him and touched his shoulder.

Karan flinched as if her touch had burned him and slapped her hand away violently, his face filled with disgust. 'Don't touch me, you bitch, or I'll break your hand.'

Kunti said desperately, 'Please, just speak with me for a moment. Karan, I'm your ... we are ... we are family.'

Karan stopped in his tracks and stared at her, shock written all over his face. He looked her up and down incredulously, and for a tiny moment, Kunti saw a child's vulnerability in those hard eyes. Then it was gone, replaced by anger.

'My family?' he asked sarcastically. 'Which side? Must be the crack whore's because there's no telling who my father was.' His face contorted with contempt as he came closer to Kunti. 'How are you related to the crack whore?'

Kunti didn't know what to say. She had seen Karan angry before, but never like this. When she had revealed to him that she was his mother the last time, he had been bitter and upset, but respectful. He had behaved in the manner expected from a Kuru prince. This Karan, whose mouth spewed filth and body recoiled from her touch, she couldn't fathom. She didn't want to lie to him and yet she couldn't bring herself tell him the truth either. She said sadly, 'I've been looking for you for a very long time, Karan.'

Still contemptuous, he moved his face threateningly close to Kunti's. She noticed that despite being so young, he was as tall as she was. He said, 'Should have looked harder, bitch. You're eleven years too late.' He turned around and stalked out of the room. Goalie stared at Kunti with wide eyes before hurriedly running after Karan.

You're too late. Kunti's tears flowed down her cheeks as she remembered a scene from a few millennia back. A memory that had haunted her ever since. She had stood weeping on the far side of a battlefield as Karan had turned to her, splendid in his royal robes and jewellery, with his gold plated bow in hand, and said bitterly before bowing and walking away, 'You're too late.'

Chapter 13

At first, when the four women had gotten back to their plush chambers in the zoo toilet that evening, they were quiet. Amba and Gandhari sat on their beds and meditated with utter relief on the quiet walls around them. Kunti lay down, sniffing and heaving, as if she had spent all of her tears but none of her sorrow, and Draupadi paced the room slowly, wringing her hands behind her back, unable to unwind.

From a large window that was obviously invisible from the outside, she saw the sun setting in the sky. Draupadi's eyes blinked as she considered how much it had changed. In her day, sunsets had been soothing, their weak, pale orange light floating lightly upon tired faces back from toiling in fields or markets. Birds would stop chirping wearily and the crickets and frogs would start in their stead. Sunsets in her day had been moments for quiet reflection and respite before the pleasures of the fire-lit night began.

This sunset was different. Its bold, reddish hues slashed across a bright orange sky almost angrily. This was a sunset that seemed to be preparing for battle, egging the mortals upon whom it shed its anxious light on towards more destruction and chaos.

Then again, thought Draupadi, maybe she was the anxious one.

She looked over at Kunti, who had been behaving completely out of character since hearing Narad Muni's news about Karan. It was as if flood gates, standing strong for thousands of years in front of her heart, had now burst open, allowing a giant river of emotion to wash over her. This new Kunti, so full of open sorrow, was unrecognizable. Draupadi, feeling somehow responsible for her turmoil, wished she had never asked Kunti to come along for this trip. Had she known about Karan's situation … She sighed. 'It has been anything but an easy day.'

Gandhari let out a bark of laughter. 'That's putting it mildly. It's been a journey through hell.'

Amba shook her head. 'I know it's been a lot to take in for one day but I wouldn't call it hell.' She turned to Kunti and said softly, 'It's been especially difficult for you, seeing Karan like that and having him speak to you the way he did.'

Kunti peered up at them from her bed. Her eyes were bloodshot from crying non-stop, but her voice was steady as she said, 'No words can describe it. It rips a mother's soul apart to see her child suffer. If I could take on his karma, his debts … his pain and suffering, I would. In a heartbeat.'

She got up. 'But I can't. All I can really do is to try and make things better for him. The last time I allowed him to push me away. This time, I won't let that happen. This time, I'm going to make a difference in his life. It doesn't matter if he never forgives me. Before I leave, I must help him. I don't know how, but I must try.'

Gandhari nodded. 'Good idea. We will help you. God knows I have seen enough of the mortal world to know that I wouldn't like to see very much more of it. There is so little beauty left in this place. Gone are the forests and the orchards, the deer and the song birds. Gone are the streams and flowers.

Gone are the colours of the market and the smells of nature. I didn't expect to meet with such an ugly world.' She sighed, a small tear threatening to overcome a disappointed eye. 'And so our time is better spent in a purposeful way. What do you say, Amba, Draupadi?'

Amba smiled vaguely. Draupadi, after a brief spell of panic, forced herself to breathe deeply and think. After all, this trip had been her idea, and no matter how shocking their first day had been or how guilty she felt about bringing Kunti along, she certainly had *not* had her fill of the mortal world. She had no objection at all to Kunti and Gandhari spending the next twenty-nine days at the orphanage if that made Kunti feel better. But she had other plans.

'Now, let's not get disheartened, ladies,' she said. 'Kunti, I applaud you for your resolve to improve Karan's life while you're here. I will strive to help in any way I can. But I intend on discovering more about this world. I have so many questions that need answers.' She began to pace again. 'Where are all the birds? They have to be somewhere because I can see their droppings everywhere. Why was it so freakishly cold inside that eating house? Why is everyone in such a hurry? How do people climb up and down those tall buildings? And, most importantly' – she twisted uncomfortably – 'how do I take off this damned bra?'

Amba and even Kunti, for all her sorrow, cracked a smile. Gandhari's lips twitched but she held back.

Draupadi looked at them with earnest eyes. 'Let's not get disillusioned with the mortal world after just one day. Let's give it another chance. Soon, it will be time for us to go back and enjoy heavenly comfort as we did before, and these days and nights will be relived only in memory. Let us not waste this opportunity to experience something, *anything* before going back to eternal sameness. Even if none of it turns out to be good, at least it will be different.'

Amba stood up and faced the others. 'I agree with Draupadi. Let's also not forget that amid the chaos we encountered today, we also met with kindness. We met someone who welcomed and helped us and asked for nothing in return. Humanity still exists obviously, even in this Kalyug, and we should seek it out and let it shield us from the chaos.'

Draupadi suspected that Amba's enthusiasm may have had more behind it than just Zafar's humanity, but at this point she needed the support. God forbid one of them called Narad Muni prematurely. She was not going back yet! She turned to Gandhari and Kunti. 'Yes. Let's do that. Zafar, the kind man' – she tried not to look at Amba – 'has invited us to his home tomorrow. Let's go and see what happens. I promise we will go to the orphanage later,' she added in Kunti's direction.

'All right,' said Kunti, her air of grief not entirely dissipated but in control once again. She had a restrained look that Draupadi recognized. It was the Kunti she had lived with for so long, the one that had been trained to hide her thoughts and plans behind a genial, careful face. Draupadi felt a sharp twinge of sadness for her helplessness in what was obviously a hopeless situation. Karan's destiny was his own and, try as she may, Kunti wasn't going to be able to change it in a few days. No, she'd be better off with a couple of distractions to occupy her mind. Draupadi looked at Gandhari and raised an eyebrow.

Gandhari's usually disdainful, confident demeanour was gone and in its place was a worried, slightly fearful frown. She took a deep breath and said, 'This world, it is, well, it is a scary place. I will do as you ask but promise me that we will stick together, and at the first sign of danger, we will go back.'

Never one to shy away from danger, Draupadi nodded a little impatiently. 'Yes, of course. I promise.' She exhaled, resolutely put on a cheery face and started looking around. 'And the ... what did he call it? Ah, phone. Yes, let me have it' – she picked it up from a table – 'for safekeeping. And let's find that rice pot, for heaven's sake. I'm starving!'

She looked around for the rice pot and realized that it was beginning to get quite dark in their chambers. The sun had disappeared behind the horizon and tiny spots of light from the zoo structures behind the trees barely reached their invisible window. Night was fast approaching and there didn't seem to be any stars or a moon in the sky to allow them meagre light.

Draupadi cast her gaze around, squinting her eyes in the almost-dark. No firewood, no fireplace, no fire holders. Nothing that even remotely looked like it could be set on fire. She muttered, 'What should we do for light? Any ideas?'

Gandhari replied, with just a tiny note of superiority in her voice, 'We can do without it. Let us quickly memorize the layout of the chambers so we can feel our way around later.'

Draupadi snorted in a most unqueenly way. 'I won't believe for a second that the old man feels his way around in the dark when he stays here. There must be some provision for light. I'll call him and ask.'

She looked squintingly at the phone and found the button that he had told them to press to find his voice. She pressed it once and put it on her ear, heard nothing, so pressed it again a few more times.

Eventually, Narad Muni's annoyed voice came screeching from inside the device, 'Enough, enough! Stop pressing buttons, I have delicate ears. What is it, woman?'

'There is no provision for a fire here. We need light,' shouted Draupadi at the top of her voice into the phone.

'Then put on the wall switch!' Narad Muni sounded even more irritated, if that was possible, than his usual self. 'And *don't* call me again tonight. I'm *busy*.'

'What's a wall switch?' Draupadi shouted hurriedly. But it was too late. The phone had gone dark and stared silently back at her. She exclaimed in anger and pressed the button again. A little light and a few numbers flickered on the surface of the phone but no Narad Muni answered her, no matter how many times she pressed the button.

'Damn you, old man,' Draupadi shouted and, in a fit of temper, flung the phone at the wall.

'No!' Gandhari screamed and launched herself at the flying phone. In the dim light, however, she misjudged the distance between herself and the phone and landed on top of a chair that fell sideways with a crash and took her tumbling to the floor with it. Meanwhile, the phone hit the wall with an ominous thud and clattered somewhere out of sight on to the stone floor.

'You fool! You stupid, stupid *fool*,' Gandhari shouted hysterically at Draupadi. 'That was our only way to contact him. If it's broken, we're stuck here!' She began to crawl on the floor, frantically feeling around for the phone.

Draupadi would have probably acknowledged that it wasn't the wisest decision to throw the phone had Gandhari not reacted so wildly. That she had, however, only served to further enrage Draupadi. Enough was enough!

She snarled into the dark at Gandhari's shadowy form, 'How *dare* you insult me? This is the second time you have called me a fool and, by God, it will be the last.'

She ran towards Gandhari and tripped over her loose skirt, losing her balance and falling to the floor. Meanwhile, Gandhari stood up straight and snarled back, 'You want to fight? Come here and I will show you a fight!' She started making her way towards Draupadi, who was scrambling to stand up.

'I'll show you first!'

'Draupadi!'

'Gandhari, no!'

Amba ran to Draupadi and Kunti ran to Gandhari before they could reach each other and tried to hold them back. But they were smaller and weaker than their charges and were easily thrown off.

The two women met in the middle of the room, grabbed each other by the hair with one hand and the throat with the other. They pushed and shoved and grunted as they struggled with each other. Draupadi slapped Gandhari with all her might and tugged hard on her hair, her hand coming away with a fistful of Gandhari's long, beautiful, wavy locks. Gandhari in turn squeezed harder on Draupadi's throat until she began to feel light-headed.

Behind them, Amba and Kunti tried to pull them away, loudly lamenting, 'This is madness!' and 'Stop it, you'll kill each other!' to no effect whatsoever.

As she felt Gandhari's fingers vice-like on her windpipe, Draupadi realized she was going to lose consciousness if she didn't do something quickly. So she gathered up every ounce of strength she had left, put her palm on Gandhari's chin and pushed her away hard.

Gandhari lost her grip and fell back with a loud *thud* against the wall, and suddenly the room filled with light.

All four women gasped and turned around. The crystal sculpture hanging from the ceiling was illuminated from within by what seemed like the light of a hundred bonfires.

'It's Krishna!' exclaimed Kunti.

They dropped to their knees at once and bowed their heads. Draupadi cursed herself silently. This was it. He was here to tell them that they had made a royal mess of matters, and that they were unworthy of staying. He was going to take them back. Tears filled her eyes, not from the throbbing pain she felt in her head and neck where Gandhari had gripped her, but from despair.

'No,' she moaned. 'Please don't take us back, O Krishna! I'm sorry. I'm so sorry.'

She looked up at the light, tears streaming down her eyes. 'Give me another chance. I will control my temper, I promise.'

Gandhari was crying as well. 'I'm sorry. I should know better. It's just as well you're here, O Krishna. Take us back, for this Kalyug is turning us into monsters!'

'*No!* Take her back. Leave the rest of us here,' implored Draupadi, pointing towards Gandhari.

'Shhh, Draupadi,' Kunti whispered. 'Enough.' Her face bore a tragic expression as she looked up at the light, resigned to her fate.

Only Amba had remained silent. She was staring at the light curiously. It was brilliant indeed, but there didn't seem to be anything moving inside it. 'Krishna?' she ventured softly and then when she got no response, got up and looked at the light more closely. 'Krishna? Is that you?'

Draupadi and Kunti met each other's gaze for an uncertain moment. Draupadi then spoke in a croaking voice, 'Krishna, why are you not answering us? Are you angry? I'm sorry.' She looked at Gandhari and, as much as it pained her to apologize, said, 'I'm sorry, Gandhari. I'm responsible for our safety and I acted rashly and' – she gulped – 'foolishly. Forgive me.'

Gandhari glanced at the light quickly and replied in a tight voice, 'I'm sorry I insulted you. Forgive me also.'

Draupadi nodded and looked away hurriedly. Even looking at Gandhari – with her dishevelled hair and bruised red cheek – was unbearable. How she wished she had left her behind in heaven. Too late for that. The best she could hope for now was to keep the peace until their trip was over and ensure that neither Gandhari nor anyone else cut their time short.

She looked back up at the cold, unresponsive light. 'There, see? We've made peace. Forgive us, Krishna,' she pleaded softly.

The light said and did nothing. Not a flicker, not a sound. They looked at each other, puzzled.

Then Amba, who was already standing, reached for a chair, pulled it under the crystal sculpture and stood up on top of it. She stretched her hand out and touched it tentatively. Kunti and Gandhari gasped at her audacity. Draupadi watched carefully as the sculpture moved gently at Amba's touch.

Amba touched it again, this time giving it a small push. It swung, taking the light that shone inside along. 'It's cold,' murmured Amba, 'and hard. The light is coming from within the sculpture.'

Draupadi frowned. Then something occurred to her. She got up and looked at the wall against which she had pushed Gandhari. A small, flat white square was stuck on it at about shoulder height from the floor. When she went closer, she saw a small protrusion sticking out of the square. She touched it gently. Nothing happened. She pressed it, and with a gentle click, the light in the sculpture disappeared, plunging the chamber into darkness.

The women gasped again. Then, as Draupadi pushed the protrusion once more, the sculpture lit up as before, illuminating the room. She pushed it a few more times to be sure, plunging the room in and out of darkness and finally filling it once again with light.

'The wall switch,' she murmured incredulously. 'This is what he meant. That' – she turned to the light sculpture – 'is what we use for light. It's not Krishna.'

She looked at the others and after one brief, dazed moment, all four of them burst out laughing.

They took turns climbing on the chair to touch and push the light gently, each of them whispering their amazement and incredulity. Cold fire. What surely could it be but magic? It defied explanation and everything that they knew to be natural.

Draupadi ran into the outer chambers, found the wall switch and turned on the light in the other crystal sculpture. It burned with the same cold brightness. The light of a hundred bonfires but with none of the searing heat, pungent smoke or unforgiving ferocity of flames.

'Amazing,' she whispered. What new miracles await us tomorrow? she wondered. She decided to make sure that the phone was not broken and placate Gandhari, for there was obviously so much more to this world than they had seen that day.

She fixed a conciliatory smile on her face determinedly and walked back to the others. Luckily for her, if there was one force even more indomitable than her temper, it was her charm. After all, she had successfully juggled five men continuously for the better part of her mortal life. Compared to that, Gandhari was going to be a walk in the park. She hoped.

Chapter 14

They walked in a single line up three flights of narrow stairs to Zafar's home. He lived in a blockish, grey building with an open staircase in the middle that connected six homes, two on each floor. Zafar's building was one of many identical ones, each surrounded by a patch of grass overrun by parked cars that looked just like Zafar's car. This particular one had a sad-looking tree in front of it, and Draupadi spotted a couple of crows in the branches. Ironically, they gave her hope.

Zafar, leading the group, stopped in front of his door with a wide smile. 'I'm so glad you could join us today. My mother and my sister are looking forward to meeting you all.' He knocked loudly.

The door swung open a moment later and a pretty woman, barely more than twenty summers, with an upturned nose, a round face and bouncy hair falling to her shoulders grinned broadly when she saw them. 'Well, well, well. *Ammee*, come look at Bhaiya's gorgeous new friends!'

Zafar rolled his eyes and turned to Kunti. 'Please don't take any notice of this girl. I have no idea who she is. At some point, my *polite* and well-mannered sister, Sania, will show up.'

He waved off Sania, who stepped back giggling as she eyed Draupadi, Amba and Gandhari and said with a teasing look, 'Wow, you guys look like models. Not bad, Bhaiya, you're moving up in life.' She giggled again as Zafar glared at her while herding them into the room. Then, she looked at them and waved. 'Hi, I'm Sania. I'm his much younger, more attractive and far more interesting sister.'

Zafar snorted, 'You wish.' He turned to Kunti. 'Sania is in college, studying to become a fashion designer. Although you would never know it from the clothes she wears herself.'

Now it was Sania's turn to snort. 'Have you *seen* what you're wearing? I'm cutting edge, baby,' she said as she waved a hand over her clothes. She was dressed in a figure-hugging black top that looked as if it had been slashed by a knife, with tassels hanging over her shoulders and short – very short, thought

Draupadi – light blue pants that ended snugly at the tops of her thighs. Her legs were almost completely bare. A fact that Gandhari was taking note of disapprovingly.

Draupadi smiled. She liked this bare-legged girl. She reminded her of herself when she was young. Of course, Draupadi *looked* as young as Sania right now, but she had none of this fresh-faced, innocent and playful spunkiness any more. A long life and an even longer afterlife had taken it out of her.

Amba looked around the modest sitting room, which was simply but elegantly decorated with stunning depictions of landscapes. She touched one of them – a field of flowers – hanging on the wall and was a little surprised when all she felt was cold glass. 'It looks so real,' she murmured, 'I've never seen a painting that could so perfectly replicate reality.'

Gandhari walked over to where Amba stood and touched a depiction of jagged, brown mountains in the background against a strikingly blue sky. In the foreground, within a grassy valley, was a rugged-looking shepherd in a blue tunic with the same fair complexion as Gandhari. He sat surrounded by a mass of sheep as they grazed lazily around him, his light brown eyes surveying the dramatic landscape.

Her eyes lit up as she stared at it for a long moment with a nostalgic smile and whispered, 'I thought I would never see this again. It's—' Her throat caught and she turned towards Zafar and asked, 'Is this Gandhara?'

Zafar frowned and looked a bit puzzled as he replied, 'You mean Peshawar ... yes, it is. In Pakistan.'

Gandhari asked, 'Have you been there?'

It was Zafar's turn to nod and reply, 'I have. Went there a few years ago for a story. It's got a really rugged, stark landscape. Used to be one of the most beautiful places in the world.'

Gandhari's face fell. 'Used to?'

Zafar sighed. 'Well, I don't know if you keep up with the news, but there's been conflict raging there for decades – much of it has been razed to the ground. Bad drought in the rural areas, virtually no law and order outside the city. It's not a very pleasant place, to say the least.'

Gandhari's face fell and she was barely able to hold back her tears as she turned once again to the depiction. She stared at it for a few long moments before closing her eyes with a deep sigh. A tear rolled down one cheek.

Amba quickly stepped in front of Gandhari and pointed at another depiction, of a gypsy woman smoking a pipe against a backdrop of sand dunes.

'This one looks so real,' she said.

Zafar glanced at Gandhari worriedly for a moment but then followed Amba's gaze and said, 'It is. It's a photograph, actually. Photography is one of my passions. Landscapes are considered passé these days, but Delhi is such a noisy, concrete-filled city that I like to fill our home with the scenic and natural parts of the world. They bring a sense of peace into the space.'

Amba looked up at him. 'These places, these scenic, peaceful and natural places still exist?'

Zafar smiled at her. 'Yes, absolutely. You have to leave the madness of the city to find them, but they're there, untouched by the noise, people and pollution. You should know, right? You probably come from one of them.'

Amba blinked, but recovered quickly. 'Yes … yes, of course. I only asked because … well, we haven't travelled much. And you – you made this?' She nodded at the picture and smiled.

'I photographed it, if that's what you mean,' said Zafar softly, unable to take his eyes off her.

'It's beautiful,' she murmured, meeting his gaze.

Here we go again, thought Draupadi in amusement; but before she could finish the thought, a middle-aged woman dressed in a sari walked into the room. She was short and plump, and her face had probably been fairer when she was young, but now had the darkened patches so common in overweight women whose menses had ceased. Her features were sharp but surrounded by puffiness and her pert, upturned nose identified her as Sania's mother.

'Finally, a sari. They tie it differently,' whispered Gandhari so only Kunti and Draupadi, standing next to her, could hear.

Draupadi looked at the sari the older woman was wearing. Whatever small comfort she gained from seeing it at first quickly dissipated when she noticed that it was brown, with tiny, even browner flowers drawn into it. She had never seen a brown sari before. What was it with mortals wearing brown clothing on brown skin? She couldn't think of anything more boring. In her day, the only things around them that were brown were mud, tree barks and excrement.

Zafar walked up to the woman and put his arm around her 'Ladies, this is my mother, Mrs Nazli Kapoor. Ammee, these are the ladies I was telling you about, Mrs Kunti Kuru and her daughters Draupadi, Gandhari and Amba.'

'Wow, hard-core names,' blurted Sania before being silenced by her brother's fierce look.

Mrs Nazli Kapoor's fluttery eyes looked the women up and down for a brief second, probably decided that they looked respectable enough and motioned for them to have a seat. 'Welcome to our home. Zafar told me what a horrible experience you girls had yesterday at India Gate. I don't know what has happened to the men in this country any more. They've become monsters. Every day in the papers about some horrible rape or the other. Terrible, just terrible' – she shook her head – 'Allah will punish them in the next world, I suppose, because certainly no one is doing anything about it down here!'

She looked at Kunti. 'Three daughters! You must be very worried about them, Kuntiji. Your husband is at home?'

It took Kunti a moment to register her question. Husband? She had never really had one in the true sense of the word. She was married to an impotent prince for a short while. He had forced her to have sex with another man so she could produce heirs to the throne. Then he died and she barely ever thought about him. Kunti shook her head, her expression evasive as she sat down along with the others. 'My husband has passed.'

That brought her instant sympathy from Mrs Kapoor. 'Same as mine. He passed when Zafar was still in college. He was a lecturer at Delhi University. Very well-respected, but as you know, professors are not wealthy men. I really had to struggle those first few years until Zafar started working. If it wasn't for my parents and the people at our masjid, we would have gone hungry.'

'Ammee ...' Zafar began weakly, but his mother was already in the middle of what was probably a well-worn rant. She dismissed him with a shake of her head and continued, 'I had run away with my husband, you see. He was a Hindu. We were very young and just out of college. Both our parents disowned us, although his parents came around when Zafar was born. They died when the children were young, you know. But mine did not speak to me until my husband died. Twenty years without seeing or speaking to them and I showed up at their doorstep, a widow with two mouths to feed and all our savings gone in a few months. Imagine my condition—'

Zafar stood up, embarrassed. 'Right. Ammee, let's leave something for later, okay?' He turned to his guests asked, 'Can I bring you something to drink? Some tea, coffee or nimbu pani?'

Mrs Kapoor also stood up. 'Yes, yes of course. I'll make you some tea. Sania makes terrible tea so I've stopped asking her. Come, come with me to the kitchen and we can chat some more. No formality.'

Draupadi got up after exchanging a few glances with the others and followed Mrs Kapoor down a short and narrow hallway into a brightly lit room which was overrun with utensils and laden with wall cupboards. An imposing grey metal box stood to one side, and on the opposite side of the room, water boiled in a pan that was placed on top of what looked like a black plate with claws. Draupadi went over to it and ascertained that water was indeed boiling inside and there was a small blue fire directly under it. But, no wood or anything flammable was to be seen. The fire seemed to be magically coming out of the plate. 'Incredible,' she murmured to herself. She chuckled, remembering having to slave over leaves, branches and stones in the forest every time they had to move camp.

Mrs Kapoor bustled about busily, bumping and elbowing them out of the way as she moved around in the now-cramped room. 'Forgive the size of the kitchen. I know it's small but there are just the three of us at home. Oh, and Bosco, of course. *Boscuu*,' she shouted shrilly, making Gandhari jump and glance at her as if she were a little mad.

A soft bark answered her from the other room. She chuckled and continued her chatter. 'He'll come out when it's dinner time and he can smell his khichdi. Poor thing is very old now and completely blind but his nose is still as sharp as ever. He can smell his dinner from a mile away!' She busily prepared the tea as Sania came in and leaned against the door of the kitchen. She reluctantly asked, 'Should I help?'

'You,' Mrs Kapoor exhaled dramatically, 'you'll have the kitchen in flames. Can't boil an egg, this girl,' she said to Kunti, 'I don't know which man is going to marry her. She is going to be a *fashion designer*, if you please.' She taunted Sania gently with exaggerated exasperation. 'Tell them. About how you're going to be famous and how you don't need to get married because you'll be able to support yourself.' She looked back at Kunti meaningfully. 'Girls these days ... although I'm sure *your* daughters are not like that at all! They look like good girls. Decently dressed at least.' She shook her head, her expression perfectly portraying her sorrow and resignation at her own unbearable situation.

Sania looked embarrassed as she peeked at Kunti and her 'daughters'' faces to see their reaction to her mother's words. She said sullenly, 'It's not that I *don't* want to get married, Ammee. I want to marry someone who respects me and respects my work. I don't want to be a child-bearing donkey with no control over her finances or future!'

Draupadi stared at Sania as yet another memory of her mortal self rushed back into her mind. She was standing in her maiden room in her father's palace, wildly pacing up and down like one of those caged animals she'd seen in the zoo. She had just been told that she was to be married to five men because her father decreed it to be so. Without a single thought about her will or preference. Or reputation, for that matter, for being married to five men had pretty much ensured that she was spitefully called the 'queen of prostitutes' in female quarters of palaces across the land for the rest of her life. On that day, Draupadi had railed against a future without respect, a future where she would have no control over her life, a future as a mere 'child-bearing donkey'. As she looked at Sania now, she saw a glimpse of her former self in the young woman's sullen face.

'She compares having children to being a donkey, I tell you,' Mrs Kapoor said to Kunti with a big sigh and then turned to Sania. 'Am I a donkey? Having you and Zafar has been the greatest achievement of my life! I love you and want to protect you, you stupid girl, and I also want you to be happy. You can't be happy in a man's world, dressing like that and having men stare at you all the time—'

Sania bridled angrily. 'Let them stare. Who cares? This is who I am. And why can't women work? Man's world, women staying at home barefoot and pregnant, not showing skin – Ammee, these are all old-fashioned notions. Times have changed and you're still stuck in the past. Go to Zafar's office. Half the people working there are women. My class in college is mostly women. The CEOs of massive companies, major politicians, artists; seriously, the world is different now. Your world might be limited to what goes on inside the masjid—'

Zafar's firm voice rang out from the living room, 'Sania, I think you've made your point.'

Sania pursed her lips and finished defiantly, '—but mine is not.'

A painful moment of silence descended upon the kitchen, until Mrs Kapoor plastered an equally painful smile on her face and said to Kunti, 'Tea is ready. I hope you'll stay for lunch too. We always make biryani on Sundays. I hope you're not vegetarian. Oh, what's that, Zafar? Gandhari is? Well, then you'll just have to pick the meat out of the rice, beta. As it is you girls barely eat anything nowadays ... Should I put some sugar for you, Kuntiji?'

Chapter 15

Food. Ah, glorious, *real* food! Finally! This day was turning out to be so much better than yesterday, Draupadi thought to herself as she indelicately plied herself with mouthful after mouthful of the aromatic meat and rice biryani that Mrs Kapoor had made. She sucked and picked at the melt-in-your-mouth marrow that hid in the bones of the meat, nibbled the spicy dried chillies and smacked her lips as she chewed juicy pieces of fried onions that danced in her mouth with the fluffy rice. She felt the smooth goodness of a boiled egg yolk on her tongue and sighed in ecstasy. Then, as she caught Sania's quick glance in her direction, she made a mental note to slow down and not eat as if she hadn't had a bite of real food in centuries.

Despite being perched uncomfortably on a chair with her plateful of food on a table, Draupadi felt optimistic about the days to come. Families still existed, and she was utterly relieved that mortals still ate well sometimes at least.

She cast her gaze around and saw Amba, Kunti and Gandhari tucking into their platefuls of biryani with equal relish. Gandhari had even happily forgotten saying that she didn't eat meat. Mrs Kapoor ate slowly, deliberately, staring down her food as if she hated it for tasting good and making her want to eat more. Zafar and Sania ate matter-of-factly, with metal instruments instead of their hands, focused more on their guests than the food itself. Draupadi caught Zafar glancing at Amba when he thought no one was looking. She really hoped this was not going to become a problem. The last thing they needed was for Amba to get involved with a man. She should discourage Zafar from meeting them more on this visit, but the other mortals they met had been so unfriendly. She supposed, with a small sigh, she could manage to keep both of them in check. It was for less than thirty days after all. How much could possibly happen in so short a time?

'Well, I'm happy to see your daughters have healthy appetites, Kuntiji.' Mrs Kapoor smiled a little meaningfully while assessing their plates. It was difficult to tell whether she meant that as a compliment or an insult. Her next words cleared that up. 'Although it's not good to eat too much, girls, if you know what I mean. Of course, after you are married, things are different, but men these days are very fussy and these girls in the magazines and the movies are just getting skinnier and skinnier. You must have a good figure now before you get married.' She pushed her plate away from her with semi-disgust and addressed Kunti tentatively, 'Have you thought about their marriages, Kuntiji?'

Kunti wasn't prepared for the question. She glanced around awkwardly and focused on chewing her mouthful of rice. But Mrs Kapoor keep looking at her expectantly so she mumbled, 'Er, yes. I have given it some thought.' Her tone clearly implied she didn't want to pursue this conversation.

If Mrs Kapoor got the hint, she ignored it. 'And what are your thoughts? They look marriageable age. Have you got any boys in mind for them?'

Kunti glanced at Draupadi, Amba and Gandhari for help. Draupadi opened her mouth to say firmly that none of them had any intention of getting married but Gandhari, probably anticipating what Draupadi might say, quickly spoke up, 'Mother is considering some good matches, but right now she has not decided on anyone.'

Draupadi almost snorted in amusement. They were old, old women. Had any of her children survived she would have been a grandmother so many times over it was uncountable. The very thought of being married again was not only ridiculous but repellent. Five times was enough, thank you very much.

'Oh? For whom? Which of you is the oldest?' Mrs Kapoor was not going to drop it.

They looked at each other. Technically, Amba was older than all of them, even Kunti, who certainly looked the oldest.

'I am,' Amba said softly, looking at her plate.

Zafar glanced up, surprised, and then looked back at his plateful of food again.

Mrs Kapoor nodded approvingly. 'You are cooperating with your mother for an arranged marriage. That is very good, beta. Your parents always do what is best for you.' She sniffed in the general direction of Sania with a wounded expression on her face but managed to hold her tongue. Sania, for her part, already had a warning glint in her eyes.

When she was done throwing meaningful glares at her mother, Sania piped up and asked Amba with a smile, 'What kind of husband do you want?'

Amba looked a little disconcerted for a moment but recovered quickly with, 'I haven't really thought about it. Someone nice.'

'Well, there are definitely no nice guys left in the world. You're going to keep looking for the rest of your life!' Sania laughed but then stopped abruptly when she noticed that her statement had made Amba look distressed.

Zafar noticed her change of expression too and gave his sister a reproachful glance. Sania shrugged sheepishly and tried to make up. 'Amba, I didn't mean that the way it came out. *Of course* there are nice guys out there. Look at my brother, he's awesome!'

That only made Amba, and Zafar, look awkward. Sania shook her head desperately. 'Not that I meant you should marry *Zafar*. I just meant that there are generally nice guys in the world and he is just an *example* of ...' She sighed. 'Never mind. Have you guys been shopping in Delhi yet?'

Draupadi perked up immediately. She had always loved shopping and wandering around in the marketplaces of all the kingdoms she visited. Disguised as a maid, of course. Royal women usually waited for vendors to bring their wares to the women's quarters of palaces, but Draupadi found many more treasures on her secret excursions to the marketplaces. A trinket, a new fruit she had never tasted before, a rare piece of cloth from a faraway land. She loved the colours, the smells and the vibrant atmosphere that were to be found in marketplaces everywhere and how different they were in different kingdoms.

'No, we haven't.' She leaned in towards Sania with sparkling eyes. 'Is there a market in New Delhi?'

Sania's eyes widened. '*A* market? Babe, there is a market around every corner. There are hundreds, if not *thousands*, of markets in Delhi. Wow, you really come from a small town, huh?'

Zafar cleared his throat softly and Sania blinked before continuing, 'Anyway, I can take you shopping if you want. Maybe you could pick up some new clothes.' Her expression was painfully polite as she looked at the clothes they were wearing but the disdain in her eyes couldn't be missed.

Even a mortal woman thought their clothes were horrible. Draupadi silently cursed Narad Muni and his taste in women's clothing.

'Do new clothes cost a lot?' Gandhari looked intrigued but also a little worried.

'No, don't worry. We can go to Janpath, where they're pretty cheap and you can bargain like hell. I'm a really good bargainer.' Sania smiled smugly. 'Are you free tomorrow?'

Draupadi didn't bother asking any of the others. 'Yes, we are. We will like that very much. Thank you.'

Sania beamed. 'No problem. Maybe Zafar and I can pick you up? What do you say, bro?'

Zafar looked quite pleased as he replied, 'Sure. I have to go to office in the afternoon, so I can spend the morning with you. In fact, if we're going to Janpath, I could check out the antiques place if they have any new knives in stock.'

'Oof, you and your knives.' Sania rolled her eyes and then, after noticing the puzzled expressions of their guests, she explained, 'Zafar has a weird fascination with antique weapons. Bows, arrows, knives, swords, etc., etc. A bit creepy, I know, but he is generally a pretty non-violent type of guy.'

'Really?' Amba's eyes lit up as she looked at Zafar. 'That's interesting. I actually like weapons too.'

Sania snorted. 'You?' Then seeing Amba's slightly offended reaction, she quickly said, 'It's just ... you're so pretty and delicate. I can't imagine you holding a sword or a knife.'

Amba shook her head. 'Looks can be deceiving. I know how to wield many weapons.'

She remembered being introduced to battle weaponry the day before Arjuna took her on to the battlefield to use as a mortal shield in his quest to kill Bhishma. He had armed her with a sword and a small dagger, just in case he fell and she needed to fight her way out. She remembered standing opposite him in the Pandava army camp, a worn, elderly spinster dressed in a man's battle armour, in whose eyes a fire had been relit years after she had lost hope of revenge against the man who had destroyed her life. She had lunged at Arjuna ferociously in the practice session. He had not been a keen teacher, his mind and conscience busy trying to reconcile the fact that not only was he going to take a woman into battle, but he was also going to use her as a shield. Dastardly to say the least, but he had explained, with tight lips and a pinched face, how there wasn't much choice. They needed to kill Bhishma or would lose the war. After the rather hopeless practice session, she had been subject to a hurried and simple prayer ceremony and been declared, in front of all the soldiers, reborn as a man. They had called her Sikandi. Amba smiled. They had really been desperate at that point.

Anyway, that practice session had inspired an interest in weapons and she had spent many a pleasant morning thereafter learning how to wield them with the palace soldiers who, during times of peace, didn't have much to do and always referred to her as Sikandi anyway. She played along and continued to dress as a man. As Amba, she had been largely ignored. As Sikandi, she was given respect.

'Really?' Zafar asked her, intrigued. 'I can show you my collection, if you like. It's right here, in the other room.'

Amba's eyes lit up with excitement. 'I would love to see it.'

Zafar smiled and stood up. 'Come with me.'

'Er, do you think ...?'

'Don't you have to ...?'

'Really, Zafar, we are still eating.'

Draupadi, Gandhari and Mrs Kapoor looked at each other and politely stopped speaking, waiting for the other to go first. Draupadi noticed a slightly desperate look in Gandhari's eye. Obviously, she had the same concerns about Amba and Zafar. Mrs Kapoor, completely oblivious to the undercurrents in the situation, merely looked miffed that her meal was being interrupted.

Finally, Gandhari spoke, 'Don't you have to ask *Mother* if you can go?' She looked at Amba with a stern glint in her eyes.

Now it was Amba's turn to be miffed. Draupadi didn't blame her. She wasn't answerable to either Kunti or Gandhari.

Amba addressed Kunti firmly. 'Mother, I am going to take a look at Zafar's weapon collection. Any objections?'

Despite her own apprehensions, Draupadi was amused at Amba's tone, which warranted no argument and, in fact, got none from Kunti, who silently nodded her assent. Amba was easy-going most of the time but could be as obstinate as a badly-trained bull when she chose to be.

Draupadi watched Amba and Zafar turn and disappear behind a door down the hallway. Then, she and Gandhari glanced at each other and shared, for a brief, awkward moment, a look of mutual concern before being distracted by Mrs Kapoor, who stood up, grumbling, 'Just like him to leave like that. His father was exactly the same, never one to wait for everyone to finish. Come on, girls, help me clear up and then we can have something sweet. I might have some gulab jamuns left in the fridge. But don't have too much, remember what I said about your figures. *Men* ...' She shook her head and sighed loudly. 'But what to do? Somebody has to pay the bills. Gulab jamuns don't come for free, girls. Remember that.'

Sania made a face. 'I can buy my own gulab jamuns.'

Mrs Kapoor didn't bother looking at her as she muttered, on her way to the kitchen with plates in hand, 'Do that. And eat them – alone.'

Chapter 16

The hair on his arms brushed against hers briefly and she stepped back abruptly, barely suppressing an audible intake of breath. She shouldn't have been standing so close to him.

'And this one is from the nineteenth century. Daggers are usually easier to find. Swords are more difficult.'

Zafar stood next to a large wall cupboard which he had opened earlier to reveal a substantial collection of weapons, each carefully mounted against the back wall or meticulously arranged on a shelf. Knives, daggers, swords, axes, a battered-looking bow, a broken spear and a few others she didn't recognize. They had all obviously been polished lovingly but no amount of care could have restored them to their original beauty. Some were tarnished beyond repair or chipped. Some were in pieces, others had torn holsters or handles. He lovingly brushed an imaginary fleck of dust off the large dagger he held. His voice was low, affectionate, as if he held not an old, rusty piece of metal but a child in his hands.

'May I hold it?'

Zafar looked up at her and smiled, an intrigued light in his eyes. 'Sure,' he said, handing it to her carefully.

She took it from him and turned it around in her hands. Memories of battle came flooding back as she felt its familiar contours and that sense of command, that thrill, which always ran through her when wielding a weapon. She schooled her reaction because Zafar was watching her carefully. A small flick of her wrist and it was positioned, blade forward, for attack in her palm. Keeping a firm grip on the carved handle, she very slowly and carefully lunged at an imaginary opponent in front of her, attacking from the front, with one arm poised next to the dagger and her knees bent.

'Whoa, easy with that thing.' Zafar laughed and put his hands up in mock defence, even though he was standing out of her way. 'Funny, I always imagined a dagger like that would be held over the head and brought down in an attack.'

Amba shook her head, smiling. The slow pulse of excitement that had begun when she heard about his collection had now begun to course through her body. She could feel her heart throbbing hard against the wall of her chest.

'No, you wouldn't do that. By putting your arm up over your head, you would leave your chest open for your opponent. See?' She positioned the dagger high above her head and demonstrated.

Zafar's eyes flickered from the dagger to her chest and then, as he realized where he was looking, slid immediately back to her face.

Amba, caught up in the moment, sprang back as though preparing to lunge. 'If I were to come at you like this, then you could pull out your own dagger, bend downwards—' She mock-lunged at him very slowly with her armed hand in the air and her other hand coming up under her. She pinned her stomach with her free hand, just as her hand with the dagger was poised halfway to Zafar in mid-air. 'And stab me in the stomach.'

Zafar stared back at her. He wasn't smiling any more. He nodded. 'Okay. So if you attacked from the front, how does your opponent fend you off?'

'You sidestep and grab my arm.'

'You're holding a dagger. You could stab my arm.'

'Not if you hold my wrist and twist it upwards. Give me your hand.'

Zafar held out his hand. Amba slowly mock-attacked him from the front with the dagger. Just as it almost reached him, she stepped a little to the side, caught hold of his hand and directed it to her wrist. 'Just here. You grip my wrist tightly. No, like this, yes, and then you push my arm back and upwards with the force of your body and at the same time, use your hand to twist my wrist so I'm forced to—'

Amba jerked Zafar's hand over her head into the air with the dagger, and he instinctively stepped forward so he could catch it in case it fell on her. They ended up standing almost chest to chest, their arms joined in the air, their bodies close enough that Amba could see a tiny birthmark on his day-old-stubble-covered chin. She felt the warmth radiating from him and heard his breath, short and sharp, as it left him.

'—drop it.'

It came out as a croak. Zafar seemed not to have heard. They just stood there, looking at each other.

CLANG!

The noise, sharp and sudden, cut through the moment like a ... dagger. They jumped apart. Amba's eyes widened in alarm as she realized what had happened. The dagger. Oh dear god, she had dropped it!

They looked down at the floor next to them. The dagger had landed on the stone floor and the impact had broken the handle and the blade apart.

'I'm so sorry!'

'Are you okay?'

They had spoken together. Amba bent down and picked up the two pieces, exclaiming remorsefully, 'I'm sorry. I'm so sorry.'

Zafar was more concerned about her. 'No, it's fine. Don't worry about it. I hope it didn't hurt you as it fell?'

Amba was furious with herself as she shook her head and saw disappointment and embarrassment, mixed with concern, in Zafar's eyes as she handed the broken dagger back to him. Disappointment and embarrassment he was valiantly trying to disguise. Foolish woman, she chided herself, acting like a juvenile with no thought for prudence or the future.

'Oh hell. It's ripped your skirt. Did it get your leg?' Zafar was frowning as he peered down at her skirt.

Amba bent and felt her skin behind a long, jagged tear in her skirt. It was untouched. The loose folds of her skirt had probably deflected the dagger away from her leg.

'No, I'm not cut,' she whispered. 'I'm, I'm so—'

'Don't worry about the dagger. I can get it fixed. No, seriously,' he said at her crestfallen face, 'it *can* be fixed. It was a mistake, Amba. Don't be upset, it's really not that big a deal. I'm just glad you're not hurt.'

Amba couldn't think of anything to say, other than, 'I'm so sorry' again.

Zafar brushed it off with a smile. He put the dagger back into the cupboard carefully and asked, 'Do you want to see any of the others? You're welcome to, you know.'

Amba took a shaky breath. 'I think I've done enough damage for one day. Shall we join the others?'

Zafar considered her carefully for a moment before replying, 'Okay, if that's what you want. But seriously, it's not a big deal and you're welcome to try them out any time you want. You're obviously really knowledgeable about combat and I would love to talk some more about your moves. And maybe next time, we can try them out without almost killing each other.' He smiled.

That birthmark on his chin was even easier to see when he smiled, thought Amba as he turned away to close the cupboard. She almost ran out of the room.

Chapter 17

Women usually had one of three expressions on their faces when they emerged in company after consorting with a man. The first one, and perhaps the least common, was a look of power coupled with an almost catlike, languid grace.

This woman always demanded food and drink to be brought to her immediately, with a suggestive smile, as if to imply that her body needed nourishment after such a rigorous and taxing appointment.

The second look was one of tight-lipped resentment, usually coupled with an intense desire to bathe, tidy a room or scold anybody in the vicinity for the most minor of misdeeds. This disgusted-and-irritated-with-everything-that-anybody-does mood sometimes lasted for days after the appointment. This look was the most common, unfortunately.

And then there was the look similar to the one a dog had after getting caught rummaging in the food store. Guilt, shame and regret, coupled with an elaborate pretence of the appointment never having occurred at all. This woman fidgeted a lot, never looked anybody in the eye and almost always wanted to talk, in great detail, about the most trivial and irrelevant of things.

Which was exactly, Draupadi noted, what Amba had been doing ever since she emerged from the room down the hallway.

'I didn't taste the cardamom at first, but I tasted one about halfway through the meal. The chilli, of course, one could taste from the first bite. My favourite bit was the fried onions. I must take the recipe from your mother,' Amba rattled on as she, Draupadi, Kunti and Gandhari lounged in the sitting room with Sania. Mrs Kapoor hadn't emerged from the kitchen yet and Zafar had gone in to help her after locking the cupboard.

Sania smiled politely.

Draupadi smiled very impolitely. 'I'm happy to see that you enjoyed your ... biryani.'

Amba glanced at her, saw the teasing in her eyes and looked away quickly, her cheeks becoming a little flushed. She scanned the room, desperately searching for another topic of conversation. In one corner was a flat, wide rectangular box with a grey glass front surrounded by a black frame. It was perched on top of a rather narrow metallic stand. She pointed to it and asked Sania, 'What is that thing?'

Sania gave her another one of those which-backwater-do-you-come-from looks before answering, 'It's a TV? You *do* know what a TV is, right?'

From Amba's slightly confused look, she gathered that she didn't.

Sania raised her brows. 'Wow. How is that even possible? Even villages have TVs these days. I've seen news stories with people sitting in their huts watching Doordarshan, for god's sake. How could you not know what a TV is? Do you live in an ashram or something?'

Amba just looked even more flustered and confused so Draupadi jumped in. 'Yes.'

Good thing ashrams still existed. Tucked away in the forest, away from civilization, life in an ashram could be gloriously disconnected from society life. 'We do, actually, live in an ashram.' Draupadi smiled at Sania, thinking on her feet. 'It's in the forest near Indrapur. We've all grown up inside. There is no TV in the ashram.'

Sania actually looked a little fearful at the prospect of growing up without a TV. Her eyes were wide as she said, 'Yeah, but they didn't even tell you what a TV was? What is it, like an Indian version of the Amish or something? Even those naked sadhus watch TV these days!'

'Sania, don't be rude.' Mrs Kapoor walked into the room from the hallway. She looked apologetically at Kunti. 'This younger generation doesn't appreciate that life existed before televisions. You know, we were taught in the mosque that the TV is the root cause for the spread of evil in the world. Teaching the children to be lazy, selfish and all these ads, spreading a culture of buy, buy, buy all the time. Young people watching all these bloody, violent programmes and the, you know – very wrong.'

Kunti nodded, as if she knew exactly what Mrs Kapoor was talking about. 'Yes, after my husband passed when the girls were very young, I brought them up in a small ashram outside Indrapur. It has been a simple life for them and so they are not familiar with the outside world much.'

Mrs Kapoor looked approvingly at 'the girls' as she put little brown balls into small bowls of syrup and passed them around. 'A simple life is best, especially for girls. Now, boys are different. You need to educate them so they can earn a livelihood. But girls, the less you expose them to the evils of modern life, the better.'

Sania's head was in her hands as she muttered, 'I'm going to kill myself.'

'Please don't,' Zafar said as he entered the room with a sigh aimed at the two women in his family. 'Life would be so boring without the two of you going at each other.'

He looked at Kunti and 'the girls', carefully avoiding Amba's eye. 'My mother and my sister have very different views on women, as you can see. But don't take them at face value. My mother is far less traditional than she sounds, and believe it or not, Sania is more conservative than she looks. But of course, if they actually agreed on anything, the earth's atmosphere would cave in on itself, so they feel it their duty to keep arguing for the survival of the species.' He sat down and smiled. 'What were you talking about?'

Sania was quick to reply, 'They've never watched TV before!'

He raised his eyebrows. After a quick explanation from Sania about their 'ashram upbringing', Zafar smiled at them and said, 'How refreshing! Here, let me show you.'

He got up, picked up a slim black object and pointed it towards the TV. Suddenly, the grey glass burst into colour and turned into a painting. Only, this painting seemed alive and there were people inside it and they were moving and talking to each other and there was music in the background but no musicians to be seen. Each time Zafar moved his finger, the painting on the TV changed into something new: people fighting, singing, dancing, talking, cars crashing into each other amidst huge explosions, words and lights of different colours flashing everywhere. It was dizzying, but exciting too.

'So the concept of Television is fairly simple,' began Zafar as he changed the pictures on the TV by pressing on the black object once again.

Sania sighed. 'Should I come back in an hour?'

Zafar smiled at Sania's cheekiness and replied, 'Fine, I will make it short. Essentially, this TV box is a receiver. It receives an electrical signal from another location through its antennae, or these days through its cable, and converts whatever is being sent to it into a picture for the viewer watching the TV. The signal is transmitted through multiple sources to take it from location to location but it always has a source. That source location could be a studio or outdoors somewhere, or in the case of a television channel, the source is the channel itself. The content the viewer sees could be live, as in happening in real time, or pre-recorded, as in it was recorded previously, edited and then transmitted later. Each channel, which has a number, represents a different TV station. Each TV station is competing for the viewer's attention by trying to put forth entertaining content, which is funded mostly by advertisers, who in turn try to support programming on the most popular channels so that their products receive brand recognition and, in turn, are chosen by viewers in the market. Does that make sense?'

Zafar looked around hopefully, only to see five utterly confused faces, including his own mother's, staring back at him. A very amused Sania cleared her throat and asked, 'May I?'

Zafar rolled his eyes and handed over the black thing to her. 'Fine.'

Sania held up the black thing and showed it to everyone. 'This is a remote. Got it?'

Five heads nodded.

'This is a TV. Got it?'

Heads nodded.

'Good. When I press this remote, the TV comes on. When I press different buttons, I get different channels. Each channel has something different for me to watch. Some have stories, some tell me the latest news from around the world, some are about music, some are about travelling, some are about cooking, etc., etc. Basically, I can watch whatever I am interested in.'

'Now, you see those people inside the TV? They're not actually inside this box. They are somewhere else, far away from here, some are in different countries all over the world, but I can see them with this TV. Think of the TV as an extension of your eyes. With it you can watch whatever you want, wherever you want, whenever you want. And everybody has a TV in their house these days – well, almost everybody it seems – so they can all watch the rest of the world in the comfort of their own home. Isn't that amazing?' Sania smiled.

Draupadi was stunned. It was possible to see anything in the mortal world with TV eyes? 'Surely, this must be magic.'

'No magic, only technology,' Zafar piped in, smiling.

'How?'

Zafar cocked his head to one side. 'Well, I *did* try to explain the technology earlier—'

Sania interrupted sarcastically, 'And how well you did. Masterful explanation!'

Zafar ignored her. 'But *obviously*, it is a little complicated. Why don't you all come to my office tomorrow after we finish shopping and see for yourself? I did mention that I'm a TV journalist earlier but you wouldn't have known what I meant, of course. I report the news on a TV channel called NPTV. Yesterday, you met my cameraman while we were covering a story. It's really fascinating when you understand the technology behind how the camera records the footage—'

Sania groaned and turned to Draupadi. 'Could you guys just please agree to go to his office so he shuts up?'

Zafar put up his hands. 'Okay, okay, I'm done. As you can see, my sister has very little patience with anything that requires an actual IQ so I could just explain it all to you tomorrow, at the office.'

Draupadi was fascinated. She couldn't wait to find out more about how the TV worked. She looked over at Amba, Kunti and Gandhari, hoping they shared her interest and was disappointed. Amba looked distracted and Kunti and Gandhari had polite but slightly aggrieved smiles on their faces. In fact, Kunti even shook her head slightly before saying, 'I'm afraid I cannot accompany you tomorrow. I must go to the orphanage.'

Gandhari was quick to add in a loud, meaningful voice, 'Yes, and I will accompany Mother to the orphanage. Amba, Draupadi, I think you two should—'

Draupadi addressed her firmly. 'I think that is a good idea. Mother will probably get tired. You take care of her at the orphanage, Gandhari. Amba and I will join you after we have finished our visit to the TV office. What do you say, Amba?'

If Amba had the urge to look at Zafar before answering, she quickly quelled it and replied softly, 'Yes, all right.'

'What do you say, Mother?'

Kunti's eyes harboured a little concern when she glanced at Draupadi, but she quickly blinked it away when she saw the determined look on Draupadi's face. 'Yes, yes, that is fine. Join us there when you have finished and, uh, take care.'

Mrs Kapoor smiled kindly at Kunti to reassure her. 'Don't worry about them, Kuntiji. My Zafar is there with them. He will take good care of your girls.'

If Draupadi hadn't been sitting right next to Gandhari, she would have probably missed her mumbling under her breath, 'I'm sure he will.'

Chapter 18

There were rows upon rows of stalls laden with colour and sparkle. Down the entire length of the street, as far as the eye could see. Clothes, jewellery, shoes, bags ... everything a woman could possibly desire, and more.

'Oh!' exclaimed Draupadi. For once, she actually felt the age she looked, a young woman thrilled at the prospect of buying a new wardrobe. Her fingers brushed against the dull grey fabric of her loose shirt. She would burn it later.

Amba's eyes were lit up in excitement too. Part of the reason might have been the presence of a certain someone who, along with his sister, had picked them up outside the zoo this morning and now stood next to her, of course, but Draupadi couldn't worry about that right now. There was some serious shopping to be done.

'Okay, so this is our strategy,' Sania said conspiratorially to her and Amba as they stood at the beginning of the clothes street, or as Sania had called it, the 'fashion street' in Janpath market. 'We walk by in front of each stall and look at the clothes. The men will invite you inside. *Don't* go in, or they'll jack up the prices immediately. Stand outside and look bored to death, as if you're doing the guy a favour by even looking at his clothes. If you like something, you turn to me and say something like "look at that, it's decent I guess, but I doubt it will fit me" or "that might match my pants but it's so ugly" or "my mom would kill me if she saw me in that thing", okay? Then I'll ask the guy what the price is. Whatever he says, look shocked and say "seriously, that's way too much" or even just say "seriously?" as if you can't believe it. Then we will start to walk away, slowly, looking very put off. The guy will panic and call us back with a new, lower price. *Don't* walk back otherwise he won't budge further. Instead, we'll stand at a distance with our backs half-turned away saying we can't buy it until he quotes a price that is acceptable to us. Then, and then only, we walk back to him half-heartedly, as if we're doing this against our better judgement, and say that we'll take it but only if he gives us a fresh piece, from the back. Oh, and never take out all your money and count it in front of them, otherwise they'll get a pickpocket on you before you can buy anything else. Just take out the exact amount you need. Got it?'

Not really, thought Draupadi, but she nodded her head, as did Amba. Gandhari had carefully counted the money last night and suggested they divide it equally amongst themselves. She had been very worried that Draupadi and Amba would spend it all on clothes. Looking at this street and all its wares, Draupadi admitted she might have been proven right had she allowed them to carry it all. Either way, she was glad Gandhari wasn't with them on this expedition. Zafar had dropped her and Kunti off at the orphanage after remarking on how they must really love animals, this being the second day he was picking them up from the zoo. Upon which they had needed to make up yet another tale about how they were staying with an ashram member who lived very close to the zoo but they didn't want to impose. Draupadi sighed. She just hoped she could remember all the elaborate excuses that seemed to be piling up with each conversation.

Sania smiled. 'Good. Now, Zafar, it would really help if you periodically said "are we done yet?" and "let's go, I'm bored" whenever we are bargaining. The bored male companion is an excellent negotiating tactic.'

Zafar didn't look like he needed any encouragement for that. 'With pleasure.'

They began to walk by the stalls one by one, Sania pointing out pieces of clothing which might suit Draupadi's figure or Amba's complexion in furtive murmurs. The men standing in front of the stalls solicited them in much the same way as vendors in the markets of her time used to, beckoning them over with promises of lower prices and better wares. Sania ignored each one haughtily, casting appalled glances at the clothes they offered. Draupadi couldn't help but smile at the girl's penchant for the dramatic.

She came across a stall which, instead of tailored clothing, sold long pieces of cloth with colourful designs. Finally, something she was familiar with! Draupadi walked up to a piece of bright, multi-coloured cloth with a bold floral pattern on it and picked it up, admiring its beauty. Then she remembered Sania's instructions and made her face void of any expression. She looked at Sania and said, 'Look at this, it's decent, I guess, but I doubt it will fit me.'

Sania's obvious pleasure that Draupadi had followed her instructions was soon replaced by bewilderment when she looked down at the garment that Draupadi was holding. 'It's a sarong,' she declared.

The stall's puzzled vendor, a young man, looked at Draupadi and said, 'No size. One size fit all. 500 rupees.'

Sania ignored him. 'Beach wear? Don't you think you should buy something to wear in the city while you're on holiday?'

Draupadi frowned. 'I *was* planning to wear this in the city. It's perfect for this weather. We wear this kind of thing all the time in hea—the ashram. Only, we don't have such lovely patterns.' She smiled as she opened up the cloth enthusiastically. 'You drape it over your legs, under the belly button. It's pretty, falls well over the hips and you can adjust it in many ways that are very appealing.' She smiled.

Sania made a face. 'O-kay. And what do you wear on top?'

Draupadi looked around and saw a small wisp of yellow cloth hanging in the stall. She picked it up and held it over her breasts. 'You just wrap this around on top and tie it at the back,' she said, as if that were fairly obvious.

Sania's eyes widened, 'And nothing else?'

Draupadi thought for a moment and then said, 'Well, you could take another small piece of cloth and drape it over your shoulders if you wanted to be modest.'

Sania's eyes widened even more. 'You expect me to believe you walk around in the ashram wearing nothing but a handkerchief over your boobs and the rest of it bare for all to see?'

Draupadi shook her head. 'No, our legs are covered—'

'And are there *men* in the ashram?'

Draupadi nodded.

Sania looked shocked. 'And they don't like, *look* at you?'

Now it was Draupadi's turn to be confused. What kind of a question was that? 'Of course men look at you if you're attractive.'

Sania let out a rush of air in a shocked half-giggle. 'Well, you'd better not wear anything like that in Delhi, unless you want to be dragged into a dark alley and raped. This is a big, bad city and men will take any exposed skin as a sign that ... well, in their twisted minds, it's like you're *asking* to be raped or leered at or felt up by their horrible, groping hands as they pass you on the street or in a market. I once had a guy grab my breast and yank it when he was cycling past me. Worst is when they come up behind you in a crowded bus and rub their crotch against you because you can't even move, y'know, so you just have to elbow them or pinch really hard or make a big scene. Most of the time, though, they'll just move away and go rub up against another girl right in front of you. Yeah, I know, I know ...' She nodded knowingly as Draupadi's eyebrows arched. 'It's sick and shameless, I get that. But that's life in good ol' India. Except, it would seem, in your ashram, which sounds like the Bahamas or something.' She ended her monologue with a roll of her eyes.

No wonder these mortal women covered up their bodies and wrapped their breasts in armour, thought Draupadi. They were scared of men attacking them. She remembered the group of men who had encircled Amba in the park, and that too when she was entirely covered in dull, baggy clothes. 'Disgusting,' she murmured. She gave a furious glare to the vendor standing next to her, making him reel in fear and stammer, 'Okay, 200 rupees' at her, gesturing desperately towards the sarong.

She flung it back at him and turned to Sania. 'In that case, since I know nothing about dressing for this kind of world, I'm in your hands. Will you select some things for me?' She looked over at Amba – still in rapt conversation with Zafar – and said, slightly irritated, 'And for my sister as well?'

Sania needed no encouragement. She beamed and said, 'Oh, of course, I *love* telling people what to wear!'

She swept around with the air of a newly-appointed army general and took charge, waving Draupadi and Amba – whom she separated from Zafar with a firm 'you can talk about your rusty knives later' – from stall to stall, barking at the vendors, holding clothes up against them and keeping a non-stop chatter going. 'You, show me that. No *that* one, you imbecile. Here try this on, Amba. No, like this – What do you mean 800? Am I *mad* that I'm going to spend so much on a crappy bag? *Cheats*, all of them are. You're lucky you have me with you. It'll look good on you but remember to only wear it with the white skirt. Do those shoes fit? Bend your toes, he doesn't have a bigger size – You have this in more colours? Yes? Then don't just stand there, *show* me! Zafar, look bored! No, no, we can't go yet. Remember, you can *never* go wrong with black, specially for a party or an evening out. No, we don't want it. 150? Okay, we'll take it for 100. Oh, it looks so pretty on you. Get one more in another colour. This look is really trending right now although I don't know why. Only a drag queen could pull it off ... You'll need matching earrings with that. Oh, your money's finished? Okay, never mind, I'll buy these for you. No, no, I insist. Zafar, give me 200 rupees.'

Zafar fished out the money from his wallet and handed it over timidly, his face in awe of his sister's shopping prowess. Then he grinned and said, 'You know, you're a lot like Ammee sometimes.'

Sania threw him a glare and said, 'Oh please, I'm nothing like her,' paid the man and handed Draupadi the earrings, looking extremely pleased with herself.

There was a moment of silence while she inspected the many bags laden with clothes, shoes and accessories. She exhaled and murmured, 'God, I'm good' before smiling and saying, 'Now, remember to wear everything *exactly* the way I told you guys, okay? Zafar' – she turned to him – 'you may drop me home, now that the boring part of the day is to begin.'

Zafar smiled with good humour, bundled them into his car, stuffing the shopping into the back with all the grace of a man who has never ironed anything in his life and dropped Sania home before driving to a very tall, metallic-looking building on the side of a busy road.

'This is the NPTV office,' he said, manoeuvring the car into the building gate as the women craned their necks to assess its dizzying height and, more importantly, wonder if and how they would actually scale it.

Draupadi had to ask, 'Do we ... have to climb up to the top?' It would take days!

Amba said nervously, 'I'm not very fond of heights ...'

Zafar glanced at her before saying, 'Don't worry. You can't really feel the height when you're inside. Just stay away from the windows' – and then to Draupadi – 'we'll take a lift up to the twenty-fifth floor.'

Before Draupadi had time to wonder what a lift was, the car entered a dark tunnel and wound downwards in a sharp, continuous circle that lasted for a while and left her feeling slightly nauseous. They were in a massive underground chamber where endless rows of cars of different colours, shapes and sizes were parked neatly between grey pillars.

'Are we under the ground?' asked Amba, looking worried. She was obviously not very fond of enclosed spaces either.

Zafar's reply was in a comforting tone. 'It's the basement car park. Don't worry, there is lots of air and we'll be in a lift in under thirty seconds.'

He quickly parked the car and ushered them into a cool glass chamber with two strange-looking metallic doors. One door opened as he pressed a switch on the wall and he guided them into it. Once inside, they stood in a small box, three sides of which were half grey metal at the bottom and half glass on the top and beyond which they could see nothing but a dirty black wall. Next to the big door, which closed upon their entry, were a series of numbered switches. Zafar pressed '25' and jumped back, in shock, as both Amba and Draupadi let out ear-piercing screams.

Chapter 19

'The wall,' screeched Draupadi, pointing at the rapidly moving dirty black wall beyond the glass, 'it's falling, we have to get out!' She hung on for dear life to a metal railing at her waist as the box moved beneath her feet. She threw Zafar a deathly look and said, '*Do* something.'

She looked around the inside of the box, saw the panel of numbers and flung herself at them, pressing them frantically. They lit up eerily, but the box didn't stop moving. Behind her, she heard Zafar say sharply, 'No, no, don't press them.'

Amba grabbed Zafar's shirt to steady herself and looked up at him in panic. 'What's happening?'

But before he could answer, the black wall fell away and in its place was ... the outside. The box they were in was climbing upwards very fast, and through the glass, they could see the streets, cars and people fall further away from them. It was as if they were a bird soaring into the sky, leaving the ground and everything on it – the noise, the traffic, the dirt – beneath them. Draupadi caught her breath and stood transfixed, staring out of the glass as the box climbed higher and higher until the people on the street became the size of insects and the outline of the vast city, with its countless buildings and structures, stretched and sprawled against the hazy afternoon sky before her eyes. It was breathtaking, thought Draupadi as she put one hand on the glass and peered out in fascination. So this was the 'lift' that Zafar had been talking about. This was how mortals climbed up and down these tall buildings. She had always envied birds their view from the sky. Who would have thought the day would come when mortals could live in the sky too?

Amba, on the other hand, gave another short scream and hid her face in Zafar's shirt. 'Get me down, get me down,' she whimpered desperately.

Zafar put his arms around her and sputtered, 'Don't worry, it's only a lift. Just, just stay calm, okay? It's going to be over soon. We're going up to the twenty-fifth floor. Well, now that you've pressed them, we're also going to the eighteenth, nineteenth, twenty-first, twenty-third and twenty-fourth floors. But it won't be very long. Hang in there.'

He blinked in a flustered way and looked down at Amba with apologetic eyes. 'I'm sorry. I forgot about the glass. I should have warned you ...'

But Amba, whose back was now turned away from the view of the outside, was distracted, having just realized she was being held, quite tightly, in Zafar's arms. She jumped back, gave Draupadi – who was still staring through the glass – a furtive glance and stood rigidly facing the metal doors with one hand over her eyes.

Zafar pushed his hair back in awkward confusion. 'Look, again, I'm really sorry. It didn't occur to me that you would have never been in a lift before. I would have explained it otherwise. Don't worry, it's perfectly safe.'

'I'm fine,' Amba whispered tightly. 'Just ... please get me out.'

Zafar nodded just as there was a little 'ping' sound and the lift came to a slow halt. A dulcet female voice calmly said, 'Eighteenth storey,' and the door opened.

Amba ran out as if her life depended on it. Once outside, she turned around and faced the two still standing inside, Draupadi intent on the view and Zafar staring at Amba with wide eyes.

'Are you coming?' Amba asked in a shaky voice.

Draupadi tore her gaze away and blinked. The doors were open and Amba was standing outside, panting like a wild deer after being chased by a tiger. Zafar stood at the door, obviously undecided about whether to go with the frantic woman outside or stay with the dazed one inside.

'Is it over?' she asked Zafar, disappointed.

Zafar looked incredulously at her, as if wondering how this woman could be screaming her head off to get out of the lift one moment and then look upset about getting out the next. He frowned and answered, one eye still on Amba, 'Not really. This is the eighteenth floor and we're going to the twenty-fifth. But, I think, under the circumstances' – he nodded towards Amba – 'it might be better if we just climb up the stairs from here.'

After another look at Amba, Draupadi agreed. She got out and followed Zafar past a few beige-coloured corridors that led to a staircase.

Seven floors were climbed in tense silence until Amba broke it on the twenty-fifth storey. 'I'm sorry. I'm not normally like that. I—I'm afraid of heights.' She smiled a little ruefully. 'And being underground, it would seem. Never tried that one before.' She looked up at Zafar with a twinkle of humour in her eyes. 'And, if you must know, I'm petrified of lizards.' She visibly shuddered.

Zafar smiled back, relieved. 'That's nothing. I'm afraid of the dark.'

Amba grinned. 'Really?'

'Really. And pressure cookers. Always avoid the kitchen when Ammee is making dal. And cats.'

Amba cocked her head. 'You're scared of cats?'

Zafar grinned sheepishly. 'Yup. There's something really creepy about the way they look at you. And that purring sound they make…' He shivered dramatically.

Amba giggled in a twirly way that was very unlike her. 'Well, then you're definitely worse than me.'

And here we go again, thought Draupadi, who had walked ahead. This needed to be nipped in the bud. She turned and said, 'You know what I really hate?'

Amba and Zafar looked at her inquiringly.

'Time wasters,' she declared. 'Now, are we going to see this TV thing or not?'

Zafar, taking the hint, became serious and shepherded them through a few more beige corridors until they entered a large hall. It was full of TVs of different sizes, some on the walls and others upon long grey tables that were also laden with parchment and strange-looking contraptions. Next to them were blue chairs on wheels and people – men and women who looked like they hadn't slept in days – striding around quickly and noisily, barking at each other. Bright white lights glared down from the ceiling, giving everyone a sallow, shadowed look and the smell of stale food and burnt tobacco hung in the air.

Despite that, Draupadi could immediately feel the energy that enveloped the place. There was a spring in the step of a pretty young girl who passed her carrying an armful of small grey boxes. There was a twinkle of excitement in the eye of the middle-aged bearded man as he sent a group of people scurrying crazily with the words 'There's a press conference in thirty minutes.' There was even a liveliness about the way that the rows of people sat in front of their TV-like contraptions, frowning and busily pounding away at protrusions on the tables. Even though everyone around them looked tired, unkempt and frazzled, they seemed to have a common sense of purpose, as if what they were doing was really important.

'Welcome to the newsroom,' Zafar said and smiled as he waved a hand over the room. 'We cover stories from all over the world here to air on our own news channel. Best team in the business. This is where I work.' He seemed proud of that fact.

He pointed to the bearded man who had initiated the press conference scurrying and who was now leaning dangerously back in his chair, running one hand through his already-dishevelled grey hair and sipping a black liquid out of a cup with the other. The expression in his puffy, dark eyes and his unshaven face told everyone around him that he was in a foul mood.

'That's my editor, Harish.' Zafar eyed him a little apprehensively. 'I don't think I'll introduce you guys just yet—'

But before he could finish his thought, Harish caught sight of Zafar and almost immediately began to scream bloody murder. He swivelled around in his chair and shouted across the room, 'Zafar, you bastard, where the *hell* have you been?'

Zafar replied calmly, 'At home. I'm on leave.'

Harish looked extremely irritated at that. 'Till when? Who the hell gave you leave when the shit has hit the fan with the new anti-corruption enquiries? They're all going down. I need everybody right now!'

Zafar stayed calm. 'Till next week. You gave it to me, Harish. I had to use my leave days before they expired, remember?'

Harish looked like he was going to burst, but then suddenly, he chuckled ruefully and leaned back in his chair again. 'Shit.' And then, as if a thought occurred to him, 'What the hell are you doing in the office? Got nowhere to go, bastard?'

Zafar smiled. 'I'm showing my friends around and I've got to collect my expenses from Mansi. I'll come back tomorrow and get on to the story.'

Harish smiled tiredly. 'Good man.' He nodded awkwardly to Amba and Draupadi and then turned his back on them.

'Don't mind him,' murmured Zafar softly as he turned to them. 'He's actually a nice guy. News is just like that. The people at the lifestyle programmes section are much friendlier. I'll take you there.'

They followed him out and a few corridors later entered a similar hall, one that was filled with wooden tables and orange-coloured chairs. There were plants and brightly coloured paintings everywhere, and the people, though lively, seemed more relaxed than those in the newsroom. They milled around, chatting and laughing. There were many more women than men, and most of them looked well-dressed and freshly bathed. A large group of women, noticing Zafar, called out to him enthusiastically, each one trying to outdo the other with high-pitched, elongated 'Hi's and coquettish waves. Zafar waved back with a slightly embarrassed smile but, much to Draupadi and Amba's relief, kept walking. There were groups of women like that in the heavenly court too. Nobody ever walked into one and left unscathed.

The hall exited through glass doors into a large outdoor terrace which had a charming garden with benches in it. Seated on one of the benches were two women; one of them was young and very pretty, dressed in tight pants and a strappy black top with big silver hoops in her ears and plenty of what women in Draupadi's time liked to call 'whore's paint' on her face. The other was an older woman, slight plump and dressed in a brightly coloured sari with chunky gold jewellery around her neck and in her ears. They were talking to each other animatedly.

In front of them and pointed directly at them was a black contraption, almost as tall as a person, with a very large head, a big, glassy round eye and three spindly legs. Behind the contraption stood four people who looked very busy, either peering into the back of the contraption's head, holding a cushioned pole high over the women's heads or holding what looked like large pieces of shiny cloth in the air and periodically inspecting a tiny TV screen placed on a chair off to one side. Thick black string linked everything together and ran all over the floor in a messy web.

Zafar said with enthusiasm, 'Oh good, there's a shoot going on in the balcony. It'll help you to understand TV. We can watch it from inside. Just remember not to make any loud sound or it'll get caught on camera. That' – he pointed at the black contraption – 'is the camera, by the way. The cameraman is standing behind it, along with the sound technician and the production assistant, and that girl next to the monitor, that little TV on the chair, is the director.'

When they got closer and stood behind the glass door, Draupadi noticed that the image of the two women on the bench was being replicated exactly in the monitor. It was like watching exactly the same scene that was happening in front of them, but minus everything else around it. The balcony, the people behind the camera, the office, none of it could be seen. Inside the monitor, only those two women existed, talking on a bench in a garden.

'Interesting,' whispered Draupadi. 'How does the TV, I mean the monitor, capture their image?'

Zafar smiled. 'It's not the monitor that captures their image, it's the camera. The camera sees the scene with its lens, like an eye, and then transfers the image via the cable – you see that black string-like thing connecting the two? That's how the image travels to the monitor, which shows it to us. The image is also recorded on a tape, which can be taken out of the camera and played in an editing room, where they organize all the material, add content and basically create the programmes we see on TV in our homes. Amazing, isn't it?'

It was beyond amazing, thought Draupadi. It was one thing to harness fire, build chariots without horses and live in sky-high houses. But to replicate the human form so accurately that not only could you see every curve, every dent in its precise colour and shape, but you could capture the way it moved and expressed itself. And then to show that likeness to people all over the world at the same time! Draupadi found herself truly appreciating, for the first time, how far mortals had come since she had been one. Next they'd be telling her mortals could fly!

Zafar looked extremely pleased to see the wonder on Draupadi's face and enthusiastically took them around the other offices, explaining how images were edited in tiny, freezing cold rooms with massive contraptions in them. He showed them how images were broadcast across continents in rooms where the walls were covered in TV screens and even how images were made without cameras in rooms full of even more kinds of TV screens. He showed them 'studios' where people talked directly into the cameras under the heavy glare of lights, rooms where 'tapes' were stored from floor to ceiling in cupboards and rooms lined with beds for those unfortunate people who had no time to go home and sleep. TVs and people were everywhere, along with plenty of hustle and bustle.

Finally, they stopped outside yet another studio with a TV screen outside it that was showing the NPTV channel. Zafar turned to Draupadi and Amba and grinned. 'I could show you lots more, but you probably need a break, right?'

Amba smiled and admitted, 'Well, I could use a break. Not that I don't find it fascinating, of course,' she added politely.

Draupadi was engrossed in watching the TV screen, where there was a programme about elaborate-looking jewellery going on, and didn't reply.

Zafar nodded and said, 'Okay then, should we go down to the canteen for a coffee?'

Amba nodded but Draupadi kept watching the TV.

'Draupadi?'

'Huh?'

'You want to come to the canteen? For something to drink?'

Draupadi replied distractedly, 'You go ahead. I'll come later.'

Zafar frowned. 'But you don't know your way around.'

Draupadi looked at him and blinked. She couldn't pay attention to what was being said on the TV while he was talking. She wasn't ready to adjourn yet. 'I'll find my way. The canteen, right?'

'Right. Okay then,' said Zafar, and he turned to Amba, 'shall we?'

Amba frowned at Draupadi and looked undecided for a moment. But then she turned and went with him.

Draupadi stood in front of the TV perfectly engrossed in the programme about the rising prices of precious gems for a while. Then, suddenly, she felt an urgent tap on her shoulder and turned to find a red-faced, short little man looking irritatedly at her.

He said in a nasal voice, 'You're not supposed to be here, you're supposed to be waiting inside, in the holding area. And why haven't you got your hair and makeup done yet? Never mind, come with me, it's almost your turn.'

Draupadi looked at him in confusion. 'What?'

'I *said* it's almost your turn to audition. The last one is just finishing hers. We've been waiting for you in the holding area as the email brief *clearly* specified. If I didn't happen to come out, you would have missed it.'

He handed her a stick-like contraption, which she had previously seen the people in the TV point at each other's mouths while speaking, and a tiny black hook-like contraption attached by a long thin cord to a small black box.

What was it with all the contraptions in this world? Did no one do anything with their hands any more? she wondered as she took them without a clue as to what he expected her to do with them. He didn't give her time to ask, quickly ushering her into the studio doors while grumbling non-stop under his breath.

Draupadi walked into the large studio automatically, wondering what the little man was going on about. What was an audition? Who was waiting for her and, more importantly, why? She looked around for someone who might know where the canteen was when the most astonishing sight caught her eye.

She was in a large arena bathed in rays of bright lights emanating from the blackest ceiling. In the centre, sitting on a chair and looking frail, scared and confused was a sari-clad young woman of around eighteen summers. Next to her, an empty chair and around her, in a semi-circle, sat what must have been up to a hundred people in elevated corrals, all looking at the young woman intensely as she shrank from their gaze. Voices bickered and heckled from the crowd incessantly, safe in their anonymity. The woman looked up at the audience around her like a rabbit in a cage.

Draupadi was immediately transported back thousands of years, to her swayamwara. The scene had not been much different. Hundreds had heckled and stared at her from corrals as she had emerged, a bride-to-be petrified at the thought of the unknown fate that awaited her, a target of the crowd's lust, resentment and frustrations.

She saw another woman in high-heeled shoes with the same black stick in her hands moving unsteadily among the crowd, trying desperately to moderate and direct the audience's voices towards a constructive discussion about the young woman sitting in the centre – whom she referred to as Vaishali – and her apparent predicament, which Draupadi couldn't make sense of amid all the shouting.

'Please, let's discuss this one by one. Please put your hand up if you want to speak. Please stop shouting,' the high-heeled woman said apprehensively as she absently pointed the stick away from her mouth. No one paid any attention to her whatsoever. A man yelled, 'How do we know you're not a professional prostitute?' at Vaishali and then immediately sat back and kept quiet before the high-heeled woman could identify or reach him. Vaishali cowered further and closed her eyes for a moment in painful acknowledgement of his words.

Anger swelled inside Draupadi. How dare he? She took a step towards the man when a hand stopped her in her tracks. 'Wait,' whispered a male voice from behind a large camera right next to her. 'You'll get your turn. Her audition ends in a minute. Then you're on. Did they give you your headset?'

Headset. Did he mean the hook-like contraption the little man had given her? Probably. 'Yes,' she whispered back.

'Are you wearing it?' the man behind the camera asked.

'No. I don't know how to wear it,' she replied.

'You first-timers,' he muttered with a soft sigh as he deftly took the headset from her hands and fitted the hook, with a click, around her ear. Then he attached the black box to her waistband at the back. It was uncomfortable, but Draupadi was too distracted by Vaishali and the high-heeled woman in the arena. Both looked like they were desperate to get out of there.

'Okay, she's wrapping up. Get ready,' said the man.

Suddenly, a female voice boomed overhead and brought the chaos in the arena to a halt. 'Cut! Okay, thanks, Sneha. You can leave the stage. Next anchor audition, please.'

'Okay, that's you,' whispered the man hurriedly. When Draupadi didn't respond, he pushed her slightly and said, 'Go.'

Draupadi was confused. Did they want her to go and take high-heeled Sneha's place? It certainly sounded like they did. She tentatively took a few steps forward until she stood a few paces away from Vaishali at the centre of the arena.

'*This* is the next anchor? Great,' the voice from nowhere boomed sarcastically again, sounding much like one of the announcements made occasionally by the demi-gods in the heavenly court. 'Say something for the sound check, please,' the voice spoke again.

Draupadi was quiet. Was it talking to her?

The voice returned, irritated and impatient. 'You, in the horrible grey skirt. I'm talking to you. Do you have a voice?'

Draupadi thought her skirt was horrible too but there was no need to be rude about it. 'Yes, I do have a voice,' she spoke defiantly into the air.

'O-kay, then – your clothes are completely wrong and why the hell didn't you get your hair and make-up done? Never mind, we don't have time to change anything now. We're going to test your headset. Hold on,' the voice said.

Suddenly, Draupadi heard a tiny voice in her ear, as if an insect was sitting inside it and talking to her,

'One, two, three, testing. Can you hear me?'

Amazed, her hand flew to her head, where she felt the headset in the folds of her hair. Clutching her head in wonder, she replied, 'Yes.'

'Great,' the insect replied. Then the demi-goddess-like voice was back in the arena. 'Okay, we take it from the beginning. Madam Anchor, time to use your voice. Face the teleprompter on camera four.'

Draupadi looked around and saw, in between the corrals of the arena, the menacing, single-eyed stare of five giant black cameras, each marked with a black number at the bottom. More were positioned at various spots around the arena, pointing in different directions. Under the camera marked '4', there was a TV screen-like contraption with words on it. Was that the teleprompter? She faced the camera and waited.

The demi-goddess voice announced, 'Okay, ready? Stand by. Point the mic towards your mouth, for god's sake! Cue the music. Roll tape. And – *action*.'

Draupadi held up the mic as she heard loud music, and then a man with a large headset around his head mysteriously appeared behind camera '4' and held up his fingers in a counting gesture. She watched him count down from five while the music played and then roll his hand frantically in a circular motion as it ended, looking at her expectantly. Was she supposed to do something?

She stood and waited for something to happen. The man began to look panicky and pointed forcefully at the teleprompter and then his mouth.

She squinted at the screen he was pointing to. There were words on it. Was she supposed to read the words? She began tentatively, 'Welcome to *Us, The Women*, a show about what it means to be a woman in India today. Join me, Arshita Gopal, as we talk about the latest issues in the news this week.'

Draupadi stopped, confused. Arshita? Who was that? Should she tell them she wasn't this person?

The man behind the camera was pointing frantically at the teleprompter again with wide-eyed panic. Probably not. She continued to read the moving words, 'We have here in the studio with us Vaishali, from the village of Katputli in Rajasthan. Her story is one shared by uncountable women in India and all over the world.'

Draupadi could feel Vaishali's discomfort as she shifted in her seat behind her. She continued to read. 'When Vaishali was just sixteen years old, her family had her married to Ram Kumar, a man twenty years older than her who had told them he worked as a vegetable seller in the nearby town. Little did Vaishali know that her marriage would turn into her biggest nightmare. After her wedding, Vaishali was kept locked in a dark outhouse behind a dhaba in the town of Golipur and raped repeatedly by her husband and the owner of the dhaba, Manoj Kumar, and used by them as a prostitute to service numerous truck drivers who stopped at the dhaba. This went on for almost six months until she became pregnant. Upon finding out about Vaishali's pregnancy, Ram Kumar threw her out on the street to fend for herself.'

Draupadi felt her breath catch in her throat as she spoke. 'With no money to get home, Vaishali went to the police station and told them her story. She was informed by a police officer that there was no proof against her husband and her best option was to get an abortion and continue to prostitute herself because her family would not take her back. Vaishali suffered a miscarriage soon after.'

Draupadi barely heard the insect voice in her ear say, 'Now read the last part and then go sit and talk to her.'

Draupadi was shaking now as she read, in a hoarse voice, 'Vaishali's situation is not unusual and she was probably not the first, or last, of Ram Kumar's victims. Thousands, if not millions, of girls in India today have a similar story but are too afraid or ashamed to seek help. Many of them end up on the street, forced into prostitution and begging to survive. Others are often sold into slavery by their so-called husbands and even separated from their children. Vaishali is here because she hopes the government, the police force and society in general can address these issues. Let's see what she has to say.'

The teleprompter went blank and Draupadi blinked. She looked over at Vaishali, who sat shrunken and overwhelmed in her chair under the gaze of an auditorium full of people. Draupadi walked over to her and sat down. Vaishali's embarrassed eyes looked at her almost in fear, as if she expected Draupadi to judge her, just like everyone else who heard her story had done.

Draupadi leaned over, put her hand on top of Vaishali's and squeezed it, saying angrily, 'Bastards.'

If there was a gasp in the room, she didn't hear it. Her only thought, her only instinct was to protect this young girl. She said in a shaking voice, 'You have been through hell.'

Vaishali's tears ran down her face as her lips quivered in response. Draupadi shook her head. 'No one should have to go through what you did. The fact that you are here with your head held high, when any other woman would have buckled under the shame and pressure, tells me that you are braver than any man I know. I salute you, Vaishali.'

Draupadi knelt down on the floor, amid further gasps around her, so she could meet Vaishali's gaze under her hanging, weeping face. She stared deep into the girl's eyes and said, 'The pain is fresh right now. They look at you as if you're a vile thing, don't they? They scream "whore" with their eyes even if they don't utter a word with their lips. Even though none of it was your fault, even though it was all against your will, they judge you, like a common prostitute. I know your pain.' She dropped her gaze for a moment as her voice faltered.

Then, she looked up at Vaishali again and said with conviction, 'It will dull with time, I promise you. Soon, you will look right back at them, daring them to speak their mind. Eventually, the pain will settle into memory and you will live the life meant for you. Look at me, Vaishali,' she said as Vaishali avoided her gaze.

The girl lifted her red, brimming eyes to Draupadi, who almost whispered, 'It will be all right. But now you have a chance to speak for the others who will follow the same path unless something is done about it. The girls who are playing in their house yards right now, who are helping their mothers in the kitchen, who are studying alongside their brothers and sisters, who have no idea how terrible their future is going to be. Are you ready to talk, for their sake, and tell your story? Are you ready to fight, for your honour and theirs?'

Vaishali paused and considered Draupadi with some surprise for a moment. Then she sat up straight, wiped her tears away with her sari and spoke with a resolute voice, 'I'm ready.'

Draupadi nodded and squeezed her hand. She took a deep breath and stood up, facing the audience and saying in an almost growling voice, 'Vaishali will tell her story now. If anybody is offended by her, they may leave now. If you stay, you will be respectful or you will deal with me.' If there was one thing she had learned during her time as a queen in a warrior clan, it was how to issue a threat. The people sitting in the front of the audience almost cowered under her gaze and there was a lot of shifting in seats.

Then, the sound of a single pair of clapping hands cut through the tense silence. A few more joined in and soon the entire audience united in applause, smiling approvingly at Draupadi.

Not entirely sure if these mortals understood that she had been threatening them, Draupadi nevertheless acknowledged the applause with a nod. Maybe this was part of the exercise, she thought. Either way, she hoped she wouldn't have to put any of them in their place as she turned and, once again, gave her attention to Vaishali to ask her questions about her experience. It was obvious that things had gotten even worse for mortal women since she was here last, and this time around, she was going to do something about it. God help anyone who tried to stop her.

Chapter 20

'Sugar?' Zafar held out a little white parcel over her parchment cup.

Amba noticed the fine hairs on his wrist against his crisp white shirt and his clean, well-groomed fingernails. She had always liked it when men kept their nails trimmed and dirt-free, even though it was uncommon in her day. The mortal men she had met when she was alive were mostly warriors who prided themselves on well-built shoulders and thighs rather than clean hands. Not that she had met that many men, having spent most of her life in the women's quarters of various palaces belonging to her relatives and family members. Always the guest, Amba had been treated with respect wherever she went to live. But that respect had always been tinged with contempt. As a life-long maiden, she had stood at the bottom of the hierarchy of royal women.

'Yes,' she said tentatively, having no idea what coffee was. Around them sat people drinking from similar cups in a large room, much like the eating house Zafar had taken them to previously. Men and women mingled freely and noisily around them and she took a moment to appreciate that such a thing was the norm in the mortal world now.

She watched Zafar mix the liquid in her cup, his eyes focused on his task. He was different from the men she had met in other ways too. He didn't leer at her or order her around as so many had done when she was a young maiden or pity her as so many had done when she had grown into an older spinster.

Zafar looked at her with respect. Spoke to her as if her opinion mattered. His manner, his voice, his person was never contemptuous or pitying. The admiration in his eyes, well, she had noticed it, of course. She may have never been around men much but she knew, just like all women did, when a man found her attractive.

It felt ... good. Nothing could ever come of it obviously, she quickly thought to herself, but she hadn't felt desirable, coveted or ... powerful in such a long time. Not since the day Bhishma unceremoniously snatched her away at her swayamwara. After that, despite being lauded for her beauty across the land, despite desperate letters of undying love from her suitors, despite her father's power and influence, it was either marry Bhishma, or be a spinster. And he had refused. She had tried everything in her power to change his mind. Begged, raged, blackmailed and even tried and failed to seduce him at one point. Amba smiled at the memory of his clumsy hands roaming her body as she pretended to enjoy it. It had ended abruptly and, in retrospect, quite comically, with him holding his dhoti and running away and her screaming after him like a shrew. She couldn't imagine now why she had so desperately wanted to be the bride of a man she loathed. Perhaps it was because she felt powerless.

So, this feeling right here, right now, she thought as she took a sip of the sweet, milky liquid Zafar had made for her, was—

'Good. It's very good,' she mumbled softly.

'You like it? Personally, I'm more of a coffee person than a tea one.' Zafar smiled warmly, his long fingers played with the rim of his cup before raising it to his lips. 'How about you?'

Amba felt her breath catch a little and her thighs clench a little as she watched the tips of his fingers absently encircle the rim again and again. Stop behaving like a pubescent girl, she chastised herself. Flustered, she sat up straight, squeezing her legs together to force her insides to behave. 'Tea, coffee, sorry, which one is this?'

Zafar's smile waned. 'Coffee.'

Amba shakily laughed out a deep breath. Be easy, be calm. 'Yes. Coffee. I like coffee.' She cleared her throat.

Zafar looked concerned at her sudden, anxious behaviour. 'Are you sure? You don't have to have coffee or tea. I can get you a soft drink or juice or beer—'

'No, no. I like this, I really do.' Amba closed her eyes for a moment in frustration. Now he thought there was something wrong with her. She needed to rescue this conversation. 'So, how old are you?' What? What a stupid question. She cringed inwardly.

'Er, I'm twenty-nine,' Zafar replied politely as he took a sip of his coffee. 'How about you?'

A few thousand, she thought to herself. Although she couldn't be sure, since she had no idea how many years she had been in heaven. Obviously, that answer wouldn't suffice. Amba tried to consider how old she looked. Probably somewhere between seventeen and twenty-six summers. She should already have been a married woman by the standards of her own time. But many of the girls she had seen in Zafar's place of work, and of course Sania, were about that age and seemed unmarried. Obviously, times had changed.

'I'm twenty-six.'

Zafar nodded. 'So, do you have any future plans, apart from marriage? Working, studying?'

Amba thought quickly and gave the answer she hoped would inspire the least further questioning. 'I prefer to stay at home with my family.'

Zafar didn't seem surprised as he nodded again. 'Is that by choice or is it something your mother prefers? Would you like to work or study further?'

Obviously her uninspired answer had not done the trick; but before she had a chance to think of another uninspired one, Amba blurted out, 'No, I never wanted those things. I always just wanted to get married and have children. But sometimes things don't turn out the way you wished for.' She instantly regretted her words.

'Nonsense,' Zafar said and smiled at her incredulously. 'Why shouldn't things work out? You're young and beautiful. Intelligent. Trained in hand-to-hand combat.' He chuckled and cleared his throat. 'You're incredible. Don't put yourself down. Any man would be lucky to have you ...' His voice trailed off as he began to look a little embarrassed.

That good feeling began to return. Amba smiled. 'Thank you. I guess I feel a lot older than I really am and waiting for the right person to come along is always frustrating.'

Zafar returned her smile, now far more at ease than before. 'I know what you mean by feeling older than you are. Sometimes I feel like I've seen too much. One of the pitfalls of being a journalist, I guess. Too much suffering, too many people starving or dying or being tortured and violated. Too much callousness. People in this city will watch a man being mowed down by a car on a road and will still honk their horns because they care more that the road is being blocked and they're late for work than the man who is dying right in front of them. It's sick. I have to remind myself on a daily basis *not* to get desensitized to it all because the day that happens, I'll not only be lousy at what I do for a living but also lose my soul. Getting disillusioned and bitter is easier than having to deal with all the shit, excuse my French, around us and that's the main problem with the media these days.' Zafar shook his head sadly. 'We've all just seen too much and are now a bunch of disillusioned zombies. Once in a while something will catch the public's interest; a particularly heinous crime or a particularly inspiring movement and we'll all jump at it, make lots of noise and literally create hysteria. But then, of course, the hype will die down and nothing will have changed.' He shrugged and gave a half-hearted smile. 'It is the Kalyug, I guess. If you're the religious type.'

Amba looked down and carefully replied, 'I guess it is. Are you the religious type?'

'Me? No.' He laughed. 'Hindu dad, Muslim mom, no chance. Religion has been more of a pain than anything else in my life. I'm a firm atheist and short of God popping up in front of my face and telling me otherwise, I'm staying that way.'

Amba nodded politely and took another deep breath. These passionate speeches were getting her flustered again but she just couldn't seem to help it. He looked so ... so ... passionate, and his eyes flashed so ... passionately, and the way his hands moved around and his body leaned in towards her and the way he spoke with his calm, firm voice was just so ... passionate. All right, all right, enough with all the passion, Amba scolded herself. This was the problem with being a virgin at her age. She should have just made love to one of the many former mortal men who had approached her when she first entered heaven. At least then she could have maybe had a normal, adult conversation with an attractive man without melting into a lusty mess.

'Are you religious?'

She snapped out of her thoughts and found him looking at her speculatively. She thought for a moment and said, 'Not religious. But I know God exists.'

A smile played on Zafar's lips as he said teasingly, 'See, so many people say that. That they *know* God exists. How? Have you had a conversation with him? Did he reveal himself to you at the top of a mountain while no one else was looking and ask for something obscure, like the sacrifice of your favourite handbag?'

Amba returned his smile and teasing tone. 'I have spoken to him actually.'

'Really? And did he talk back?'

'He did.'

'And what did he say?'

Amba chuckled. 'He said that this Kalyug is getting out of hand and he intends to destroy all mortals shortly, if you must know.'

Zafar threw his head back and laughed, and Amba felt that bittersweet clench again. She abandoned hope of controlling it this time and watched, without inhibition, as his shoulders shook and his eyes crinkled up and his breath came out in delighted gasps.

Zafar looked at her and said light-heartedly, almost to himself, 'You're incredible.' Then he leaned forward and said earnestly, 'Look, I know we haven't known each other very long, but I think you're amazing and would really like to get to know you better.'

Amba smiled shyly and was about to reply when she heard Draupadi's voice. There was something wrong with it. It was distorted and angry and sounded like she was shouting at someone. Amba instantly sprang out of her chair and looked about anxiously. She couldn't see Draupadi, yet her voice seemed to be coming from within the room. 'Draupadi?' she said loudly as her eyes scanned the room quickly.

'Draupadi?' this time more fearfully.

'Look.' Zafar pointed to a large, flat TV on the wall. There, reflected from within its frame was Draupadi's moving image. She was in a large arena, surrounded by an audience of people and she was arguing heatedly with one of them – a balding, middle-aged man with a beard – beside whom she stood pointing a rounded, black stick at his mouth.

Amba was horrified. What was Draupadi doing inside the TV box? She moved closer to the TV and Draupadi's voice, although still a little distorted, became more audible.

'You call yourself a guardian of good values, but it is people like you who hold society back from progressing.' Draupadi looked directly down into the man's eyes as she spoke forcefully while he bristled with humiliation. 'Perhaps there will come a time when you won't be so comfortably judgemental about other women. Perhaps that day will come when one of the women in your own family will be touched by rape.'

Draupadi tilted her head and waited for the angry response that she fully expected to receive. She stood tall, her stance accentuating the curve of her waist despite her baggy clothing, her hair falling dramatically past her shoulders, leaving the contours of her face illuminated by light. She looked magnificent, a true warrior queen.

Amba looked over at Zafar, who had stepped closer and was looking at Draupadi with an intrigued smile on his face. She met his gaze questioningly and he mumbled, 'I have no idea what she's doing in the studio auditions, but she seems to be doing great. Let's watch more.'

Amba nodded and turned her attention back to Draupadi and the now red-faced man.

'You think you're so smart, you young girls,' the middle-aged man responded angrily. 'The women in my family don't go outside in skimpy clothes that reveal their arms and legs and half their chests. Talking to strangers and taking public transport, eating at public restaurants and even drinking alcohol. Females like this are *inviting* men to look at them in that way. Women in my family are modest and they stay inside the house, where they belong, where they are safe.'

Draupadi's eyes glittered as she replied in her husky voice, 'Inside the house, where they belong … I can see that even while mankind has scaled the skies to live among the birds, has conquered disease and discomfort, has made advancements that would seem unfathomable and unimaginable to someone from a previous age, not much has changed for womankind.' She looked around the arena. 'Does anyone disagree with me?'

The few people that Amba could see sitting around Draupadi seemed far too scared to disagree with her in any way for fear of having their heads bitten off. Zafar must have thought that too, for he chuckled and looked over at Amba. 'She's quite something, your sister. Powerful stuff. She has an amazing presence and voice. The camera loves her.'

Amba nodded, still confused about what was happening but happy that Draupadi seemed to be safe for the moment. She was also a bit disappointed – no, a bit relieved, she told herself resolutely – that her moment with Zafar had been interrupted. Just as well, she thought and then said brightly, 'Should we go and see her?'

Zafar nodded, a little disappointed, as he looked at her. 'We probably should.'

Chapter 21

Draupadi looked around the arena. She guessed that at least half of the audience was probably wary of her by now, but she pushed on. She made her way towards a woman who was raising her hand, as she had loudly told everyone to do when they all started yelling towards her at the same time, when she heard the voice in her ear say, 'Okay, you can stop now. That was great. Leave the studio and wait outside the door for me. I want to speak with you. Don't go anywhere, okay?'

Then the same voice boomed in the studio, 'Cut! Okay, that's a wrap everyone. Thank you and pack up, please.'

Draupadi felt someone's hand on her ear as her earpiece was deftly taken off and she was herded quickly towards a door. Over her shoulder, she saw Vaishali being herded out of another door. She would have liked to speak to her, at least say goodbye.

'That was really good!' A pretty, short woman, probably around thirty-five summers, walked confidently towards her as she left the studio. The woman was dressed in tight black pants and a stringy red garment that clung to her upper body and left her arms and shoulders bare. Despite standing a head shorter than Draupadi, the woman looked up at her authoritatively and smiled. Her eyes twinkled with wit and intelligence and held none of the awe or trepidation Draupadi usually found on people's faces when they looked at her. She liked this woman instantly.

'I'm Angela,' the woman said and Draupadi recognized her voice as the same demi-goddess one she had heard in her ear and in the studio. 'Sorry about the clothes comment, but seriously, you have a great figure and that outfit does nothing for it. No offence taken?'

Draupadi shook her head in resignation and smiled down at Angela. 'If you give me clothes like yours, I'll burn these right now.' She wiggled uncomfortably, resisting the urge to adjust herself. She looked at Angela's breasts, which looked relatively unrestrained. 'Tell me, are you wearing a bra?'

Angela laughed at the informality of the unexpected question. She looked down at her own chest and said, 'No.

Thankfully, my boobs are not that big so I can get away with a small tube top. It's so much more comfortable than a bra.'

Draupadi wondered what a tube top was and where she could get one. She would have asked but Angela continued enthusiastically, 'Okay, so I really liked what you did in there. A bit too preachy and opinionated, the tone a bit too angry, but overall I see a lot of potential. You have to remember that your job is not so much to pass judgement on everything as it is to collect the viewpoint of everyone else. But I like your style, your voice and your presence and *love* the way you interviewed Vaishali. It was almost as if you knew *exactly* what she had been through!'

I do, thought Draupadi, but she nodded along quietly as Angela continued, 'Super relatable. And an awesome segue into the interview. Got the audience on your side right away. They loved you!'

Not by the end of it, Draupadi thought to herself, especially after she chided a woman for asking Vaishali how many men she had serviced during her time in the outhouse. 'How does it matter?' she had exclaimed loudly at the woman. 'Whether it was one or one hundred, that is not the *point*.' She had then given the woman a withering glare that had her stammering an apology a few moments later.

She watched Angela continue in her enthused voice, 'I think you'll do really well after some training. So, we could start with a probation period and then move you up to a full-time position once we get approval from the management. You can sort out the logistics with HR. What do you say?' She smiled brightly up at Draupadi.

Draupadi had no idea what she was talking about. 'Say about what?'

Angela looked a little perplexed. 'About the job. To be the anchorperson for *Us, the Women*. Do you want it?'

'A job,' Draupadi repeated a little stupidly. 'You're asking me if I want a job? Doing what I did in there?'

Angela looked even more perplexed now. 'Ye-s. A job. The one you just auditioned for, Arshita.'

Oh right, Angela thought she was Arshita. Now it all made sense. Draupadi smiled a bit sheepishly. 'You see, there has been a slight misunderstanding … my name is not Arshita. I just happened to be visiting here with Zafar Kapoor' – whom, thankfully, she could see entering the hallway with Amba in tow – 'and a man found me out here, thought I was Arshita and sent me into the studio.'

Angela was looking at her as if she were mad.

Draupadi shrugged her shoulders, her smile becoming even more sheepish. 'It all happened so fast—'

Zafar walked right up to them and spoke to Angela playfully. 'She's going to need to speak to HR and sort out her package before she makes any decision. I hope you're not bullying my friend here?'

Angela eyed Draupadi. 'Bullying? No. But I would just love to know who exactly your friend is.'

'You haven't been introduced? That's strange, considering she just auditioned for you.' Zafar was confused.

'Isn't it?' Angela continued to eye Draupadi.

Zafar looked from one to the other and said, 'Angela De Souza, producer of a long line of very successful talk shows here at NPTV. Ms Draupadi Kuru, currently a tourist here in Delhi with her mother and sisters.' He looked over at Angela and smiled cheekily. 'And may potentially become a resident?'

'Draupadi Kuru' – Angela looked over at Zafar – 'seriously?'

Zafar's eyebrows rose questioningly as he replied, 'Seriously. Is that an issue?'

Angela shrugged. 'No, just saying – wow, o-kay.' She blinked a few times and turned her still-confused-but-ready-to-get-on-with-it gaze to Draupadi. 'So, Ms Draupadi Kuru, since you are obviously not Arshita, you probably didn't read the brief about the programme. This is a TV talk show. We will be doing one episode a week where we will address a women's issue in society today. It could be violence against women, forced marriage, female foeticide ... basically any issue that addresses women and that we think needs changing. We will call in victims, advocates, women on the street, anyone who has experiences to share and opinions to give and the anchorperson will interview them, tell their stories, get audience reactions – basically have a constructive discussion to try and bring these issues to the TV audience at home. The show will reach millions of people so hopefully we can create awareness about how women are treated in our society.'

Draupadi had to ask, 'Millions of people will be able to see *me* in their TVs at home?'

Angela nodded.

Draupadi couldn't wrap her mind around that idea. 'Everything I say or do? Will I look like myself?'

Angela turned to Zafar and asked, 'Is she for real?'

Zafar mumbled irritatedly, 'Cut her some slack, she's from an ashram.'

Angela looked back at Draupadi and shrugged. 'Well, that explains the clothes, I guess.' Then she put on a look of forced patience and said politely, 'Yes, that's right. Millions will see and hear you, exactly as you are in real life. You can really make a difference to society with this show.'

Draupadi's mind was reeling. She could be seen by millions of people. 'And these millions of people, they're all in Indrap—I mean, they're all in New Delhi?'

Angela shook her head and sighed dramatically in a way that suggested she was not used to dealing with small-town girls. 'About 300 million or so of them are in Delhi. Another 900 million or so across India and a few million more non-resident Indians around the world who subscribe to the channel. Of course, not all of them will be watching *Us, the Women*, but many of them will. We can really only get an idea of the numbers once we start airing the show. So, do you want the damned job or not?' She crossed her arms and began to tap her foot insistently.

Draupadi couldn't even fathom the idea of such scale. It was too much. She couldn't take the job for obvious reasons – she wasn't going to be around to do it – but the fact that something like this could even be a possibility for her in this day and age, that was really something.

Angela's sudden, and meaningful, cough made it clear that she expected an answer without delay; and so Draupadi said the first thing that came to mind, 'I can't decide now. I'll have to think about it.'

Angela looked at Zafar. 'Is it about the salary? We can discuss that, you know.'

Zafar looked cautiously from one to the other before saying, 'I think it's maybe a lot to think about and would involve a lot of life changes. Also, she probably needs to speak to her mother as well.'

Her mother? Oh right, he meant Kunti. Perfect foil. 'Yes, yes, I'll have to speak to my mother. I can't make such a big decision without asking her.' Draupadi did her best to simper like a young girl.

Acting was never one of her strong points and Angela raised an eyebrow at her tone. But she nodded and replied, 'Fine. Get back to me ASAP though.' She looked at Zafar and said, 'You follow up, okay?'

Zafar nodded and said, 'Yes, ma'am' cheekily, making Angela smile as she walked away from them.

That was when Draupadi noticed Amba staring after Angela with what looked suspiciously like jealousy on her face. She looked from Zafar to Amba speculatively as she remembered that they had walked off together to the canteen a while back.

'So, sister, where have you been? Busy?' she asked Amba a little tartly.

Amba levelled her eyes with Draupadi's and could see the suggestion in them. She lifted her chin and replied in much the same tone, 'Not as busy as you, sister.' She nodded her head towards the studio.

Draupadi smiled. Amba, usually mellow, could fire up when the occasion demanded. Draupadi personally loved to rile her up whenever she got the chance, but now was probably not a good time. She touched Amba's arm as a peace offering and said, 'Shall we go find Gandhari and ... Mummy?'

Amba's eyes twinkled in response. She turned to Zafar and asked, with a tiny bit of familiarity that wasn't there before, 'Will you take us there?'

Zafar responded with an equally familiar look and murmured, 'Of course. I'll just quickly go get my cheque from HR. Wait for me at the lift outside the entrance, okay?'

They nodded. Draupadi waited until he was out of earshot and then turned to Amba.

'All right, what's up with you and TV boy? You do realize we're going back soon, don't you?'

'I do. And nothing is up with us.' Amba's tone was guarded but firm. 'We simply talked a little and it was – fun.' She looked straight ahead towards the entrance of the office, as if she couldn't get there fast enough.

Draupadi, never one to avoid confrontation, pushed on, 'Then why are you both crooning at each other like a pair of besotted lovers? It's obvious he will fall in love with you given the slightest encouragement, but I'm not worried about him. I'm worried about you.' She looked at Amba and said half-jokingly, 'I don't want to spend an eternity in heaven with you swooning and sighing every day.'

Amba smiled wryly. 'Aren't you the selfless one? I'm fine. You have nothing to worry about.' With that, she strode ahead.

As she watched her far-from-fine friend walk away, Draupadi glanced upwards towards the heavenly world, as if to check that nobody was watching. If somebody was, they were in trouble.

Chapter 22

'What are you doing here, woman? Are you crazy?' Karan whispered furiously as he gripped Goddess Saraswati – aka Shashiben – tightly by the arm and pulled her out of the tiny hut and on to the street. Kunti and Gandhari followed closely behind. From the back of the ramshackle structure they had just left, children of all ages and sizes scrambled out, their arms full of packages, and ran away in different directions, disappearing easily into the maze of alleys around them.

Kunti, Gandhari, Shashiben and a fuming Karan stepped out on to a crumbling mud street in the centre of which ran a stinking open drain. This was one of a myriad of similar alleys and streets which constituted the settlement they were inside. On either side of the drain, for as far as the eye could see, were more dilapidated single-room structures made of wood, cardboard, canvas and tin, pressed together as tightly as possible so as not to waste a grain of space. They were too rickety to even be called huts. Their pokey doors were covered with dirty cloths which provided little privacy for the people in the poorly-lit rooms within. Filth was everywhere. The air was heavy with the stench of rotting food, human and animal excrement, sweat and homespun cigarettes.

Kunti had much on her mind but it was impossible to ignore the scene around them. Here was a place where the Kalyug was alive and thriving. People were everywhere, selling their wares or managing children or cleaning their living spaces or just sitting around, many of them spitting right on to the street as they went about their business. Women appeared from behind filthy curtains to throw putrid brown water into the drain while others, who got splashed by the water, cursed them with the foulest words imaginable. Young naked children defaecated directly into the drain mere steps away from where their mothers washed their cooking utensils. This slum, as Shashiben had called it, was unbearable and she couldn't imagine how mortals could live in such dirty conditions, virtually on top of each other, with barely enough room to breathe. There had been extreme poverty in her day too, but even the poorest of the poor had lived with more dignity than this.

Earlier, on their way here to find Karan, Shashiben had carelessly pointed out the prostitutes, as if they were a tourist attraction. They stood outside their huts or sat at their doors, dressed mostly in torn petticoats and sari blouses or ragged shifts, a look of utter detachment on their faces. Their vacant eyes either stared into space or followed the movements of people around them, seeming not to register much. Shashiben had shrugged and cackled, 'In this area, most of them use a drug called crack, although they have other ones too. They smoke it to numb themselves. Only problem is that it's very addictive so they need to keep having it regularly, and soon all their earnings go into buying more of it. It's a vicious circle and they're trapped in it.'

'Why do they smoke it if they know it's bad for them?' was Gandhari's perplexed question as she had looked around in horror.

Shashiben chuckled and said wryly, 'You know, there was another queen long after you who said something equally stupid. Her name was Marie Antoinette. They cut her head off.' She grinned at the combination of bafflement and fury on Gandhari's face and continued, 'They start to smoke it because it makes them feel better. It momentarily takes them away from their hell of a life and gives them a little respite from their inner feelings of shame and self-loathing. You wouldn't know what hell is, of course, coming from up there.'

Gandhari had shot back, 'As a matter of fact, I do. I spent my entire life with my perfectly good eyes covered in a blindfold. I lived to send all my children to the funeral pyre. No mother should have to bear that. It was hell for me.'

Shashiben had looked at her keenly in the eye and then at Kunti. 'All you mothers with your angst. I'm sick of all of you moaning about losing your children when half the time it's you who are floating them off in rivers or pushing them into battle. No' – she shook her head firmly when Gandhari opened her mouth to argue back – 'don't waste your breath.

What do I know? I'm just a godforsaken goddess. Literally!' She had cackled at her own wit as they arrived at the hut where she had been told Karan would be.

The scene that followed once they stepped inside would forever be etched inside Kunti's mind. They had seen a group of young boys and girls, all dressed in ragged, filthy clothing, sitting on the floor next to a large pile of purses, wallets, briefcases and plastic bags. They were playfully arguing with each other as they passed around and inhaled a large rolled-up joint and drunk a foul-smelling spirit from an unlabelled bottle. Karan seemed to be one of the older ones, for there must have been children as young as five in the room.

The group took one look at the three women and scrambled quickly, shouting at each other to pick up the bags and cursing. Karan had shouted instructions as he quickly grabbed Shashiben and hauled her out.

Now, he shepherded them down the street quickly, furtively looking around and over his shoulder, as if a demon was going to spring out and attack them from the shadows. At the end of the street he pushed them into the entrance of a tiny, dark alley that was virtually undetectable between two huts. Kunti felt herself stepping over something slimy and smelly but she kept her eyes ahead towards Karan, who spun around in the gloom and faced them, almost spitting with rage.

'What the fuck is wrong with you?' He turned on Shashiben and asked, 'Why did you bring them here? They'll kill me if they find me with you.'

Kunti gasped, 'Who will kill you?'

Karan ignored her but Shashiben answered instead, 'The local gang members who peddle the drugs and pimp the prostitutes. They also use street children for begging, stealing and transporting drugs. Among other things.' She looked at

Karan. 'You should know better, boy. You're not like the rest of them.'

Karan laughed bitterly. 'Who's going to protect me, old woman? You? Her?' He pointed to Kunti derisively.

Shashiben's eyes glazed over into her familiar carelessness as she said, 'She wanted me to help her find you. I thought it would be useful for her to see you in your element. You're going to be a big *dada* in the gang at this rate, aren't you? You've certainly got the brains for it. Should be very proud of yourself.'

Karan rolled his bitter eyes. 'I don't answer to you. I don't owe you anything.'

'Then why did you bring us into this alley?'

Kunti didn't realize she had spoken until everyone looked at her. She looked deep into Karan's eyes. 'Why didn't you just run away with the others? You put yourself in danger to lead us to safety. Why?'

Karan seemed determined to ignore her as he said to Shashiben sourly, 'Go back to the orphanage and take this bitch, who claims to be my family but has been missing for eleven years, with you. I don't want to have anything to do with her.'

'I know why you did it,' Kunti pressed on. 'Because you're a good boy with a good heart, even if you don't believe that right now. I didn't know where you were till now' – Kunti stepped closer to him and firmly put herself in his way so he had no choice but to look at her – 'but I know now and that is what matters. I'm not going to give up, Karan. I'm going to help you.'

Karan tried to sidestep her but she blocked him. 'I'm also going to keep coming back every day to find you. And you can call me names and try to scare me off, but it's not going to work. Now that I've finally found you—' She stopped. Now that she'd finally found him – what was she going to do? She had no idea about the specifics yet, but she couldn't make empty promises. 'I'm going to help you,' she repeated weakly.

Karan finally looked at her. His young face, as tough as it seemed to be, looked confused for the first time. He asked in a rough voice, 'How? Can you take me away?'

Kunti's heart burned with guilt and regret. She was only here for less than thirty days. 'I wish I could. But I have nowhere to take you.' She couldn't bring herself to tell him how long she was here for.

Karan's eyes went cold and he laughed a bitter, ironic laugh. 'So much for dreams of rich relatives. You're as poor as I am. Just my luck.'

He put his face closer to hers, his tough-boy act firmly back in place, and hissed, 'Fend for yourself old woman. You're not tricking me into feeding you.'

'I'm not tricking you, Karan. And I don't need you to feed me or take care of me,' Kunti began earnestly, but Karan's attention was diverted elsewhere, behind them. She turned to look and saw the smaller boy who had been with Karan in the common room, Goalie, standing at the far end of the alley and signalling furiously.

Karan's face fell into a mix of fear and purpose as he whispered, 'Ustaad.' He quickly looked at Shashiben. 'Hide.' Then he darted off at a speed one would think impossible for a boy of his age. He ran to Goalie and they disappeared into the maze of dark alleyways.

Shashiben pushed them back roughly into a dark doorway behind a foul-smelling sheet and put a finger over her mouth. They could hear voices, men shouting to each other and footsteps – at least five or six pairs of them – running towards their alley. They heard most of the footsteps run past, as the men shouted at each other to 'find them' and 'look in this one', but for one man who, breathing heavily, darted into the alley where they stood and came a few paces short of the doorway in which they were hiding.

Kunti closed her eyes and willed her heart to beat less loudly as – for a moment that seemed to stretch far too long – the man looked around, saw nothing except a quiet, empty alley, turned around and ran back the way he came. The shouting and footsteps receded into the distance, and Kunti let out the breath she had been holding.

Gandhari made a small, strangled noise and Kunti realized that she had forgotten her presence. She hadn't uttered a word during Kunti's exchange with Karan, which was very unlike her usual opinionated self. That soon changed as she looked at Shashiben and muttered, 'This is ridiculous. You shouldn't have brought us here. We could have been seriously hurt. Get us back to safety immediately!'

Shashiben glanced over at her and said, in a voice dripping with amused sarcasm, 'Yes, of course, your majesty!'

Chapter 23

'*How* can you allow it?'

Shashiben's eyes widened, as if she couldn't believe what she was hearing. She snarled back into Kunti's furious face, '*Allow* it? You think I have control over any of this? What do you want me to do? I get enough money to cook one lousy meal a day for thirty-five children. Do you know how many children show up every day for that meal? Over a hundred! I give the food to the youngest ones and refuse the older ones or the ones who have adult family members. Those kids have to leave and try to find work. The street gangs recruit them to beg and gradually, as they get older, involve them in gang activities. All I can do for kids like Karan is provide a shelter at night. Unless I can provide them with food and an education, I can't protect them from these gangs. Kids need full stomachs and an occupation, and these men offer them both. Along with drugs and drink and money to spend.'

She sat down on one of the two unbroken chairs in the orphanage common room and looked down at her lap, a deadened expression on her face. 'I have contacted the trust, the authorities, appealed to charities in the area, met countless bureaucrats, even tried to reason with the gang members.' She shook her head. 'Never try that, by the way. Almost had my throat slit.'

She glanced back up at Kunti, who paced the room in front of her. 'Nothing lasts. I get a donation but the money runs out. I get new volunteers, but they get scared and stop coming because of the crime and prostitution in the area. I get a charity involved, but they want to run the place like a business. This is not a business, this is an orphanage. The only staff I have is an old cook who is an alcoholic and keeps his share of food aside before he feeds any of the children. I haven't been paid a salary in over fifteen years.'

She closed her eyes, sighed and leaned back in her chair. With her eyes closed, her wrinkled, old face looked as frail and broken as her body. 'I'm tired. All I can do now is pray for Yamraj to release me.'

Kunti kneeled down next to her and put one hand over hers. 'I'm sorry. You have been through a lot. But you cannot give up now. What will happen to these children once you are gone?'

Shashiben laughed bitterly. 'What do you think? No other fool is going to live here on one meal a day and no salary. Once I go, this orphanage will go too and your precious Karan will be sleeping on the street.'

Don't cry, Kunti told herself. It would be a complete waste of time to cry now.

She started crying nonetheless. Softly, into Shashiben's lap.

Shashiben stroked Kunti's hair absently. Her eyes, bitter a few moments ago, seemed to suddenly light up with a tiny spark again as she looked down upon Kunti's shaking head. She glanced at Gandhari, who sat on another chair in the room and seemed to be quite detached from the situation, looking resignedly at her hands. Then she looked back at Kunti and smiled – just a little. 'Unless ...'

Kunti looked up at her quickly, by which time Shashiben's eyes had purposefully resumed their bitter, deadpan look. Kunti whispered from a sodden, red face, 'Unless?'

Shashiben shook her head dramatically, dismissively, as if the 'unless' option wasn't worth a consideration after all. Kunti squeezed her hand and looked beseechingly at her.

Finally Shashiben seemed to succumb, as if against her better judgement, and said, 'Unless someone else were to take over from me. Someone younger, more energetic, with new ideas that might really make a difference to kids like Karan.'

Kunti nodded furiously and murmured, 'Yes, yes,' and then after a moment, 'But who?'

Shashiben looked up at the ceiling. 'Who indeed?' And then, her eyes came down and rested upon Kunti, their meaning and implication perfectly clear, 'Who indeed?'

Kunti registered her meaning and reeled in surprise. 'Me? But I have to leave in a few days.'

'You don't have to leave. Not if you don't want to—'

'What nonsense!' Gandhari exploded from a few feet away as she got up and walked towards them. 'Of course we have to leave. We've been given only thirty days here. And moreover, even if she could stay, she would be giving up heaven forever. She would be stuck in an endless cycle of rebirth for eternity until the mortal world comes to an end.'

Shashiben shrugged. 'It's going to happen pretty soon, from what I hear.'

'Very funny. And anyway, that's not the point!' Gandhari exclaimed. '*You* will be comfortably ensconced once again in your goddess realm when you are released, so you can have no idea what it would be like for someone else to make that sacrifice. It is too much to ask of anyone. She cannot consider it even if it were possible, which I'm pretty sure it isn't.'

Kunti merely looked at each of them in turn as they spoke, her eyes showing nothing but surprise at the idea. It was certainly too much to ask of anyone. Even if it were possible, which Gandhari was pretty sure it wasn't.

Was it?

Surely not.

She didn't get a chance to ask because just then Draupadi and Amba walked into the room. They looked just a little put off with each other, parting ways and walking to opposite ends of the room. Amba went to a small dirty, window looking out on to the front yard and Draupadi came to join them.

Her first reaction, when she realized that Kunti had been crying again, was compassion. Then came irritation … how did their simple, recreational mortal-world-visit get so complicated?

She became even more irritated when she glanced over at Gandhari, who sat fuming and shaking her head in a corner.

'Now what?' Draupadi had just sat through an excruciatingly long car ride, where she'd been obliged to witness TV boy swooning non-stop over Amba, only to get here and find Kunti in emotional agony once again and Gandhari, who she wished for the thousandth time that she had left behind, was obviously being a nagging, self-righteous bore as usual.

Shashiben cackled her usual laugh as she looked Draupadi up and down. 'You're the one that was married to the five brothers. I saw you studying next to your brother when you were growing up. You were much more intelligent than him, you know.' She tsked softly. 'Such potential wasted.'

Draupadi, never one to refuse a challenge, returned Shashiben's assessing stare haughtily. 'So you're the avatar. In my day, avatars were better looking. They smelled better too.'

Shashiben laughed, her eyes twinkling with good humour at the rebuttal. She tossed her chin towards Amba, standing at the window, and asked, 'What's wrong with her? Not enjoying her little adventure?'

Draupadi shook her head a little. 'I think she might be enjoying it a bit too much.'

'Ah. Must be a man.' She looked back down at Kunti, her expression softening a little. 'Anyway, think about what I said.'

'She doesn't need to think about it.'

Shashiben ignored Gandhari and slowly stood up, her body creaking and cracking as she did. 'You'd best be getting to wherever you're sleeping now. It's almost dark, and trust me, you don't want to be out on the roads after dark in this city. Once the mortal men start drinking, they become like masth elephants. Where are you staying?'

Kunti answered, 'At the zoo. We will walk back if you tell us the way.'

Shashiben looked over Draupadi, Amba and Gandhari with their beautiful faces and young bodies. 'Walking would be a bad idea. I think I had better find you an auto rickshaw. It's the best way for you to get around the city, as long as you are careful. Come with me.'

Chapter 24

Draupadi flung herself on to her bed exclaiming, 'What a day!'

She was exhausted, rattled and disoriented, partly because it had been a long, eventful day but mostly from being jolted around in the back of the 'auto rickshaw' they had taken to return to the zoo. She had a new appreciation for Zafar and his car now, although she was also pleased at being able to get around the city without depending on him. Indraprastha seemed to be huge now and there were so many people around. The noise and chaos never seemed to let up. Every sense was bombarded constantly by something or the other. And while it was exciting, there seemed to be very little relief from all the excitement except when one came back to one's own abode.

The expressions the others wore suggested a similar relief at the respite from the Kalyug playing out outside. They had each lain down on their beds with tired sighs, and for a while, no one said anything.

Then Gandhari sat up and fidgeted with her clothing. 'I still can't believe she would suggest such a thing.'

Draupadi, still lying on her bed and staring at the gilded ceiling, swallowed a sharp retort and asked in the most even tone she could manage: 'What did she suggest?'

Kunti sat up slowly on her bed and sighed. 'Gandhari, there is no point still being upset about it.'

Kunti looked at Draupadi and said, 'Shashiben told us that after she passes on, there will be no one to look after the orphanage. It'll probably close down. The children, including Karan, will be left on the street, at the mercy of the drug lords, brothels and street gangs. It would be a terrible situation.'

Groaning softly, Draupadi sat up and returned Kunti's troubled gaze. She sighed. 'It *would* be a terrible situation, I agree. But what could we even do in the short time we have left here?'

Kunti looked away and replied faintly, 'Shashiben suggested that it could be prevented if someone took over from her. But mortals wouldn't want her job, so she suggested that, well, that I stay back and take over as the warden of the orphanage.'

That made Amba sit up and pay attention. Draupadi frowned. 'That isn't possible. And besides, Krishna expressly said not to get involved in the mortals' affairs.'

Gandhari acknowledged Draupadi's words with exasperated gratitude. '*Thank* you! That's exactly what I said.'

Draupadi ignored her and spoke to Kunti in a gentler voice, 'I know it must hurt you to see Karan the way he is, but you know you can't stay back with him. You do know that, right?'

Kunti replied, 'I know, I know. I just wish I knew what to do.' She stared at Draupadi with tormented eyes. 'Today he asked me if I could take him away. When I said I had nowhere to take him, you should have seen the desolation in his eyes. I told him I was going to help him' – she dropped her head into her hands – 'but I have no idea how to do that.'

'There is nothing you can do, sister. This is the Kalyug and Karan chose to be reborn,' Gandhari said harshly. 'He had the option of staying in heaven. This is his choice.'

Kunti looked at Gandhari with an uncharacteristic fire in her eyes. 'Nobody chooses to be born into his circumstances. He is only a child, with no idea why this is happening to him. How can you see what you saw today and still be so cold?'

'What I saw today, what I have seen since I got here, is a world gone mad. It is ugly, chaotic and cruel. Mortals seem to be no better than animals in this world, living in their constructed jungle. This is not a world I recognize.' Gandhari looked wary and agitated. 'This is most certainly not a world I would choose to be born into. Or want you to be living in, my sister.' She ended with an emphatic look for Kunti.

Kunti replied with equal fervour, 'A mother would gladly live under Mara's own roof if it meant she could be with her children.'

Gandhari looked shocked. 'You mean you would actually consider staying back here?'

Kunti frowned. 'No. Yes. I don't know.'

'You can't be serious. To give up heaven forever—'

Draupadi interrupted firmly, 'Enough. This discussion is going nowhere very fast. Kunti, you are the best mother I know. Better than all of us put together. I have no doubt that you would brave a demon army for your children, but right now, it's not like you have the choice.'

Kunti stayed silent, staring down at her bed sheet.

Draupadi continued gently, 'I suggest you make the most of your time here. Spend your days with Karan, keep him out of trouble. It's the best you can do under the circumstances.'

Kunti looked at her and whispered with conviction, 'That's not enough. If I can't stay with him, I'll have to think of something else.'

Gandhari expelled a loud breath, her eyes still wide. 'I can't believe what I'm hearing—'

'I think you've said enough, Gandhari,' Amba interrupted quietly. 'Spare us your sweeping judgements.'

She gave Kunti a sympathetic glance before saying to Gandhari, 'Not everyone sees the world you see. For every bad experience we have had, there has been a good one to counter it. I don't think you should be so quick to dismiss the mortal world.'

Gandhari laughed harshly. 'Of course you would say that. Don't think we haven't noticed your fondness for a few, or should we say *one*, mortal in particular. Get up to something interesting when you were alone in the bedchamber with him yesterday?'

Amba scowled and tossed her head. 'It wasn't a bedchamber and he was showing me his weapons collection. That's probably more interesting than anything you've ever done when alone in a room with a man.'

Draupadi let out a snort of laughter and even Kunti spared a small smile, which of course she quickly hid when she saw the inflamed look on Gandhari's face.

Draupadi said with shaking shoulders, 'You deserved that, Gandhari.' She then smiled and asked cheerfully: 'Now, is someone going to ask me how my day was?'

Kunti smiled affectionately at her. 'How was your day?'

Draupadi told them what had happened in the studio and how she had been offered the anchorperson job for the TV show, which of course there was no question of accepting, she hurriedly clarified before Gandhari could say anything. She also told them about Vaishali and her story.

'How horrible,' remarked Kunti.

Draupadi nodded. 'I know. It's not much better for women like her than it is for those orphan kids of yours. This is what surprises me so much about this world. On the one hand, there are women like Angela, who seem to be on par with men in every way, but on the other, not much seems to have changed for women like Vaishali. There is such a vast disparity between the two that it confounds me.'

It seemed to confound everyone else too, for no one apparently had anything to say about it. Kunti and Amba seemed distracted with their own thoughts and Draupadi was pretty sure Gandhari was sulking.

She sighed and lay down, once again staring up at the ceiling, unable to stop thinking about Vaishali. Her heart went out to that girl. As she dozed off, she wondered if there was something she could do to help her before she left.

Chapter 25

'Look, Zafar, I'm flattered that the, the … *who* thought I was good?' Draupadi frowned at the phone.

Zafar's voice rang out of it. 'The producers.'

'Right, the producers, whoever they are, but—'

'They're the ones who produce, who make the TV show *Us, the Women*. You met one of them yesterday. Angela.'

Draupadi nodded impatiently, as if he could see her. 'Yes. Look, please thank her for the offer but I can't accept it.'

His voice was insistent. 'No one is asking you to take the job. She just thought you might like to see your performance. Aren't you curious to see what you look like on TV?'

She *was* curious, even though she knew full well that it was a snare. She ran her gaze around the chamber, watching the other women as they got dressed. Kunti and Gandhari were off to the orphanage again this morning, Gandhari having apologized to Kunti at some point during the night and also having vowed to support her. As for Amba and herself, they had planned to take an auto rickshaw around the city. Until the phone clanged with Zafar's voice waiting inside it.

She watched as Amba absently combed her hair, pretending not to listen to her conversation. It would probably not be a good idea to have her and Zafar spend too much time together. Oh god, now her thoughts were beginning to sound like Gandhari.

'Well—'

Zafar cut in quickly, 'Draupadi, come in and take a look, that's all she's asking. Should I pick you up later? Outside the zoo again?'

Oh, what the hell, thought Draupadi. 'All right.'

She could hear him smiling. 'Great! Is—is Amba going to come too?'

Draupadi smiled as she glanced over at Amba, still slowly, deliberately combing her hair next to the window, looking delicate and beautiful as the morning sunlight bounced off her glossy locks and chiselled cheekbones. What man wouldn't want her, thought Draupadi. Besides, Amba was a grown woman who more than deserved a little excitement. It was Draupadi's job to guard her on this expedition, not parent her.

'Yes, she'll be with me.'

He was waiting for them on the road, leaning against his car, when they walked out of the zoo. They had worn their new clothes, Draupadi in tight black jeans with a red t-shirt that Sania had picked out for her, and a colourful patchwork bag slung over her shoulder, and Amba in a long, flowing, blue skirt paired with a tight, but modest, white top.

A piercing whistle rang out as they walked to Zafar's car. Draupadi turned to find a group of men standing to the side ogling them with saucy smiles and suggestive comments. She glared at them but smiled to herself after she turned her face away. Finally, somebody noticed her! These last few days had probably been the only time in her existence that she had walked relatively unappreciated among men. Used to being feted and lauded, it had been an unwelcome change. Even Zafar, polite and discreet as he was, had an appreciative gleam in his eye as he greeted her. The world made a little more sense again.

They arrived back in the TV office amid many more ogling and appraising glances. Angela looked up from her desk as they approached and raised an eyebrow. 'Wow. Why didn't you wear that yesterday?'

Draupadi half-smiled at her, not wanting to be overly friendly since she was going to be refusing the job again shortly. 'You wanted to show me something?'

Angela's eyes lit up in a knowing way which indicated she was more than ready for the duel ahead. She stood to her full, tiny height and craned her neck to meet Draupadi's eyes. Even then she managed to emit authority and confidence as she spoke, 'I did. I wanted to show you how magnificent your performance was yesterday. You deserve to know' – she smiled, all amused charm – 'what it is that you're refusing.'

Before Draupadi could reply, Angela looked over her shoulder and suddenly barked out, 'Get the tape ready,' which sent two younger women scurrying off quickly.

Then she turned back to them, her tone becoming charming once more. 'Can I get you some coffee?' she asked with a hospitable smile, as if they were guests in her home.

They shook their heads.

'Right. Come along, then, let's get this show on the road.'

They followed her down several busy hallways until they reached a cramped, dark room with one wall almost covered in TVs of different sizes. Machines covered another wall, and in the centre were two long tables covered with even more TV screens and machines. People sat along these tables, idly leaning back in their chairs and chatting with each other. When they saw Angela, however, they sat up and quickly returned to their tasks, pressing buttons on the machines in front of them and staring with ferocious concentration into the newly flashing screens.

Angela swept the room with an amused stare before turning to her guests. 'Meet our production crew. Masters of what we call LBDF ... Looking busy, doing fuck-all.' She spoke to a meek-looking young man sitting nervously on the side, 'You, new production assistant, roll the tape.'

Zafar directed Draupadi and Amba's gaze to a large screen in the centre of the wall, which suddenly came to life with flashing numbers and a beeping tone. Then, music filled the room and the words 'Us, the Women' flashed on the TV.

Angela remarked, 'This is just for reference, we haven't cut an opening montage yet.'

Draupadi nodded as if she knew what that meant. Then she started in shock as she saw herself on the TV. It was unreal. There she stood, tall and proud, even in her dull, boxy clothes, her wavy hair shining, framing a face full of compassion one minute and anger the next, with eyes that burned with conviction as she told Vaishali's story. It was as if she was talking directly to herself, standing with Zafar, Amba and Angela in the small room, entreating them to feel the same way about what had happened to Vaishali as she did. She watched her expression turn to indignation when she talked about the injustices and humiliation that Vaishali had been made to suffer, as if they had been done to herself and not someone else.

'See what you did?' said Angela softly. 'You brought the viewer into her story. Made them root for her. And you. You made it personal.'

Draupadi was transfixed by the image of herself, now speaking empathetically to Vaishali, bringing her to tears one moment and then making her flush with courage the next.

Then she was walking around, speaking to audience members, her voice authoritative as she coaxed a shy, young woman to give her opinion but lambasted another older one for her judgemental notions.

And then, as quickly as it had begun, it was over and the TV screen turned black as her image faded away.

'But that wasn't the whole thing,' protested Draupadi. She wanted to see more.

Angela turned to her and said, 'No, we edited it. This is just a teaser, a compilation of your best bits.'

She took a deep breath and continued impatiently, 'Look, you can't teach people how to do this stuff, especially not people who look like you. You're beautiful *and* relatable ... that's almost unheard of. A little bit of training needed, obviously. I mean, Oprah wasn't built in a day. Some cool clothes and a slap of make-up and you're looking at prime-time gold, baby.'

She gave Amba a quick, dismissive glance before saying, 'Look, I know you're from a small town, traditional family, yada yada, but this gig pays big time. I could make you a *very* attractive offer. Enough for you to relocate, get a nice pad, buy a set of wheels, maybe even some bling, if you're into that kind of thing ...' She cocked her head to one side and smiled coaxingly. '... am I moving the needle at all here?'

Draupadi's completely baffled face blinked at her for a moment and then turned to Zafar. 'What?'

Zafar was thoroughly amused. 'She said that you're very good. You just need a bit of training. If you agree to take the job, she is willing to pay you a lot of money. Enough for you to live a good life in Delhi.'

Draupadi looked back at the blank TV screen and tried to take it all in. Seeing herself from the outside had been overwhelming. Her face, her expressions, her body and the way it moved – it was so real. The fact that this likeness of her existed separately now, suspended forever in that moment in time with a life of its own was ... amazing!

She turned back to find Zafar and Angela looking at her expectantly and with Amba staring at her very apprehensively. Remembering that she still needed to give them an answer to whether she'd take the job or not, Draupadi hesitated. It was out of the question, of course, no matter how fascinated she was by all of this. She needed to let them down firmly.

She said with a slight note of regret in her voice, 'Thank you, but I can't. Sorry.'

Angela rolled her eyes but her face was adamant as she asked, 'Why not?'

'I have to go back to, uh, the ashram. I can't stay here.'

Angela frowned up at her angrily, the determined look never once leaving her face. 'How can you want to go back to a bloody *ashram* when you could have—No, never mind. Forget I said that.' She breathed deeply, obviously calming herself down. 'Look, it's a lot to take in, big decision etc., I get that. I've got a proposition for you.' She looked at Zafar, trying to garner his support. 'We shoot a pilot. If after you see it, you're *still* not up for it, I totally respect that and I'll totally back off.' She took a step back with her palms facing Draupadi, as if to emphasize her point. 'But at least give it a damn shot. Just shoot one episode with me.'

Draupadi, for the life of her, had no idea what this woman was talking about. She looked at Zafar again.

Zafar grinned and turned to Angela. 'You need to speak English, Angela. Most people think a pilot is someone who flies an aeroplane.'

Draupadi asked, 'What's an aeroplane?'

Angela looked up at the ceiling, seemingly for heavenly assistance. 'Jesus Christ.'

Zafar gave her a meaningful glare before replying, 'An aeroplane is like a really big car but it's shaped like a bird, with wings, and it flies in the sky very fast, carrying a lot of people inside it. Usually, aeroplanes ferry people to and fro between places in the world that are far from each other or have seas or oceans separating them. Pilots are the guys who drive the planes, just like I drive my car.' As usual, he seemed quite pleased with the explanation.

Draupadi willed her tone to be casual. 'Flying in the air?'

Zafar nodded. 'In the sky, very high up so they don't bang into the birds.'

'With people inside?'

'Yup. Depending on the size of the plane, it could carry anywhere from three people to three hundred people.' Zafar smiled. 'You can see aeroplanes at the airport. I can take you there, if you like.'

Mortals *could* fly! 'Yes, thank you. I would really like that.' She grinned at Zafar, probably for the first time, barely able to keep her excitement in check. Then a thought occurred to her. 'Or I could take an auto rickshaw!'

'Great idea,' Angela interrupted with sarcastic enthusiasm, her face clearly indicating that she was at the end of her tether. 'Now, may I get this conversation back on track here?'

She turned to Draupadi and said, 'A pilot is the first episode. Okay, hang on, let me try again. A pilot ... We just get you to do *exactly* what you did before, but this time for longer – for one hour precisely – until you finish the discussion. So you speak to Vaishali, tell her story, take questions *exactly* as before,' she repeated. 'But this time, we dress you up a little, give you a few tips on how to handle the audience, teach you a bit about keeping the show on track, etc. and *then*' – she smiled painfully, as if to a child who would try the patience of a saint – 'we go back, edit it and turn it into a TV show. You only have to show up for a few hours on one day and follow instructions. No commitment beyond that.'

Draupadi frowned. 'One day? That's all?'

Angela looked firm and nodded. 'That's it. No more. After that, if you don't like what you see, I'll never bother you again.'

Amba piped in, 'And what if she does like what she sees?'

Angela gave her an irritated glance before saying to Draupadi, 'If you like what you see, then we'll discuss options.'

Amba's eyes narrowed. 'Like what?'

'All right.'

They all turned to Draupadi in surprise. She smiled. 'I'll do it. Just one day, we do the same thing as last time, right?'

Angela grinned. 'Right. Awesome!'

Amba wasn't happy. 'Are you sure?'

Draupadi nodded. 'Yes.'

Amba gave her a look that clearly meant they were going to discuss this later, in private, before Angela whooped and shook

Draupadi's hand vigorously. 'You're doing the right thing. It's going to be great!' Then she turned to Zafar and said, 'She needs to sign some stuff. Could you take her up to HR?'

'Sure,' he replied.

Angela smiled. 'Thanks,' and looked at her watch. She exclaimed in surprise and said to Draupadi in a rush, 'Okay, well, I've got to run for a shoot now but Zafar will take you up to HR and get you to do the paperwork. I'll sort out the date for the pilot shoot and get the details to you ASAP. Probably next week sometime. You guys going to be coming to the office again? We can hang out, get to know each other since we might be working together' – she smiled sheepishly and crossed her fingers – 'hopefully!'

No chance of that happening beyond next week but Draupadi liked this tiny, pushy chameleon of a woman, so she said, 'Well, we hadn't planned to come back here but yes, it would be nice to, uh, hang out.'

Angela thought for a quick moment before her face brightened with an idea. 'Hey, what're you guys doing on Saturday night? There's a Gautam Thakur fashion show at The Raj Hotel and the after-party downstairs in the nightclub later. Want to come?'

Zafar said enthusiastically, 'Good idea. I got Sania an invite for it since she's studying fashion. I could get a few more if you guys are interested, and we can go together.'

Draupadi looked at Amba, whose face was politely conflicted. On the one hand, it was obvious she wanted to spend more time with Zafar, but on the other, she didn't exactly want Draupadi 'hanging out' with Angela. Oh, what the hell, thought Draupadi. They could finally find out what a hotel was, at least. Draupadi smiled and replied, 'We would love to go.'

'Awesome, see you on Saturday, then.' Angela gave them a dazzling grin and was out of the door.

Zafar turned to his companions with a good-humoured roll of the eye. 'Packs quite a punch for someone so small, doesn't she?'

Amba replied with uncharacteristic sarcasm, 'She sure does.'

Chapter 26

'Name?' asked the stout, serious-looking man who squinted a little myopically at the piece of parchment on the table.

Draupadi remembered the soothsayer and said, 'Ms Draupadi Kuru.'

The man looked up at Draupadi, Zafar and Amba with a vacant expression, as if to wait and see whether they were serious or not. Then he had to ask, 'Is that your real name?'

'Yes.'

He looked mildly irritated. 'Once I write it down, I can't change it. Then I'll have to get a fresh form.'

Draupadi felt her temper rising. 'That is my real name.'

He dully wrote it down. 'Married?' He didn't look up.

'No.'

'Single?'

Zafar answered, 'Well, if she's not married then she's single, right?'

The man looked up at him with a deadpan look. 'She could be separated, divorced or widowed.'

Zafar, usually the picture of patience, looked irritated. 'Single.'

The man addressed Draupadi again. 'Age?'

A few thousand years. 'Twenty ... five,' she replied. Bit older than she looked, probably, but an advanced age always meant a little more respect.

'Educational qualifications?'

Well, she had had a tutor till she started menstruating but she doubted she could tell him that. 'What are the options?'

The man didn't look up. 'Higher secondary, bachelor's degree or master's degree. Or post-graduate diploma.'

Draupadi shrugged inwardly. 'The last one.'

'Subject of diploma?'

She huffed and looked at Zafar. 'Is all of this really important? I'm just coming back for a day.'

'Subhash,' Zafar addressed the man, 'can she fill out this stuff later, if she takes the job? She's just shooting a pilot.'

Subhash blinked at Zafar. 'I need to have her details before she can sign the indemnity form and I give her the advance payment.'

Zafar nodded placatingly. 'Yes, I understand but Angela doesn't need to know her educational qualifications right now, so let's just have her sign the indemnity. Oh, and she doesn't have a bank account in Delhi' – he turned to Draupadi – 'right?'

Draupadi decided to agree with him and nodded.

Zafar turned back to Subhash. 'So you'll need to give her the advance in cash.'

That request finally broke Subhash's blank expression and he looked up, thoroughly irritated, at Zafar. 'Cash requires more paperwork.'

Zafar's eyes narrowed. 'Dude, you'd rather deal with me or Angela?'

A flash of terror briefly lit Subhash's eyes. After that, he was subdued enough to waive the paperwork, getting Draupadi to quickly sign her name before handing over a thick wad

– actually, several thick wads bound together with stretchy bands – of money. 'I only have hundreds, for petty cash,' he mumbled.

Draupadi weighed the money in her hands. It was probably ten times as much as Narad Muni had given them for their entire trip. 'What's this for?'

Zafar smiled. 'It's half the payment for shooting the pilot. You'll get the other half after the shoot, on that day itself.'

Draupadi looked over at Amba, their eyes widening at each other over the sheer amount of money she would be paid.

Zafar noticed their surprise and said softly, 'This is only a token amount, Draupadi. Hosting a show like this once a week is a very lucrative job. You should seriously think about it' – he held up his hands when she looked at him – 'but like we said, no pressure.'

He smiled good-naturedly, his eyes wandering over to Amba. 'Okay, um.' His eyes softened and so did his voice. 'I guess I'll see you on Saturday.'

Amba nodded up at him. 'Yes.' She smiled gently.

'Can I' – he looked from Amba to Draupadi and back again, unsure about whether to ask or not – 'speak to you for a moment?' He looked slightly embarrassed now as he added, 'In private?'

That got Amba a little flustered. 'I, er—'

Draupadi cut in. 'We really should get going.' She looked at Amba with a raised eyebrow.

That got Amba annoyed. 'Yes, but I'd like to hear what Zafar has to say. After all, he's been really' – her eyes focused on the money meaningfully – '*nice* to us, hasn't he, sister?'

Draupadi would've argued if Zafar hadn't been looking at her. 'Fine. Excuse me while I go count my money.' She rolled her eyes.

Zafar was relieved. 'Okay, although don't count it out in the open. Put it away in your bag now and I'll get you a meeting room where you can have some privacy.'

They followed him through a series of hallways until they came to a less crowded, narrow hallway with lots of identical-looking doors, each marked with a sign that said 'Meeting Room' followed by a number and then a coloured box, which was either red or green, depending on the door. Zafar led them to a door with a green box and turned it to make it red. Then he held the door open for Draupadi. 'You can sit here. There's a water cooler on the side if you're thirsty. We'll just be next door.'

'Take your time.' Draupadi couldn't quite mask the irony in her voice as she strode in and shut the door behind her. She looked around at the dark wood table and the beige-cushioned chairs, sighed and decided to count her money after all.

Meanwhile, Zafar led Amba to another meeting room close by and shut the door behind him, saying softly, 'Sorry, I just had to speak to you. I feel we didn't quite finish our last conversation.'

Amba's heart was already beating very fast when she walked in, but at those words, it started racing. She nodded, unsure about what to say.

Zafar's heart might have been in a similar state because he took a deep breath before he continued, 'As I was saying, I really like you and—and I'd like to get to know you better.'

Not a good idea. She only had a few days in this world and it wouldn't do to start getting involved with people. She didn't want to hurt him. Or herself. Still, she stayed quiet, avoiding his gaze, unable to come up with a suitable response.

Zafar waited, but when she didn't say anything, he felt compelled to continue, 'Unless, of course, you don't feel the same way about me.'

She shook her head quickly and met his eyes for a moment. Then she looked away again.

'Does that mean no, you don't feel the same way or no, you feel the same way?' He smiled.

Amba shifted on her feet. 'I, well, I really can't say, Zafar. I'm not used to talking about this sort of thing.'

Zafar nodded, thought for a moment and then smiled flirtatiously. 'Fair enough. Then maybe I can make an educated guess. I'd say you don't *not* like me. In fact, I'd probably go as far as to say you might even enjoy my company a little.'

Amba couldn't help smiling back. 'Only a little. Very little.'

Zafar's smile broadened. 'Hey, I'll take that. Best I can hope to get from a lady who is so totally out of my league.'

He cocked his head with a wicked look and her heart stepped up its pace, which was remarkable because it had been racing to begin with.

'I didn't tell you how nice you're looking today, in your new clothes.'

Amba wished he would stop looking at her like that. 'Thank you.'

'Want to have another coffee with me sometime?'

'No.'

He blinked. 'Why?'

'I didn't really like it.'

Zafar's grin was back. 'Then next time I'll get you hot chocolate. It's a sure shot. All girls like hot chocolate.'

'I'm not like all other girls.'

A spark lit Zafar's eyes and he became serious as he said softly, 'No, you're definitely not.'

The room seemed to have inexplicably shrunk. His presence seemed to overwhelm it. Her heart, damn it, went into a sprint and her breaths came in short spurts. Zafar, his grin replaced by a searing stare, took a step closer to her. 'Amba, I ...'

He was going to kiss her. She was sure of it. Not a good idea. Really bad idea. She had to do something, anything, to stop him. She felt like throwing up. No, she couldn't do that, it might put him off her. But that's what she wanted, right? Not really, oh god, he was going to kiss her.

He stopped in front of her and looked deep into her eyes. Then, he said softly in a hoarse voice, 'Just give me a chance,okay?'

She looked up at him and barely managed to nod. Now, he was going to kiss her.

Zafar cleared his throat, put his hand on her shoulder and gave it a gentle squeeze, saying, 'Great. So the coffee is on. Or hot chocolate, whatever. I'll call you, okay?'

She nodded. He was going to kiss her now, right?

He took a step back with a deep breath and grinned again. 'We'd better go get your sister out of that room. She looked like she was going to kill me when she saw it.'

He wasn't going to kiss her?

'Oh hey, when we get a chance, I must show you this sword I bought. Nineteenth century. You'll love it,' he said over his shoulder as he opened the meeting room door and turned the box on it back to green. Then he stood aside so she could come out.

No, he wasn't going to kiss her.

Amba stomped out of the room and past him. Thank god, she thought to herself angrily. She would have hated it anyway. No point complicating things. Just as well. Her lip trembled.

'Amba, this way.' Zafar indicated the opposite direction from which she was walking.

Embarrassed and angry at herself for feeling and behaving like a petulant, inexperienced girl, she swivelled around and pointedly ignored him as they walked to get Draupadi out of the other room. She was fine without his kisses. He didn't know what he was missing. He could go to hell for all she cared.

He opened a door and she stalked into it. When her eyes met Draupadi's, a small tear inadvertently welled up in one of them. Draupadi's eyes narrowed but Amba quickly shook her head a little. They could talk later.

Zafar apologized to Draupadi for keeping her waiting. She accepted his apology with a tight lip, her worried gaze never leaving Amba. 'Can I drop you both home?'

'No,' Draupadi said categorically, 'we'll take an auto rickshaw.' Her eyes brooked no argument.

He didn't insist, thankfully, and took them to the road where he hailed an auto rickshaw, rigorously interviewed the young driver, fixed the payment amount and gave him strict instructions about directions in a stern and almost threatening tone. Then he said, 'See you Saturday' and waved goodbye as the auto rickshaw sped away, the driver muttering to himself sulkily.

'All right,' gasped out Draupadi as they were jostled violently to the left in a bid to overtake another auto rickshaw on the road, 'what happened?'

Amba watched as an oncoming bus sped towards them only to swerve at the very last instant to avoid running them over and said, 'Why did you agree to do the pilot thing?'

Draupadi blinked impatiently and cursed the driver as she held on to the metal rod behind his seat. 'Are we talking about you or me?'

Amba shouted to be heard over the loud honking of the truck speeding along next to them, 'I don't want to talk about it. We're talking about you.'

Draupadi shouted back, 'I agreed because it's just one day and I enjoyed it.' She shrugged. 'The you-know-what doesn't hurt either. More clothes for us!' She chuckled.

Amba ignored the last bit, looking away thoughtfully for a moment before turning back to Draupadi with a worried expression on her face. 'Aren't you getting too involved? Making promises you can't keep?'

Draupadi replied deliberately, 'I'm going to have some fun for a day and forget about it after that.' She looked carefully at Amba, her eyes full of meaning. 'You have to ask yourself the same question, my dear.'

Amba stared at her for a moment. Then she looked away, a considering expression on her face.

Draupadi cursed the driver again as they were thrown off their seats, the auto rickshaw literally flying over a bump on the road. Then she sat back and watched him muttering in response, leaving Amba alone with her thoughts. She didn't need to say any more there.

Her own situation wasn't as simple as she had made it sound. The truth was she had really enjoyed her experience in the studio. And the money was good, more than enough to live comfortably in Indrap—Delhi. If, that is, she wanted to make a life for herself in the mortal world. She smiled as she imagined what Gandhari would say if she knew her thoughts. Fool, she would call her again.

She sighed. Giving up heaven is huge. Too huge, she thought, for rebirth would be so uncertain. They would probably make her be reborn as one of those dung beetles next time, just to spite her. Not worth it to suffer in future lifetimes just for the excitement of one as a TV show host.

No, she better not fool around with the system. A thirty-day trip was all well and good, but this world was still deep in the Kalyug and she was better off in her cloudy paradise. She sighed again as she thought about the conversation she would need to have with Angela on Saturday. That woman was not going to be easy to put off. She would have the tenacity of a hunting dog, and even though she had never seen it, probably the temper of a banshee as well. She reminded Draupadi of herself.

A screech, a bump and she lurched forward and knocked her forehead on the metal rod she was holding. '*Once* more,' she snarled at the driver, making his eyes open wide and his nostrils flare in fear, 'and I swear I will *skin* you alive, do you hear me? I'll be *damned* if I die before my thirty days are up!'

Chapter 27

The days passed by all too quickly after that.

Draupadi ventured out to see the city with Amba time and again and was continuously amazed to realize how vast it was. Each part of the city differed in small ways. Some parts had massive buildings while others were slums, and still others were relatively tranquil colonies with stately houses, much like the guest palaces that had graced Indraprastha in her own time. Some parts of the city had ruins dotted around the landscape, which were quite unlike anything they had ever had seen: large domes, geometric patterns and words in mysterious languages. They usually stood in sparse and neglected parks and gardens that were the only relief from the heat, dust, dirt and noise that followed them everywhere.

They visited large buildings of worship and were awed to see the sheer scale of the temples, each serving a different religion or community, each with its own architecture, design and style of art. They were surprised to find out how many different religions and belief systems coexisted peacefully at such close quarters. Here in Delhi, they were told, people in neighbouring houses could worship different gods, eat different food, wear different clothing and still be friends. The only thing that distinguished people from each other in the city, said one vendor who served them roasted, spiced sweet potatoes on a street corner one day, was money. Those who had it, he said as he spat out a black stream on to the road behind him, could live well in the nice bungalow colonies, travel and enjoy the comforts of life, irrespective of caste or religion. Similarly, no matter how high your caste or privileged your background, if you had no money, you lived as a pauper in a slum somewhere.

One day, while walking past a large gathering around a ramshackle stage in one of the poorer neighbourhoods, they even came across a performance about Draupadi herself. On stage, a sallow-faced young woman dressed in a gaudy red sari and covered in shiny baubles was squinting and crowing at the audience about how the Great War at Kurukshetra had been fought because of Draupadi's desire for revenge against the Kauravas for disrobing her in court. The real Draupadi, in utter shock and disgust, was forced by Amba to leave the gathering before she got up on stage herself and gave the woman a piece of her mind.

She let loose on Amba instead. '*Me*? They think *I* was responsible for the Great War? How typical, blame it on the woman! No one talks about *their* ambition or the fact that my darling husbands wanted their own revenge for being kicked out of Hastinapur and then Indraprastha into the blasted forest, where they had to pick leeches off their skin and eat berries for twelve years. I could've screamed at them about revenge until the cows came home, but a fat lot they would have done about it had it not suited their own purposes. I can't believe they made it *my* fault. No *wonder* nobody will name their daughters after me any more!'

Amba clucked and soothed, making all the right noises, but for the most part, her mind kept either replaying her conversation with Zafar in the meeting room or preparing what she was going to say to him on Saturday night. She was attracted to him, obviously. Her inability to control herself around him, the fact that she had desperately wanted him to kiss her and then gotten angry when he didn't – there was no point denying it any more. It was as if her loins had suddenly woken up, after thousands of years, and realized that they were still alive. They reminded her of that fact every night before she went to sleep, parts of her unhelpfully pulsating as she tossed in bed thinking about the knife-play with Zafar, or the way he drank coffee, or the kiss that he never gave her.

She would have to withstand the temptation of getting involved with him, naturally. Not only did she not want to lose her heart to him, but she didn't want to hurt him either by making promises and then disappearing. No, she would be strong and tame her wretched body.

Kunti meanwhile had managed to contain her sorrow long enough to figure out how she could help Karan in the short time she had left in this world. On Shashiben's advice, she had gone to meet the headmaster of a free boarding house and school run by a charity for boys of Karan's age. As she walked into the compound, she tried not to let the sight of a group of older boys dragging a younger boy by the collar into a building nearby discourage her. In the office, she had met a tall, burly man of about sixty summers with intense, disillusioned eyes, a partly puffy, partly sunken face that suggested too much drink and a harsh way of speaking. He had told her in no uncertain terms that unless Karan was completely committed to staying there until he finished his education – which would be at least six years but probably more – there was no point in her applying on his behalf. His biggest problem was runaways – boys who could not take the pressure of a disciplined life or the bullying that they inevitably faced from the older boys. He had no time or money to waste, and so she had to make sure that Karan had all his papers and attitude in order first.

Back at the orphanage, she had cornered Karan and told him about her proposition. He had laughed and coarsely told his friend Goalie to 'tell this nut job of a lady that the walls of "schools" like these see more fucking than a brothel and that I would rather die of starvation in this slum than be buggered by that headmaster and his cronies.'

Kunti found that there was no reasoning with Karan either; he would simply end up stalking off and disappearing into the neighbouring alleys. His attitude towards her grew a little softer with each passing day, but he still refused to speak to her directly, always using Goalie or Shashiben as a go-between.

Shashiben, of course, kept up her meaningful glances and unhelpful comments. 'Well, you could change things, if you *really* wanted to' was a well-worn refrain, as was 'Unless you show commitment, why should he?' That line of reasoning always ended with Gandhari turning on Shashiben in a temper. Kunti suspected that Shashiben had begun to say such things expressly for the sake of riling Gandhari up for her own amusement. Things were going nowhere very fast.

Before they knew it, Saturday was upon them. Kunti pleaded out of the evening with Sania and Zafar, saying that she intended to spend the whole day at the orphanage and would return to Narad Muni's cabin late. She insisted that Draupadi and Amba carry on without her and that Gandhari go with them. She refused to heed Gandhari's protests, saying that while she was very grateful for the support, she couldn't help but think that Gandhari needed some time to enjoy herself too.

'Go on,' she said to Gandhari kindly, but determinedly. 'Have some fun, just for one evening. You deserve it.' To herself, she breathed a small sigh of relief when Gandhari reluctantly agreed. It meant a few hours of respite from the constant verbal duel between her and Shashiben.

And so it happened that when Zafar and Sania pulled up their car in front of the closed gate of the zoo that evening, they found Draupadi, catlike in her tight black jeans and a black top that bared her arms and neck, Amba, in a little black dress, and a slightly nervous Gandhari in an almost-ankle-length white skirt and ill-fitting, but modest, black top that Draupadi had insisted she borrow so she didn't look out of place.

'Good girls,' whooped Sania excitedly. 'See, Zafar, they listened to me. You can never go wrong with black. You guys look stunning. I am so proud of myself! Now all you need is a touch of make-up and a spritz of perfume, both of which I happen to have with me, of course.' She fished these things out of her bag dramatically, looking thoroughly pleased with herself as she dabbed a reddish clay-like substance on Draupadi and Amba's lips, some powder on their eye-lids and cheeks and sprayed a pleasant, oceany smelling liquid on to their necks, behind their ears and, with a tiny wink, into their cleavages. Gandhari disdainfully shook her head to refuse with a look one might give a concubine who had the audacity to show herself at court.

Zafar couldn't take his eyes off Amba, who felt a flush climbing up her neck to her face and became flustered as she scrambled, as quickly as possible, into the back seat of his car. This was such a bad idea, she scolded herself once inside. Zafar was clean-shaven and handsome in his fitting, smooth black shirt and smelled of fresh lemons and warmth. She should have gone with Kunti to the orphanage. How was she supposed to resist him if he insisted on looking so good!

If Draupadi noticed that Amba looked agitated or Gandhari looked irritated, she ignored it. A fashion show, Sania was explaining over her shoulder as Zafar drove the car, was a show where fashion designers – people who designed clothing – put their newest wares for display. Women, called models, wore the clothing and walked down a ramp on stage so people could see the clothes up close. There were new looks for each season, and all the important people in the city usually attended the event. This particular designer, Gautam Thakur, was one of the most famous fashion designers in the country. Sania was breathless as she talked about how lucky they were to be able to get invites for the show and it would never have been possible if Zafar was not a journalist with a big TV channel.

'Gautam Thakur is fashion royalty!' she exclaimed.

'Royalty?' Draupadi asked with interest. 'He is a prince as well?'

Sania shook her head. 'No, he isn't. But there probably will be a couple of princesses there. The royals love wearing his clothes in their private time. They have to wear all those chiffon saris and big emeralds in their public pictures and appearances, of course. It's the uniform.'

Draupadi's eyes lit up at the thought of meeting a current princess. She began to wonder if they would be anything like herself when her thoughts were interrupted by a spectacular sight.

The car drove on to a porch illuminated by thousands of tiny lights suspended, seemingly, in mid-air below the ceiling, designed to look like a shimmering golden cloud. Draupadi's eyes widened as a man dressed in an elaborate purple turban walked up to the car and opened the door for them.

She got out and was ushered through a large doorway into a breathtakingly beautiful room, larger than an arena, with a high, domed ceiling decorated in elaborate murals and gilded pillars everywhere. Larger, more dazzling versions of the illuminated crystal sculptures in Narad Muni's chambers hung from this ceiling, their bright warm light coating everything with an extravagant brilliance. The floor was marble of the whitest white and the walls were draped in delicately painted silks, enormous, gold-framed paintings and undulating carvings in gold leaf.

'A palace,' murmured Amba, giving voice to Draupadi's thoughts. 'It's splendid.'

Sania giggled. 'Oh, this isn't a palace, honey. It's a five-star hotel. The Raj Hotel.'

So this was a hotel, was their unspoken thought as Draupadi and Amba gave each other a meaningful look. Definitely nothing like a temple, thought Draupadi as she looked around with wide eyes and a dropped jaw.

Music, a light and inconsequential tune, played in the background. Women, their faces enhanced with the same 'whore paint' as theirs, were dressed in colourful, shimmery saris, or tunics with heavy jewellery, or tight and slinky black clothing. They tottered along on impossibly high-heeled shoes that looked uncomfortable at best and ankle-breakingly dangerous at worst. Men either wore thick and shiny fitted tunics or slinky, black clothes with almost as much jewellery as the women. Everyone's hair was coifed, their faces shaved and their hands and feet soft and groomed. Their expressions screamed superiority, their demeanour one of contempt towards those who served them.

The atmosphere in here was completely different to anything Draupadi had experienced in the mortal world so far. This place reeked of lavish wealth and luxury and seemed completely out of touch and separated from the noisy, dusty and hot, impoverished and chaotic world outside. Draupadi looked behind her at the large ornate doorway they had just walked through and realized that there were armed guards outside it, standing discreetly to the side. To keep the Kalyug at bay, she thought, for those who could afford it.

She saw a woman in a short black dress walk past them and check out Amba up and down. Then, when Amba smiled tentatively at her, she looked away haughtily. Amba caught Draupadi's eye and whispered with a chuckle, 'Looks like everyone's a princess in this palace.'

Draupadi returned the chuckle amd said, 'Some things never change.'

Zafar had an amused look on his face as he watched Sania melt in with the ambiance, her stride becoming a little saucier even as her face took on a look of bored disdain. She ushered them into a large hall, as ornate as the last. This one had a lit-up walkway in the centre, which was surrounded by hundreds of cushioned chairs. Loud, unfamiliar music, if it could be called that, blared loudly even though there were no musicians or singers in sight. People, all dazzlingly-dressed, milled around and Sania's face lit up when she recognized some of the faces.

'Oh!' she exclaimed. 'There's the designer, Gautam Thakur,' she said, pointing to a delicate-looking man excessively dressed in a tight pink tunic that was covered in gold embroidery with large gemstones sewn onto it.

'And that's Pramila Devi. She's the princess of Amarpur. Gorgeous, isn't she? She was named "Royal of the Year" by PQ magazine.'

Zafar grinned in amusement. 'No doubt because of all her charitable endeavours.'

Sania smiled, but said, 'Ha, ha,' in a deadpan voice just to put him in his place. That only served to widen his grin.

Draupadi watched Pramila Devi as she talked to another woman. Yes, she was pretty; but as far as princesses went, she was a disappointment. She wore a delicate-looking peach-coloured sari with rubies dripping from her ears, neck, fingers and wrists. Her air was one of awkward nobility and her manner seemed distinctly ingratiating towards the woman she spoke to.

'Who is she speaking to?' Draupadi asked Sania.

Sania looked disinterestedly at her companion, an older, shorter, stouter woman in a garish, gold-coloured sari. 'That's the older Mrs Gopal. She's Arun Gopal's wife.'

Zafar explained: 'Arun Gopal is a media mogul. He owns TV channels, magazines, websites, you name it. One of the most powerful men in the country. He controls most of the information out there.'

Sania chimed in with, 'He's not that interesting. His wife is' – she nodded at the woman – 'one of the leaders of the spiritual-socialite scene.'

'What's that?' asked Amba.

Sania shrugged. 'It's one of the *in* crowds these days. They throw parties featuring some self-styled, flavour-of-the-month guru where they all wear cream saris and sing bhajans and listen to speeches about living a simple life and loving everybody, which is the opposite of the way they *actually* live, but I guess it's all about sitting there and *looking* pious.' She shook her head. 'Not my thing. I personally prefer the activist-socialite scene. Zafar knows a lot of those types.'

Zafar smiled. 'Activist-socialite?'

Sania replied, 'You remember the interview you did with that industrialist's daughter who told you she was a spokesperson for the conservation of the Asian elephant? How much time do you think she's actually spent with Asian elephants? I'll tell you; two minutes, and that too while sitting in a safari jeep, chugging cold mineral water and slapping on sunscreen and insect-repellent. It's all the rage now to be championing some cause or the other – street children you're too disgusted to touch, animals that are preferably furry and high up in the food chain, alternative energy sources that you never use and research to cure diseases whose victims you'll never meet because you're too afraid you'll catch it.'

She smirked. 'Again, it's all about corporate sponsored parties where everyone gives intelligent-sounding speeches, but still, at least activist-socialites provide a little cool factor to these events. They're definitely my socialite-of-choice. Much more useful than the spiritual-socialites or even the pseudo-intellectual-socialites who get ghost writers to author books and "talks" for them and, worst of all, the designer-socialites' – she shuddered – 'who slap their names on everything from jewellery, handbags, clothes, shoes to perfumes and homeware and never give the real designers – young, unknown people like me – any credit.' She shook her head but was too enthused by her surroundings to stay disgusted for more than a single moment.

Zafar laughed. 'I never knew there was such a large menu of socialites to choose from. Let's go sit, shall we?'

But before they could move, Gautam Thakur, the fashion designer, turned and caught sight of them. His eyes widened as he walked across quickly, his face set in an ecstatically astonished expression. As he came closer, Draupadi could see that his gaze was fixed on Gandhari. He swept up to her, ignoring the others – even when Sania uttered a meek but excited, 'Hi, Gautam' – and admired her from the top of her head, which was significantly higher than than his, to the tips of her toes.

'Wow!' he said in a soft, dulcet voice which had a deliberately feminine tone to it. His hand waved down the length of her with high drama. 'A goddess, a warrior queen, a fair Amazon! You, my dear, take my breath away! Tell me you're a model. Tell me one of the others got sick and you are modelling in my show instead. Please, tell me!'

Gandhari, who was significantly taken aback by his behaviour, looked uncertainly from him to Zafar and Sania, as if they could potentially save her from this mad man. She stammered, 'No, no. I'm here with them.' She waved vaguely at Zafar and Sania, hoping to divert his attention.

Gautam Thakur looked at them briefly, decided that they were not worth his attention and turned it back to Gandhari. 'You must model for me. That untamed hair and fresh face. God, I haven't seen unthreaded eyebrows since I was in school. Your eyes, your skin and your poise, the way you stand – you're the muse I've been looking for! When can we talk, darling?'

Draupadi, though she personally couldn't understand what he saw in Gandhari, was thoroughly enjoying her discomfiture. Gandhari, for all her haughtiness and know-it-all attitude, was not the best at taking compliments or flirting harmlessly. Her smooth, fair skin was getting more flushed by the second as she struggled between being pleased at his praise and annoyed at his impertinence. Knowing Gandhari, it would probably be her annoyance that would win. And it would undoubtedly make her say something rude, which would probably result in them being asked to leave; so Draupadi thought it wise to step in and say, 'Hello. My sister is a bit shy, but I'm sure she would like to talk to you later.'

Gautam Thakur looked at Draupadi and his expression became a little bored. 'You're sisters?'

Draupadi nodded and tilted her head towards Amba. 'Yes, the three of us.'

He looked at Amba with the same unimpressed look. 'Well, the three of you look *nothing* like each other. Your mummy must have been a very naughty girl.' He smirked, amused by his own wit. 'But that is completely beside the point. Now see, I've lost my train of ... ah, yes' – he turned back to Gandhari and his raptures returned – '*you* must come to the after-party, darling. It's downstairs, at the club. We can talk there.'

'I already invited them,' came Angela's voice as she walked up to them and smiled at Gautam Thakur. 'They're with me.' She was dressed in a black dress that looked as if it had been painted on to her body, beginning halfway down her breasts and ending at the tops of her thighs. Every other part of her was bare, except for her feet, upon which she wore a pair of strappy, ridiculously high-heeled shoes. Surprisingly, she seemed fairly stable perched atop them.

Gautam Thakur squealed softly and kissed the air next to Angela's cheeks exclaiming, 'I should have known! One muse has brought me another!'

'You mean I've been replaced?' Angela pouted with a smile in her eyes. 'You're turning out to be just like a man, GT. Out with the old and saggy, in with the young and firm.'

'*Never* compare me to a man, darling.' Gautam Thakur clutched his chest as he cast a quick eye around the room. 'Now, I have to run. Show's going to start soon. See you after.'

'Break a leg!' Angela called after his scurrying figure.

She turned around and smiled at the three 'sisters' with a deep breath that clearly meant she had resolved to be friendly despite her personal reservations. She said to Gandhari: 'I guess you're the third sister. Well, if getting you to become a model is going to be anything like convincing Draupadi here to become a talk show host, poor GT has his work cut out for him.' She tilted her head. 'Let me guess, your name is Sita. No wait, wrong story. Who were the Mahabharata ones? Aha, Kunti!'

Gandhari frowned. 'No, I'm Gandhari. Kunti is our mother.'

Angela laughed. 'But of course.' She smiled at Sania and Draupadi and said to Zafar, 'You do drink, don't you?'

He nodded.

'Good. Be a darling and get me a drink. I'm going to need one. Come ladies, let's sit. The show is going to start.'

'The show' involved extremely loud music that sounded like a battle being fought to the beat of insistent drums with tall, thin girls in glittery, awkward clothes and elaborate hair styles walking down a narrow stage and then turning around and walking back. After this happened a few times, Draupadi leaned over and shouted over the music into Angela's ear: 'Aren't they going to do anything else?'

Angela shouted back with a wry look, 'Better if they don't. They're showing off the clothes. Look at the clothes.'

Draupadi looked. The clothes were certainly striking, but thoroughly impractical; and after a while, her gaze shifted to the people watching the show instead. Some of them stared at the clothes and models with rapt attention, others chatted distractedly, shouting into each other's ears. A few furiously wrote down things on little pads of parchment on their laps, and a handful stood behind cameras like the ones she had seen in the TV studio. The vast majority simply held up their phones in front of their faces and looked into them instead. Draupadi wondered what they were looking at. Whatever it was, it had to be more interesting than this show, with the endless walking up and down to music. Who *walked* to music anyway? Had mortals forgotten how to dance?

Chapter 28

Apparently not, thought Draupadi some time later. Although whether what she saw in front of her could be called dancing was debatable.

In a large, darkened room awash with flashing lights of different colours and the same ear-splitting battle music, on a low, circular platform that was surrounded by high tables and stools, were a group of about fifty mortals, men and women, doing what could only be described as simulating sex. The women swayed and pulsed their hips suggestively to the music, their arms over their heads and their backs arched. The men leaned forward and thrust their pelvises towards the women in beat with the tune. Some couples did this while dancing apart and some were actually grinding their hips together. It was dancing at its most primal level, without delicacy, without artistry and certainly without a hint of subtlety.

'Reminds me of gypsy dancing,' Amba shouted into Draupadi's ear as they stood around a table on the side of the platform. Zafar and Sania had gone to get drinks, and Angela was busy talking to a group of people at another table.

Draupadi nodded. 'I saw a jungle tribe dance like this once, when we were in exile. Too bad I was with Yudhishtra at the time. I had to pretend to be shocked.'

She laughingly remembered the tribals jerking their hips at each other, much like this. Yudhishtra had been disgusted. She, on the other hand, had been secretly delighted. There was freedom in the abandon of their movements. It was powerful, liberating. She had felt sure that had Arjuna been with her at the time, he would have agreed. Although trying it, of course, would have been completely out of the question. Royal women could as daring as they wanted with their husbands in the pleasure chambers, but in public they had to be the epitome of virtue and dignity.

Amba laughed too, but Gandhari looked more than a little appalled. She turned on them with anger and disgust on her face. 'This is indecent. Let's go away from here.'

Draupadi, alarmed, shook her head quickly. 'No. We can't just leave.'

'We must,' Gandhari insisted. 'This is wrong. Fornicating like animals, in public—'

'They're not actually fornicating—'

'I don't care!' shouted Gandhari over the music. 'I want to go back to the zoo.'

Draupadi frowned. 'And how do you propose we get to the zoo? It's late at night and we have to depend on Zafar's car.'

Gandhari looked like she was going to explode. 'Then let's get an auto rickshaw.'

'We can't. It's not safe.'

'I want to go back home,' Gandhari declared, her tone a little hysterical.

For a tiny moment, Draupadi wondered if Narad Muni might consider taking only Gandhari away and leaving the rest of them here until their thirty days were up. She quickly dismissed the idea. The old man would probably be more than happy to cart them all back prematurely if they were to call him now.

She put a reluctant hand on Gandhari's shoulder and shouted soothingly into her ear, 'You're upset. Come, sit down for a moment. You don't have to look at this horrible sight any more.'

She quickly looked around and spotted, on the far edge of the room, rows of low-slung cushioned sofas around candlelit tables. She led Gandhari to an empty sofa that faced away from the dancing and sat her down. Then she calmly explained: 'Let's just wait until Zafar and Sania have spent a little time enjoying the party and then we'll ask them to take us back, okay? They won't take kindly to being ordered to drive us back when they've only just got here.'

Gandhari, now that she was facing away from the offending sight on the dance platform, soon calmed down enough to consider Draupadi's words and even half-heartedly agree that maybe they could wait a little while, just to be considerate guests. But she insisted on sitting, her back straight and stiff as a sword, and staring with a disapproving face at the wall in front of her.

That was fine with Draupadi. She got up just as Zafar and Sania arrived at the table with glasses in their hands. They sat down next to Amba on the sofa and began to talk. Draupadi turned and spotted Angela walking towards her.

'So' – Angela smiled as she reached Draupadi – 'you ever tried liquor?'

Of course she had. But Draupadi, reminding herself that Angela thought her to be a twenty-five-year-old girl who had lived in an ashram all her life, shook her head.

Angela grinned. 'Don't tell your mom or those uptight-looking sisters of yours.' She held out her glass towards Draupadi surreptitiously.

Draupadi smiled and, taking the glass, drank deeply. Amrith, the nectar of immortality, which was the only thing one ingested in heaven, tasted mildly sweet and fresh. This liquid was pungent, bitter and warmed her insides from her mouth all the way down to her belly, just like its cousin had when she was a mortal. She drained the glass and looked at Angela, who had the biggest grin on her face. 'Where can I get another one of these?'

Angela laughed heartily. 'Easy tiger. That was a double shot of neat whisky. We don't want you throwing up all over the place.'

Draupadi was mildly offended. 'I never throw up.' Well, except during her five pregnancies, but generally she was known to have a strong stomach.

Angela raised her eyebrows but walked Draupadi to a high table she referred to as 'the bar' and bought her another whisky. They stood drinking from their glasses and watching the crowd dancing on the platform until Angela spoke once more. 'You know, for a girl who has lived in the middle of nowhere up until now, you're pretty cool. Strange, when I look at you, I see a young woman, but your eyes seem a lot older. The way you speak, the way you told Vaishali's story – there's a wisdom in you which usually only comes from experience.'

Draupadi smiled vaguely. 'I guess I'm just lucky to be born with it.'

Angela was about to say something when a man of about forty summers, obviously drunk and sweating profusely, stumbled up to them and leaned close to Angela, his eyes straying to her chest. Draupadi could smell the spirits on his breath as he leered and drawled with a contemptuous smile, 'You look like a party girl. Can I buy you a drink?'

Angela didn't look at him as she hissed back, 'Fuck off.'

He grinned stupidly and leaned in closer. 'With pleasure.'

Then, he winced as the whisky in Angela's glass was unceremoniously flung into his face. As he wiped it out of his eyes, his face turned angry and he grabbed her arm and pulled her towards him, shouting, 'Bitch!'

Without thinking, Draupadi shot her arm out and gouged at his face with her fingernails. He squealed in pain and let go of Angela's arm. Angela, meanwhile, called out over her shoulder at the man behind the bar to 'call the bouncer'. Then she pushed the drunkard, who was now hurling obscenities at them, with as much force as she could. Since he was extremely intoxicated, he easily stumbled backwards, then tripped over a step and fell, hitting his head against a nearby table and landing unconscious on the floor. A few people standing around turned to look at his limp form, but no one seemed the least bit bothered by it or what had just occurred.

'What *is* it with men in this city?' Draupadi exclaimed as the man was picked up and carried off by two burly men.

'Tell me about it,' said Angela, whose expression of bored indifference was a bit too studied for Draupadi to believe it. 'They see a woman who isn't dressed like a fucking nun and think she's a whore. This is Delhi for you. The rape capital of the world.'

She brushed off some imaginary dirt from her dress and said with a bitter note in her voice, 'So many times I've thought I should just get out of this place. Go live and work in a country where I can let loose and just be myself, you know? But then I think: if all the educated, smart women left, what would happen to women like Vaishali? That would be tantamount to letting these bastards win. There is something inherently fucked up in our society that allows men to treat women like this and get away with it. Women like me, like you too, we can change it if we do it right. The media is a powerful tool. It's transformed the world so many times.'

She cast a hard look at Draupadi. 'You think I'm chasing you for a stupid job. It's more than just a job. It's a chance to make a difference to the lives of millions of women. You can be part of something really important. I don't want to push you tonight, obviously, but you should think about what this job means in the larger scope of things and what a rare opportunity this is for you to have a life that means something. That's it. Enough said. Now, can we get back to having a good time?' She smiled shakily and ordered another whisky, tossing it back the instant it was set before her.

Draupadi was taken aback. She had thought about the job, of course. About how much fun it would have been had she been able to stay in the mortal world. But she had never thought about the TV show itself and what it would mean for women everywhere. Twice on this visit, her friends had been physically accosted by leering men. What happened to Vaishali, the thought that these things happened to millions of women every day was unimaginable. That she could help fix this broken world was a revelation. It almost made the idea of ... No, she couldn't. She looked down at the floor to hide the turmoil in her eyes from Angela. It was too much to ask. Yes, it would be wonderful to have a life beyond pandering to a bunch of men and managing a palace, a life that meant something, that made a difference to womankind.

Stop it, she mentally kicked herself. A change of subject was needed to stop this line of thought. Quickly. She looked up at Angela, smiled and nodded towards the dancing couples. 'So this is how people dance.'

Angela looked amused and asked, 'Yeah. Are you shocked?'

Draupadi shook her head, relieved to be talking, and thinking, about something else. 'Not at all.'

'Good. Do you want to dance?'

Draupadi shook her head once again, but it was half-hearted and Angela knew it. 'Come on,' she said. 'You know you want to. And besides, after all that, I need a distraction too. Come on.'

Maybe it was the two glasses of whisky that she had drunk, or maybe it was the knowledge that she wasn't a princess any more. Whatever it was, Draupadi allowed herself to be led to the dancing area by Angela, who immediately raised her arms in the air and began to gyrate her pelvis in beat with the music.

Draupadi stood awkwardly for a few moments, but then, spurred on by Angela, she began to imitate the people around her. Her hips loosened and swayed, just a little. She took a deep breath, closed her eyes and tried to listen to the music. Her hips relaxed even more, her arms went up in the air and her knees bent just enough to allow her to rock in time with the tempo. When she opened her eyes, to her own surprise, she was dancing very much like those around her. It *was* liberating, to be able to do this, celebrate one's sexuality so blatantly, in front of everyone. She threw her head back, giving herself up to the experience. If only Yudhishtra could see her now. She laughed and pulsed her hips harder.

Chapter 29

'Darling, there you are! I've been looking all over for you.'

Gandhari felt her heart sink into her stomach when she heard those words spoken behind her. She had been hoping that Gautam Thakur, who had the appearance of a fickle person to say the least, would have forgotten her. Now, not only was she stuck in this hell hole of a place with mortals pretending to fornicate around her – like beasts! – but she had to put up with this man without anyone to protect her.

Her eyes desperately searched for her companions even as Gautam Thakur took the seat next to her. God only knew where Draupadi had gone, and Amba was deep in conversation at the other end of the table with Sania and two of her friends. She was on her own.

'Tell me you're having a mojito. They're divine! Now, sweetie, who are you? What is your name? You can call me GT, by the way. Everyone does. Tell me everything about you!' He crossed one leg over the other, put his chin in one hand and leaned in towards her with an exaggerated look of interest.

Gandhari noticed that his face was painted in much the same way as Sania had done for Draupadi and Amba tonight. She asked bluntly, 'Are you a eunuch?'

GT's eyes widened for a moment and then he burst out laughing. 'Oh, you are too much! No, darling, I still have all the equipment. I just use it differently.' He laughed some more.

Gandhari had no idea why he was laughing so much. There had been absolutely nothing funny about her question. She asked stiffly, 'What does that mean?'

GT chuckled and replied, 'That means I'm gay, darling. The real deal which, let me tell you, is not as common as most designers would have you believe.' He leaned in conspiratorially. 'Ninety per cent of the hand-flapping, crooning queens out there are just regular dudes putting on an act. Why, you ask? Well, most Indian women are *frightfully* prudish about having a hetro in the dressing room with them. Not because they don't want to be seen in their undies, but because they don't want him to know their measurements!' He laughed again.

Gandhari allowed herself a tiny smile. He may not be a eunuch, but she could surmise the meaning of his words from his mannerisms. There had been such men in her time as well, but in a clan like the Kurus – where machismo, virility and excellence in battle were revered – men like GT weren't given much respect. Still, Gandhari had had many eunuch companions during her mortal life, and though she never admitted it, infinitely preferred their company to that of her husband.

'Aha! She smiles.' GT clapped dramatically. 'Mona Lisa couldn't have done it better, darling. You need to be a model. You were born to be a model.'

Gandhari shook her head.

'No, no, I mean it.' He was insistent. 'You'd have to lose a few kilos, of course. Fifteen, no, I think ten will do. The stick-insect look is so boring. A haircut, some make-up and voila! You, my darling, will be a sensation. You'll take the fashion world by storm.'

Gandhari firmly shook her head again and replied, 'No, I thank you. I have retired from active life.'

GT's eyes widened and he laughed. 'Retired? You're what, nineteen? You're too young to retire from anything.'

She smiled ruefully. 'I'm a lot older than I look.' That was an understatement if ever there was one.

'Still, what could possibly have happened to you to make you want to retire from life, darling?'

What hadn't happened, thought Gandhari with a small sigh. She replied simply, 'Life has not been easy.'

The humour left GT's eyes and he lost some of his exaggerated manner as he said, in a deeper voice that was more natural, 'It never is, sweetheart. We all have challenges, gosh, I should know. But life must be lived, yes?'

Gandhari smiled sadly and nodded. 'Yes, life must be lived. The best must be made of it. And I did, for a long time. Then, I went to hea—I went to an ashram, where I was able to let go of the past and heal. Somewhat. I live there now.' She looked into his now-serious eyes. 'So, you see, I can't stay. I have to go back.'

GT raised his eyebrows. 'Do you want to go back? You've got the rest of your life ahead of you, darling. I can't imagine being locked away in an ashram, of all places, for the next, well, sixty years at least.'

Eternity was a lot longer than sixty years. Gandhari replied with not a trace of doubt in her voice, 'Yes, but you see, I'm happy there. Happier than I ever was when I was ... not retired. Except for my childhood.' She smiled nostalgically. 'Those were the happiest years of my existence. So carefree, so simple.'

GT shuddered visibly. 'You're lucky. I had the worst childhood ever. You should have seen me in school. Scrawny little gay boy. I wanted to kill myself. If the brutes around me didn't do it first.'

Then, he smiled. 'But I showed them, darling. I'm probably worth more today than all those losers put together.' He giggled but then saw that she still looked nostalgic and shook his head. 'But we're talking about *you*, not me. Tell me about your awesome childhood.'

Gandhari's eyes glazed over as, in her mind's eye, she saw rugged, snow-capped mountains in the distance against the bluest cloudless sky. A simple fortress stood at the top of a hill, surrounded by grazing lands that were dotted with farm animals. She saw handsome, hearty people with pink cheeks who laughed hard and sang loudly and called after her as she ran in the fields, the cold, crisp wind nibbling on her face. Then, day turned into night and she looked upwards to see stars, countless gleaming stars in the clear black sky. On the ground was a bonfire, next to which she sat huddled with the hag that took care of her, listening to stories about brave warriors, beautiful princesses and the handsome, dashing king who would, one day, come along and make her his queen. Together, they would rule over a powerful, peaceful kingdom. They would be happy and in love forever. They would have good-looking, devoted children who would take care of them when they grew old.

A small tear threatened to spill from her eye, and she sniffed softly, so softly that it was lost in the noisy racket that these mortals called music. Gandhari's mountains had been silent, apart from the howling of the wind, the chirping of the birds and the gushing of streams. Music had been simple and soulful, and their songs had been about true love and the magnificence of the world around them. If Zafar was to be believed, that world, her beloved Gandhara, didn't exist any more. It had been reduced to a barren land infested with power-hungry, fanatical mortals. From what she had seen of Indraprastha ever since they arrived, it wasn't much different. Such hopes she had nurtured when she asked Draupadi to bring her down here again. What a disappointment it had been. Mortals had taken all the beauty out of their world. It was an unrecognizable, grim place now and she couldn't imagine ever living here again.

She blinked away the tear and replied, 'It was a wonderful childhood spent in the mountains. I won't bore you with the details. Suffice to say that the outside world holds no appeal for me any more. I am better off in my ashram, where I can at least be at peace.'

GT gave her a long look and then smiled, his exaggerated demeanour and high-pitched drawl returning when he said, 'Well, darling, if that's how you feel, what can I say?' He took out a small piece of parchment from his garment and held it out to her. 'Here's my card. If you ever change your mind and still look as magnificent as you do now, call me.'

Gandhari took the card politely.

He stood up, adding brightly, 'Cheerio, darling. And good luck.'

Gandhari nodded. 'And to you too.' She looked after him as he walked away. Then, she peeked at the card he had given her, with his name and phone number on it. She sighed, crumpled it up and threw it on the floor. Then, noticing that Amba and Sania were no longer sitting at the table, she exclaimed in frustration. And where on earth was Draupadi? She was sick of this noise and wanted to go back to the zoo. She got up and steeling herself from the impending sight of the dancing mortals, resolved to find her companions and get out of there.

Chapter 30

You know, thought Amba, there is only so much a person can stand. For the life of her, she couldn't understand why the rules and limitations of her previous life should still apply. If she wanted to be with a man, she should be able to be with a man, even if it was for a short moment in time and left them both a little wounded.

Or maybe that was just the two glasses of what Sania called 'Moheetos' that she had drunk earlier talking. She sighed and looked around as she stood at the bar counter. Sania was busily discussing the clothes that had been on display at the show with the two friends she had run into earlier. Zafar had left to buy another round of drinks for everyone. He had been staring at her with fiery eyes all night. Every time they looked at each other, the tension between them was palpable.

Amba was torn. She knew it was more than just desire. But she didn't want to think about that right now. She wanted him, desperately. And he wanted her. It didn't have to be complicated. If they gave in to their ... whatever it was, just for a few days until she left, she was sure he'd get over it in time. As would she. There was such a thing as playing it too safe.

She wanted to give in so badly that it hurt. That was when she heard his voice in her ear.

'I need to speak to you.' His tone was steady but his eyes had an urgency that Amba recognized. She had seen that urgency in other men's eyes before. It had always put her off. Not this time. This time, she felt the same urgency growing inside her. Her head felt a little light, her body tingled and her breath came heavy and fast. Her womanhood felt as if it were permanently attached to a string that kept jerking it upwards every time Zafar looked at her or brushed against her or even when she noticed something about him, like the width of his shoulders or the curve of his lips. And how could she possibly ignore that insistent throbbing, that dull ache below, where it contracted every once in a while as if to remind her, to beg her to lead it to completion. It must be what I drank, she told herself, or the loud, primal music, or the dim, flashing lighting that were responsible for the way she felt. Anything but him or the thought of what it would feel like if—

'Amba?'

She stared deep into his eyes and knew that if she went with him now, if she was alone with him, she would know exactly what it felt like. She closed her eyes and felt, for a moment, her pleading body. Then, she nodded.

He glanced over her shoulder to make sure no one would notice them leave. Her hand was taken in a firm hold and pulled out a of door into a neighbouring, equally large arena, into a dark corner, where they were shielded from view by the backs of a large group of merrymakers.

Her back was against the cold wall. She shivered and felt the warmth of him come up close to her, blocking out the crowd, the pounding music, everything but him and the feel of his hands on her waist as he leaned in to kiss her. His lips brushed against hers at first, as if he was trying really hard to be gentle with her. She pressed her lips against his urgently, clung to his shoulders and pulled him closer to her.

'Please,' she whispered against his lips and he responded immediately, pinning her against the wall with his body and locking her lips with his in a duel that had her head spinning, her knees melting and her hips rising up to tease him.

He breathed in sharply and caught the small of her back with one hand, arching her towards him, pressing her hips to his own as his tongue parried with hers in their mouths. His other hand ran through her hair, her back and her waist as if he couldn't get enough of her. She felt him hard and straining against her belly, felt his roaming hands burn through the thin material of her dress and his mouth thrust against hers and moaned softly in her throat. It was overwhelming, it was exhilarating. It was torture.

He broke away from the kiss, breathing heavily, his hands and body reluctant to follow. He held her tightly and said in a ragged voice, 'Amba, I don't want to rush you—'

'Shhh. I want this too,' she breathed back, clinging to him, her swollen lips throbbing in protest.

Zafar shook his head and looked away, obviously fighting to control himself. He began to draw back. 'We need to talk.' His face looked pained.

'No, please don't stop, Zafar.' Amba held him back and turned his face to look at her.

He stared back at her, his eyes still reeling with passion but intent on doing the right thing. 'You don't know what you're saying. I can't take advantage of your inexperience. Let's take things slowly.'

She didn't have time to take things slowly. She was going to be gone in a few days! Amba shook her head in desperation. Never, in her entire existence, had she felt so alive. Her body, currently in an uproar over his withdrawal, had never experienced anything so powerful, so urgent. When he kissed her she felt almost outside of herself, like a reckless, unrestrained creature whose only goal was as primitive as the animals she had seen rutting in the palace gardens as a princess. She wanted him and she didn't give a damn about whether it was unwise or too soon. She had waited for this moment for far too long and she was going to have it, even if she had to lie for it.

'I'm not as inexperienced as you think I am,' she said carefully, trying hard to meet his gaze and not falter.

Zafar frowned, confused. 'What do you mean?'

Amba blinked and willed herself to keep going. To hell with propriety, to hell with being a princess. Tonight, she was going to be a woman. 'I've done this before. This, and much more. You don't need to stop.'

He did stop, however, and searched her face for signs of deceit. When he found none in her steady eyes and lifted chin, Zafar said, 'Are you sure?'

Relief. He believed her! And unlike any man she had ever met as a mortal, he didn't seem to judge her for it. His eyes remained unchanged as they looked at her, no hard glint at the knowledge that he may not be her first and even better, no knowing, cocky gleam. Just concern, and restraint, until he was sure that she was sure. Her heart filled with ... she frowned. No, that was definitely unwise.

Amba put her hand on his cheek and came closer to murmur into his ear, 'Take me somewhere we can be alone.'

Zafar looked down at her shoulder, breathing hard, still unsure.

She hadn't spent a lifetime in women's quarters without learning a thing or two. She whispered directly into his ear, 'Please.' Then, she bit it gently.

Chapter 31

The car ride to Zafar's home was made in electrified silence after he rasped that his mother had gone to Lucknow for a couple of days to visit a sick relative. Sania was still at the nightclub. They would be alone.

It was dark and quiet inside his sitting room when he closed the front door behind them with only the sound of Bosco's sleepy barking to disturb the stillness of the moment.

Zafar reached out for Amba and pulled her to him. The street light outside the window dimly illuminated half of his face as he looked down at her, his eyes full of desire, his chest heaving with laboured breaths. He looked so handsome, she thought, as she watched him lower his face towards hers. Then she closed her eyes as his lips took hers once more and his arms went around her, welding the contours of her body into his. Her breasts were pressed against his chest, her heart clamouring between them, her hands roaming his neck, his hair, his back and clinging to his shoulders for support as she felt her legs turn weak.

Zafar held her with an arm around her waist as his mouth left hers and trailed passionate kisses down her neck. She arched her head back as his other hand pulled the cloth of her dress off one shoulder, leaving it naked. He looked at her smooth skin and took a quick breath, whispering her name before he kissed it. Then, he returned to her lips and seized them with even more fervour than before, lifting her hips to meet his and pressing his manhood against her.

Amba had never felt less in control of herself. All her senses seemed to be bursting within. The feel of his body, his lips on her skin as he trailed kisses on it. Her ears filled with the sound of their combined breathing, the swishing of their clothes, that low sound he kept making with his throat and her soft moans. The smell of him, like lemons mixed with salt, mixed with the heady, fresh twang of the mint leaves in the spirits he had been drinking earlier. His mouth tasted of mint too, and his eyes were half-closed as he looked back at her, so awash with passion.

She felt her feet leave the floor as he lifted her by the waist. She instinctively wrapped her legs around his hips for support as he carried her, their lips still locked, to his bedchamber. They fell together on to the bed, his not unwelcome weight pinning her down against the sheets. He raised his head and looked into her eyes and said huskily, 'Are you *sure* you're sure?'

Amba exclaimed in exasperation and pulled his head down to resume their kiss. Then she gasped, threw her head back and moaned as she felt his hands caress her breasts, first through her dress and bra and then, as he quickly pulled the fabric away, without any barrier between them. His mouth ousted his hands as she writhed and trembled with gasps of pleasure beneath him.

It wasn't like any pleasure she had known before. This one was fickle, demanding, for it seemed that the more she got, the more she needed. Her body arched and invited him to do more as he peeled off her clothes and continued to kiss and caress her. Then, he pulled back to undress himself.

Suddenly and strangely shy at the prospect of seeing him naked, and of his gaze on her naked body, Amba turned her head to the side and through her half-open eyes caught sight of herself and Zafar in a large wall mirror on the side of the bed. She saw herself lying down, the smooth contours of her body illuminated by the same street light outside the window, her thighs wantonly parted, her skin flushed, her breasts taut, her long hair wildly splayed on the sheets, lips swollen and eyes glazed. She looked ... unrecognizable. Next to her stood Zafar, quickly undressing to reveal an equally taut, aroused body.

Amba had seen unclothed men before. She had seen holy men, the odd lover being chased out of the palace women's quarters, demi-gods who preferred not to cover themselves and, of course, men bathing in rivers. But she had never seen a naked man she was about to be intimate with. Even now, watching them both in the mirror, she felt like a voyeur, outside herself as he quickly slipped a sheath over his manhood and lowered himself on top of her. Even as she heard the whisper of skin against skin and felt his naked warmth slide on top of her and weigh her down, she couldn't tear her eyes away from watching the scene in the mirror. She watched herself straddle him intuitively and wondered who this woman even was as the dull ache between her legs turned into a violent, throbbing, wet shrew when she felt his manhood poised against her. Only then, when he turned her face towards him did she finally look up into his eyes and realize with a deep, shaky breath that this was really happening to her.

'Amba ...' Zafar looked tender as he fought to keep himself in check. 'You're so beautiful. I—'

'Shhh.' She put a finger on his lips to stop him as a tiny butterfly of fear fluttered in her belly. 'Don't say anything.' She didn't want to give in to the fear, didn't want better sense to prevail right now. 'I want you ... inside me.'

Zafar groaned and kissed her passionately as his hands found their way to her womanhood. He teased its lips, making her buck and gasp in response. Then, he held them apart to ease himself in with a gentle thrust.

Amba held her breath as she felt him sliding inside her, filling her inside more with each gentle, controlled thrust. It felt new, and wonderful, and absolutely ... 'Oww!' A sharp pain coursed through her from between her legs and brought an involuntary sob.

Zafar froze. Amba forgot the pain and stared at him, waiting with apprehension. She watched as he registered what had just happened and his face went from passion to confusion to horror.

'What the—' Zafar exclaimed as he looked down at her. He started to withdraw.

Amba held him inside her with her legs desperately and cradled his face with her hands. 'No, stay. Listen to me.'

'You're a virgin? But you said, you made me think—'

'It doesn't matter what I said or what you thought. This is what I want.'

Zafar closed his eyes and dropped his head for a moment, trying not to let his arousal get the better of his judgement. He let out a gasping breath. 'This is not how it should have happened. You deserved better. I'm so sorry. I should've waited, I should've—'

'Zafar.' Amba's tone was husky as she said his name, designed precisely to spur his passion. While she was moved by his conviction and his scruples, she had waited too long for this to let him stop now. If there was one thing her former handmaidens had diligently taught her in preparation for her swayamwara, it was how to rule a man in bed. Time to use those lessons.

'This is what I want and you're the man I want it with.' She shifted her hips teasingly, squeezed her womanhood and ran her fingernails down his back. He gasped and she smiled coyly. 'Don't you think I deserve to finish at least?'

That was all it took. His lips came down on hers and he thrust himself into her, filling her completely. So this was what she had been missing all her mortal and immortal life, thought Amba in wonder as she bent her head back, raised her hips and took him in, again and again, in a dance as old as time itself. This is what inspired every song ever written, every poem ever composed, every story ever told. This is what women giggled about in hallways. This is what men fight wars over, what lovers risk their lives for. She finally knew what all the fuss was about. The dance of sweet torment, thought Amba as she looked at Zafar's almost pained face before she gave herself up to it.

Chapter 32

'Where have you *been*? Gandhari's on the verge of losing her mind, and I can't believe I'm saying this, but I think, for her sake, we should get back to the zoo.' Just then, Draupadi saw Zafar walk in through the hotel doors after giving his car over to the doorman to be parked. Amba had just walked in a moment earlier.

Draupadi's eyes narrowed as she looked back at Amba. Her hair was slightly tousled, her dress crumpled and the paint that Sania had applied on her lips was nowhere to be seen. She looked at Zafar, who came to stand beside Amba. He had a slight frown on his face, and when Draupadi met his eye, he looked extremely uncomfortable. Amba looked up at him and a moment of unspoken understanding passed between them.

Draupadi barely stopped herself from grinning when she made the connection. Good for Amba. If anyone deserved a little action, it was her friend. Although the cheeky smile was immediately wiped off her face when she remembered that Gandhari would probably be upon them shortly.

She said to Amba, 'Okay, look, if Gandhari asks where you've been, don't admit it. She'll hit the roof. She found me dancing at the party earlier and almost started crying. I think the noise was getting to her, so we came out when we couldn't find you inside.' She spoke to Zafar, 'Sania decided to go to another party with Angela and her friends. She told me to tell you not to worry.'

That made Zafar look worried and he replied in a slightly unsteady voice, 'Okay, I'll call her later. I'll drop you back first.'

'Thank you,' Amba said to him softly with a smile. She added, a little cheekily, 'For everything.'

Zafar tried his best not to smile but a small one broke through despite his best efforts. 'Very funny.' Then, he went back to looking bothered.

Whatever was going on in his mind after what was obviously an enjoyable encounter, thought Draupadi, it was also reassuringly obvious that Zafar did seem to care about Amba. She seemed to care about him too, from the looks of it. It would be a bit of work when they got back to heaven to help Amba get over him, she realized with a tinge of regret, but they could deal with that hurdle when they came to it.

As predicted, Gandhari soon strode up to them looking agitated and angry. She exclaimed at Amba, 'Where have you *been*? We've been looking everywhere for you!' She glared at Zafar.

Amba replied in a calm voice, 'We've been sitting right over there' – she pointed at a cosy seating alcove in the corner, behind a massive sculpture – 'and talking. You may have missed us.'

Gandhari didn't back down. 'I checked that area. You weren't there.'

Zafar intervened, 'We were sitting there for some time and then we had a cup of coffee at the hotel coffee shop. Do you want to go now? I can take you all back home.'

Draupadi saw a brief struggle on Gandhari's face, which ended in a look of resigned defeat. She replied, 'Yes. Please, let's go now.'

The ride home was spent in grateful silence. When they thanked Zafar and got out of the car, Gandhari stalked off to the toilet cabin immediately without saying a word. Draupadi, however, stopped Amba before she went inside. 'Can we talk?' she asked softly.

Amba threw her a defensive glance and Draupadi quickly added, 'It's all right. I'm your friend. I'm not going to judge you. I just want to know how you are.'

Amba's face relaxed and was contemplative for a moment. Then she replied softly, 'I'm falling in love with him.' She looked deep into Draupadi's eyes and asked, 'Is that reason enough to stop?'

Draupadi's heart went out to Amba. She asked gently, 'What do you think?'

Amba looked up at the sky and then back at Draupadi. 'I don't want to.'

'Then don't. You'll have plenty of time to get over him later. Enjoy this moment.'

Amba blinked back tears. 'What if it isn't enough?'

Draupadi frowned. 'What do you mean?'

'I don't know,' Amba whispered back, allowing her tears to fall now. 'I don't know.'

Draupadi gathered Amba into her arms and held her silently. Amba's shoulders shook a little as she cried into Draupadi's shoulder but she didn't utter a sound.

Draupadi waited until she had finished, drawn back and composed herself before saying, 'You'll be all right, you know.'

Amba seemed far away as she said, 'We'll see.'

Draupadi looked closely at her. 'Are you meeting him again?'

Amba looked at the ground, her arms wrapped around her own body, and nodded slightly.

Draupadi nodded back, understanding. They went inside.

Things changed after that night. Each woman seemed to be a little different from before. Gandhari looked tired and often stayed inside the toilet cabin instead of going out with the others. When asked why, she sighed and said she'd seen enough. She took to meditating and drawing mountainous landscapes on pieces of parchment with coloured writing implements that she had bought in a market. Draupadi, who had discovered that mortals bound parchment together into the most fascinating reading material called 'books', bought some for her that contained pictures of mountains. Gandhari was very grateful, but they didn't cheer her up much.

Kunti had made many tiny breakthroughs with Karan because of all the time she spent at the orphanage and was definitely more cheerful and purposeful. Often, at night, she would discuss the orphanage's administrative matters with the others and ask them their opinion on how something or the other should be done, or tell them her ideas for securing Karan's future or finding funds so that the orphanage didn't have to close after Shashiben left her body.

Draupadi, while glad to see Kunti looking more confident and brimming with ideas, couldn't help but worry that with their thirty days running out fast she might be getting too involved and inadvertently encouraging people to depend on her presence. However, when she did express her concerns, Kunti was dismissive. Yes, she knew time was running out. That's why she needed to get things done quickly, she would say. Then, she'd rush off to the orphanage again.

Amba was in a world of her own. After her initial candidness, she became unusually reticent with Draupadi, preferring to spend most of her days out with Zafar, coming back late at night only to crawl into bed and disappear again the next morning.

That left Draupadi on her own to see the sights of New Delhi and soak in as much of the mortal world as she could. And, of course, to make what Angela called the 'pilot' for the TV show. It was quite an experience. She had walked into Angela's office one morning only to be confronted by an enthusiastic group of people who had big plans for her. They cut her hair and styled it with fantastical-looking instruments, they painted her face and made her wear new clothes. And all the while, Angela sat in front of her, teaching her about how to conduct herself in the studio with the audience, what to say and what not to say, and most importantly, how to say it.

Draupadi found herself learning more and more at the studio practice sessions, which were held one after another until Angela was satisfied with Draupadi's performance. Finally, Vaishali and the audience were brought in and Draupadi repeated her earlier performance, this time armed with the knowledge and techniques that Angela had taught her.

At the end, after Angela had said 'Cut' the audience rose from their seats and applauded loudly while Vaishali beamed at her from the chair. Overwhelmed, Draupadi could do nothing but stand silently while a feeling of utter triumph enveloped her. Later, Angela had played the show back for her, commenting, praising and criticizing Draupadi's performance. The pilot was good enough to go on TV, she said, telling Draupadi she would be showing it to the heads of the TV channel. The next morning, Draupadi was convinced it had all been a dream until she saw her hair in the mirror and the fat new wads of money in her bag.

The other thing that had been on her mind for some time, ever since she had learned that mortals could fly, was her desire to see an aeroplane. Since Amba was busy with Zafar, Draupadi went to the airport by herself guided by an enthusiastic auto rickshaw driver who, ecstatic about the large payment she had promised him, parked on the side of a road, right next to what he called the 'runway', where she saw the underbelly of planes flying just a few paces above her head before they skidded on to the ground with earth-shattering roars. She sat there for hours next to the driver and he told her all that he knew about aeroplanes – which wasn't much considering he had never been in one himself. Every time a plane flew by, Draupadi was filled with a sense of childlike wonder and awe. Who would have thought mortals would one day be able to fly? Such a thing would have been considered impossible without divine intervention in her day. As difficult and chaotic as it was, how also full of promise, of possibility, was life in this remarkable world. So unlike the celestial sameness of her heavenly abode.

Days passed, one speeding into the other, until Draupadi stopped counting how many they had left. She didn't care any more. She wanted to live every single day as if it were her last. Until it was.

Chapter 33

'Draupadi,' whispered Kunti, shaking Draupadi a little. It was dark in their chambers and she could hear Gandhari and Amba breathing steadily in deep sleep. It had been three hours since they had retired for the night.

She shook a little harder when Draupadi didn't budge, whispering a tiny bit louder, 'Draupadi, wake up. I need to talk to you.'

One eye opened and examined her in a daze. Then, seeing the serious expression on Kunti's face, Draupadi sighed and got up sleepily, whispering back, 'What is it?'

Kunti's heart was beating faster than a rabbit's and her breath came with difficulty. She knew she shouldn't panic but she was having trouble focusing. The words spilled out of her in a furtive whisper. 'Karan is going to be in trouble. Shashiben told me that his gang is going to collect a large amount of some drug tonight and the police know about it. They're going to catch them. If Karan gets caught, he'll be imprisoned.' Her eyes were desperate. 'We have to do something!'

Draupadi's eyes narrowed. 'Do what?'

Kunti had been trying to figure out the answer to that question from the moment that Shashiben told her about what was to happen that night. Shashiben had hobbled into the orphanage's common room, where Kunti was playing with a few of the younger children and waiting for Karan to show up, and had said in an unusually serious voice, 'Your boy is going to be in very big trouble.'

Kunti had pressed her for details, upon which she had revealed that Ustaad and his gang had recruited Karan and four other boys to collect a bag of some lethal drug called heroin from a man who was bringing it to Delhi by something called a 'train' to bring it into the slum. 'But a little bird told me that the police know about this transfer and that they're going to try and catch them in the act. Apparently, Ustaad hasn't paid them off this time and he's been getting a bit cocky lately so they want to put him in his place. Can't do anything around here without giving the police a piece of the pie, everyone knows that. Anyway,' she said worriedly, 'Karan and the others will probably be paid for it, but they don't have much of a choice. Ustaad will probably kill them, or worse, maim them for life if they refuse.'

Kunti remembered asking Shashiben what would happen if Karan got caught by the police and Shashiben had cackled without humour, 'Prison. You don't want to know what happens to young boys in prison, my dear. And that's if the police don't kill him tonight.'

She shuddered and tried, for the umpteenth time tonight, to stay calm. She had steered her children out of harm's way many times before in her mortal life and she could do it again. But her nerves, softened after too many comfortable centuries in the safety of heaven, were badly worn, and she hoped she could depend on Draupadi to help her get Karan out of this predicament.

She blinked at Draupadi and said, 'Shashiben says they're going to collect it behind the New Delhi railway station. We need to go there. It's dangerous, I know, but I—I have to try and warn him, Draupadi. You are the bravest person I know and I need your help.'

Draupadi looked into Kunti's eyes for a long moment and then, with another sigh of resignation, stood up without a word.

Leaving the zoo, they walked along the road – being careful to stay in the dark shadows of the trees and buildings to avoid being noticed – until they came to an auto rickshaw parked on the side against the pavement. The driver was fast asleep inside it, and the two women shook him awake and, with many threats and inducements, persuaded him to splash some water on his face and drive them to the New Delhi railway station.

They arrived at the entrance of a large complex that looked like a gigantic, covered marketplace, only much, much more crowded. Outside, the road was jammed with every kind of vehicle and pedestrian, all trying to move past or run over another in a harsh duet of honking and shouting. The place stank of concentrated urine. Inside the complex, there were people everywhere. There were insistent beggars and men dressed in red uniforms that ran up to them in an excited mob and then walked away, disgusted, when they noticed that the two women alighting from the auto rickshaw had no luggage. There were tired travellers with large bags sprawled over every inch of filthy floor space that wasn't covered with sleeping people or stray dogs, urine, excrement, spittle or rotten food. The bright white lights that shone from a filthy ceiling cast dark shadows over everyone's eyes, making them look like washed-out, walking corpses.

Kunti looked around and couldn't help thinking that if there was one scene that would personify the Kalyug that the mortal world was in, it would have to be the one around her at this moment.

'We need to go behind the station,' she said, staring around rather hopelessly at the colossal space and the sea of chaos they were in.

Draupadi nodded and said, 'Let's not go further inside. Follow me.'

Kunti followed her as she exited the building and started walking around it. The shadows here were full of even more people, most of them sleeping beggars and a few drunks mumbling loudly at them before spewing their stomachs into the open drains they slept next to. The stench was overwhelming and Kunti had to stop herself from gagging. This place smelled worse than the slum.

She looked at Draupadi, who moved with the stealth of a panther and had a fearless yet watchful look on her face, as if anticipating an attack at any moment. Kunti knew that Draupadi didn't want to be here and yet here she was, walking towards certain danger for her without a single question or word of protest.

She put a hand on Draupadi's arm and said softly as Draupadi turned and looked at her, 'Thank you.'

Draupadi shook her head slightly and half-smiled. 'We're family. I'm glad you woke me up. This place is disgusting,' she ended, wrinkling her nose.

Kunti wrinkled her own nose in agreement. She looked beyond them into the distance, past a sea of parked vehicles and people to a dark, deserted opening behind the station.

It looked like an extension of the car parking area but was overrun by debris, which probably made it too difficult to access. A single street light shone within it, giving the space a haunted, shadowy appearance.

'Do you think they'll be around there?'

Draupadi considered that for a moment and then replied, 'It's difficult to say. If all they had to do was collect a package, wouldn't it be easier to just have the boys enter that chaotic fray around the entrance and have the package exchange hands without anybody noticing?'

Kunti said, after a moment, 'Yes, but what if a payment had to be made? And the contents of the package had to be verified?'

'Then you would want as deserted a place as possible where, hidden in the shadows, you could comfortably open a package, examine it and make the payment accordingly.'

Kunti looked back into the distance. 'Then, perhaps that is where we are going.'

Draupadi looked around her at all the faces. 'Chances are that they will be hiding among the crowd right now and will only show themselves when a signal is given. Our best chance is for you to look amongst the crowd closer to the back of the building and try and identify Karan. Then we can warn him before he does anything to implicate himself.'

Kunti nodded. 'Good idea. I'll try and spot him.'

They walked closer to the deserted area slowly, in the shadows, Kunti staring at each of the faces around them carefully. There were many children around, and many of them were shrouded in darkness, which didn't make her task any easier.

Draupadi mumbled to herself: 'If I wanted to see a signal from over there, where would I put myself? Somewhere in the direct line of sight, facing in that direction but sitting in the dark and pretending to be busy doing something ... children, boys ... boys sitting and facing in that direction ...' She scanned the crowd carefully until she stopped at a group of five boys sitting in a circle on an elevated divider in the middle of the car parking area. They seemed to be absorbed in a game which involved flicking marbles into a circle in the mud. There was much backslapping and teasing, but one of the boys – the tallest one – sat facing the deserted area and kept glancing up towards it before returning his glance to the game at hand. His posture suggested he was at ease but his right hand was clenched to his side and one foot was shaking with nervous energy.

Draupadi nodded grimly towards him. 'Is that him?'

Kunti followed her gaze and her eyes widened. 'Yes,' she whispered emphatically. 'Yes it is. Let's go!'

'Not so fast.' Draupadi caught Kunti's arm with a firm hand. 'We have to be careful. The gang members and the policemen can't be very far away, and they're probably keeping an eye on the boys. We need to approach them in an innocuous way.'

But as she was speaking, Kunti noticed that Karan looked alert all of a sudden. He said something to the boys around him and stood up. The other boys followed, looking around nervously.

'They're getting up,' whispered Kunti. She tugged at Draupadi's hand desperately. 'Let me go, I have to warn him.'

Draupadi shook her head and held on tight, a worried expression on her face as she looked around urgently. 'No, Kunti. They might be anywhere. You stay here, I'll go. You'll get hurt.'

'I don't care!' Kunti turned her blazing eyes towards Draupadi and back towards Karan. All the boys had begun moving quickly towards the deserted area, stopping on the way to beg for money from passers-by but not waiting to collect it before moving on. They were obviously trying not to attract attention to themselves.

Kunti saw the figure of a man appear in the distance, in the direction the boys were headed. He carried a bag on his back and another smaller bag in his hand. He stood in the shadows, leaning against a metal pole, waiting. Karan had seen him too and started walking faster.

Kunti felt her chest go cold with fear. She had to stop him. She jerked her arm out of Draupadi's hand violently. 'Let me *go*!'

'Kunti, wait,' Draupadi muttered furiously but Kunti had bolted towards Karan. Her mind didn't once stop to consider what she would actually do when she reached him. Like a lioness whose cub was in danger, she charged blindly to protect her child any way she possibly could. Skipping clumsily over bodies and bumps in her path, she hurled forward and called out, 'Karan!'

Karan froze and whipped his head around to look at her, shocked. When he saw Kunti coming towards him, he seemed to not know what to do. His eyes fluttered in panic from her to the boys who were with him, to the shadows around him. He was scared out of his wits and looked like he was about to make a run for it. Kunti held out her hand to stop him. 'Don't go to that man. It's a trap!'

Now he looked even more scared. The boys around him looked scared too. Three of them began running towards the lone man in the distance, but Karan and his friend, Goalie, stayed rooted to the spot. Goalie pulled Karan's ragged shirt, urging him to run too but Karan kept looking at Kunti and then at the shadows, his expression one of agonized indecision.

Kunti could hear men shouting. Out of the corner of her eye, she saw could see many of them leaping out of the shadows, while others, pretending to be drunkards that lay unconscious on the ground, now sprang to their feet. There was confusion everywhere as the shouting became louder and more frantic and people darted about, chasing each other, some coming to blows as they were caught. Kunti had just reached Karan and Goalie when she heard a loud bang that echoed through the night. More such explosive sounds followed as she grabbed Karan. 'Come!'

He didn't need to be asked twice. They ran together as if their lives depended on it, Karan easily outrunning middle-aged Kunti and getting ahead of her. Suddenly, just as he was about to jump over a large drain, a burly man appeared out of nowhere and grabbed him. Cursing loudly, the man twisted Karan's arm and the boy cried out in pain as he struggled uselessly. Kunti screamed and ran as fast as she could, but before she could reach them, Draupadi leapt out of the shadows, running towards the man with a large object in her hand and smashing him over the head with it. Then, as the man crumpled to the ground, Draupadi pulled Karan, who had keeled over in pain, back to his feet.

She shouted over the clamour, 'This way.' She turned, still holding Karan, and ran. Kunti followed behind them.

Draupadi led them out of the station and on to the road and didn't stop running until they found an auto rickshaw and jumped into it. It was only then that Kunti realized that Goalie was with them as well. The four of them bundled into the back, and the driver turned to protest that only three people were allowed at a time but Draupadi gave him a deathly look and commanded: 'Drive, *now*!'

The auto rickshaw jolted to life and Draupadi ordered the driver to take them to the zoo. Quickly.

The clamour of banging sounds faded into the distance as they drove away from the scene at the station. The observation, voiced by Draupadi, that no one seemed to be following them was met with gasps of relief. Nobody said a word during the ride to the zoo. Draupadi, after a terse haggle with the driver, paid him off and they scampered inside and sat the boys down on a bench amidst the bushes after Kunti reminded Draupadi that they couldn't take the boys *inside* because of the fence that you-know-who had put up.

Karan was whimpering in pain and clutching his forearm. Goalie was crying out softly, 'They're going to kill us. They're going to kill us.'

He looked at Karan and said, wild-eyed, 'We have to run away. If they find us—'

'Don't worry,' interrupted Kunti with a confidence she didn't feel at all. 'We'll make sure nothing happens to you.'

Karan looked up at her and, wincing in pain, asked, 'How? If we go back, they'll find us.'

Kunti sat next to him and cradled his arm gently. 'Then you won't go back. Let me see if this is broken.'

It turned out that Karan's forearm was, indeed, broken. A clean break, which Kunti declared would heal in no time. She went inside the toilet and emerged with a cleaned and trimmed branch of wood and long strips of cloth, with which she gently splinted Karan's arm. He watched her carefully the whole time, until she glanced up and caught his gaze. She smiled softly and caressed his cheek without thinking. He flinched a little but stayed where he was and allowed her to do it. His eyes even softened a bit the next time he looked at her.

Kunti kept her expression confident and gentle and was careful not to express too much concern or act too affectionate for fear of unnerving him or trampling his new-found trust in her. Inside, she was see-sawing between elation at the softness in his eyes and the torment of trying to figure out what they were to do now. They couldn't stay on the bench forever.

Draupadi went inside and returned with some rice and water for the boys, which they gulped down eagerly, barely bothering to chew. After second and third helpings, they leaned back on the bench and once again began to fret about the prospect of Ustaad finding them.

An hour or two passed with very little constructive conversation. Then suddenly Draupadi's phone began to clang loudly, setting off a few howls and cackles from the nearby zoo animals. Shashiben's agitated voice rang when Draupadi answered: 'Are they with you?'

Kunti answered for them. 'Yes, Karan and his friend Goalie are with us.'

They heard Shashiben's breath of relief. 'I'm glad to hear that. There is turmoil in the slum right now. The police are raiding the brothels and drink shops and arresting gang members by the dozens. Word is that Ustaad and most of his men were killed in the shoot-out at the station.'

Karan and Goalie gasped, staring at each other, obviously wondering what this meant for them. 'Ustaad and his men are dead. Raja and the other two boys?' asked Karan.

Shashiben replied, 'In jail, along with all the gang members whom they picked up at the slum tonight. The boys will probably be sent off to a juvenile home. The rest will likely languish in prison for a while. They're saying that the police is going to make a big deal about taking down this gang. They've cordoned off the entire slum and the surrounding roads. The media is going crazy. The main road is full of TV vans and reporters right now. The inspector general himself is involved. Probably wants to get into politics or avoid an anti-corruption inquiry. Anyway,' she paused for a moment and said in a cheerful tone, 'you know what this means, right?'

Karan and Goalie weren't the only ones who held their breath. Kunti could feel her heart hammering against her chest.

'It means that the slum is going to be gang-free! For the moment, anyway. I'm sure a new one will sprout again soon. But meanwhile we can do some good work, get the children involved in constructive pastimes and really make some changes around here.'

Karan's voice was a whimper as he asked, 'We can come back?'

Shashiben answered, 'Of course. Not now. You should probably wait till the morning when most of the police have cleared out. Come in through the back entrance and I'll hide you for a few days. They've already searched the building, so I doubt they'll be back. Call me before you leave.'

With that, Shashiben abruptly hung up.

There was a brief moment of stunned silence and then Goalie jumped up and whooped. Karan joined in with excited laughter that was tempered by the pain of his broken arm. Draupadi smiled broadly and Kunti felt a small tear threaten her composure before she blinked it back and laughed along with the boys.

Kunti looked at Karan's face, carefree and childlike for the first time since she'd met him. She said a quick prayer of thanks to Krishna for restoring some of the child in him. Then, as was typical of mothers who had just gotten their children out of one tight spot, she began to worry about the next one. There was much to be done before she had to leave, the foremost of which was to ensure that the orphanage remained open so that Karan – and the other children she had come to know so well – would have a roof over their heads. After that, they would need funds to provide more food, better hygiene, perhaps one or two more caretakers. Maybe they could even organize an educational programme for the children, thought Kunti absently, so that they can be gainfully employed when they got older.

Shashiben had obviously been a dedicated warden for a long time, but after spending so much time with her and getting to know her ways, Kunti had come to feel that she was too rigid and narrow in her thinking and wasn't doing all that could be done. Kunti had been speaking to the local charities and the people who ran them. Most were willing to help, but all unanimously felt that Shashiben was too crabby and arrogant to work with.

Of course, Kunti was no closer, despite much time spent thinking, to finding another warden to replace Shashiben. Who would want a job with no salary, virtually no sustenance and definitely no prospects? Who would do it just for the love of the children? Who would do it well, with full commitment and energy? Deep in her heart, Kunti already knew the answer to those questions. Usually though, whenever that answer sprang to mind, she squashed it back down almost immediately. Today, after tasting the fruit of success, she toyed with the idea for a little while first.

Karan drew her out of her thoughts by saying a little brusquely, 'Thank you for coming to help me.' Then, after a moment, he asked, 'Why did you come? You put yourself in danger for me. Why?'

Kunti looked at him, allowing the undiluted love inside her to shine in her eyes and said simply, 'Because I love you. There is nothing I would not do for you to keep you safe and happy.' And then, the force of her own statement hit her and she was struck into temporary silence by it. Then she repeated it, more for her own benefit than for his. 'There is nothing I would not do for you.'

Draupadi had been listening carefully, and hearing that, she said softly, 'Kunti—'

'Shhh, Draupadi. We'll talk later.'

Draupadi reluctantly fell silent.

Karan stared at Kunti closely, digesting what she had just said. Then, cringing in pain at the movement, he slowly shifted towards her and gave her an awkward, loose, one-armed hug.

It took all of Kunti's will power not to wrap her arms around him tightly. Instead, she put one arm around him equally loosely and with the other, patted his shoulder. As she kissed the top of his head, a few previously unshed tears fell discreetly into his hair, and she closed her eyes to savour the moment. Draupadi smiled and Goalie looked away politely as Karan let out a sigh and made no effort to pull away.

Chapter 34

'I'm calling Narad Muni.'

Draupadi, Kunti and Amba stopped their morning ablutions and turned towards Gandhari in shock.

Gandhari was shaking as she continued, 'You've all gone completely out of control. You two' – she glowered at Draupadi and Kunti – 'were out all night last night doing god knows what, coming back in broad daylight without any explanation. You,' her stare turned to Amba and she spat out, 'you think I don't know what you're up to with that man every day? You used to be a princess in one of the most celebrated and noble royal families of our day, and now ... You should be *ashamed* of yourself!'

Amba's eyes became fierce. 'How dare you?'

'I dare because it's true. There's a name for a woman who lies back and spreads her legs for a man who is not her husband, and you know what it is because you've become one!'

Amba gasped and lunged towards Gandhari, only to be held back firmly by Draupadi, who knew that Amba was no match for Gandhari. Undeterred, Amba strained against Draupadi's grip and screeched, 'You know *nothing*. Stay away from me, you witch! I *never* want to see your petty, spiteful face again.'

Gandhari laughed bitterly. 'You have no idea how much I wish I could stay away from you ... you whore! That's why I'm calling Narad Muni, so I can be put out of my misery and not have to watch you or you' – she looked at Draupadi and Kunti – 'destroy yourselves, your future and worse, your honour.'

Draupadi let go of Amba and glared at her. 'You—'

'Enough,' said Kunti loudly. She looked at Gandhari and said angrily, 'Sister, you say too much when you're upset. There is no question of calling Narad Muni earlier than expected. You may have decided that you've had enough, but the rest of us still have work to do. You will just have to wait a few days.'

Gandhari's eyes were tearful as they looked, betrayed, at Kunti. 'You, my sister, even you? Where has your wisdom disappeared? Do you not see that you are building expectations that cannot be met, harbouring dreams that cannot be fulfilled?'

Draupadi answered emphatically, 'That's because she's alive, and hope is the companion of the living. You ... you've decided to die because you're too scared to live. You've put on your blindfold again, Gandhari.'

Tears streamed down Gandhari's cheeks. 'Maybe I have. But I prefer to be blind than have to see everything I hold dear destroyed. Sister' – she spoke to Kunti – 'you're only going to be alive for a few more days. Why do you set yourself up for a broken heart?'

Kunti began to cry too. 'Because it matters too much. Don't you see, Gandhari? I can't help myself. My son, all those children, they have no one but me. What else can I do?'

Gandhari exhaled in frustration. 'And after you leave? What then?'

Kunti looked torn but was silent, staring at the floor instead.

Draupadi intervened, 'Gandhari, let it go. Yes, each of us has changed. That's what happens when one lives in the mortal world. One is shaped by experience. Please don't call Narad Muni. It's matter of a few days. Be indoors, be disapproving, but be kind.'

Gandhari frowned through her tears. 'Some would say it would be kinder to put an end to this sooner rather than later.'

'Well, I don't agree,' said Kunti. She walked up to Gandhari and craned her neck to stare angrily into her eyes. 'If you call Narad Muni today, I will consider it the most severe of betrayals. When you lay dying in the forest fire as an old woman, blind and burned on that day so long ago, I stayed with you, holding your hand and comforting you as you passed. I could have run to safety, yet I chose to die with you, Gandhari. Now, in return I ask you – command you! – to wait in silence until he comes for us. I also ask you to refrain from insulting your companions. Will you obey this command?'

Gandhari stared at Kunti and slowly nodded reluctantly through her sobs. 'I will. I have never forgotten that day, and I will do as you bid, sister. And I will pray for you, as you did for me.'

Kunti gave her a brief hug and pulled away to say gently, 'I think you owe Amba an apology.' She turned, with a conciliatory smile, to the spot where Amba had been standing.

It was empty.

Draupadi, who had been focused on Kunti and Gandhari till now, cast her eyes around the chamber and went to check in the adjoining one as well; but Amba was nowhere to be found. 'She must have slipped out.'

Kunti took a deep breath and said, 'Well, we'll speak with her tonight. I must get to the orphanage now. Shashiben would have returned from the, what did she call it, ah, the doctor. I must see how Karan's arm is doing.'

Draupadi decided to go with her. She had taken quite a shine to Karan and his friend Goalie.

At the orphanage, they found both the boys fast asleep in one of the rooms, Karan's arm encased in a hard, white shell of some sort.

Outside, there was jubilation in the air. The media was full of the news that the slum had been cleared of one of the most feared gangs in Delhi. Their operations, which included begging syndicates, drink shops, bars, bootlegging, drugs and brothels, had been shut down. Their leaders had been killed. For the moment at least there seemed to be hope that social workers could come in, without fear, and really make a difference in the neighbourhood. In fact, one of the workers from a local charity was sitting with Shashiben as Kunti and Draupadi walked in. They were discussing new avenues to arrange funds for the orphanage.

Draupadi was both amused and surprised when Kunti, after a single look at Shashiben's guest, said, 'Ah, Sonal beta, nice to see you here. Thank you for coming and seeing us.' From that point on, Kunti proceeded to take over the conversation enthusiastically, much to Shashiben's chagrin. In fact, at one point, Shashiben even muttered, 'I'm not dead yet, you know.'

The others pretended they hadn't heard her.

Draupadi's phone rang while she watched the others talk. It was Angela.

'Oh my god, oh my god, Draupadi, you have no idea what's been going on,' she said in an excited squeal that was very unlike her.

Draupadi frowned, getting up and walking to the back of the room. 'Angela? Everything all right?'

'Everything is more than all right, babe. You're a hit! The pilot aired and we've been getting massive reactions. The ratings are through the roof. But, best of all, they've arrested Vaishali's husband and the dhaba owner.'

'What? But how?'

'After the pilot was telecast, a local women's group went and created a big shindig outside the police station and forced them to file an official FIR and take the men into custody. They've even asked for an inquiry against the officer who refused to help Vaishali *and* hired a lawyer for her to contest her case. You did it!'

Draupadi closed her eyes. Vaishali would have justice. She had helped achieve that for her. She had never known exhilaration so painful. 'Angela—'

'Don't you dare say anything or I swear I'll have the mother of all hissy fits! Think, babe. Think about what an amazing thing you did, and I'll speak to you later.'

Her voice was replaced by a dial tone and the phone went off. Draupadi stared at it for a few moments, her mind unable to grasp at any single thought. Instead, it flitted from one thought to another, one extreme emotion to the other. Happiness, sadness, resolve, regret, hope, hopelessness, they all seemed to blur together for a few moments. She looked up at the sky. Krishna, she thought at it, I know you can't or won't answer me, but I would love to know if you planned for all this to happen. And if you did, what is it you want me to do? Do I even have a choice?

'Draupadi?'

Draupadi absently turned to Kunti, who asked softly, 'Everything all right?'

Draupadi felt a despondent tear sting her eye, which was very unusual for her and a little alarming. She firmly pushed it away but couldn't stop her lip from quivering just a tiny bit as she replied, 'No. Not really.'

Kunti immediately got up and came over to where Draupadi was standing. Taking Draupadi by the arm, Kunti led her to the far end of the room where their words wouldn't be heard and asked softly: 'What's happened, my dear?'

Draupadi blurted out the whole story – the audition, the pilot, the reaction with Vaishali, Angela and her words and her own exhilaration when she had been in the studio. She shook her head sadly. 'Never did I think that a short thirty-day visit would end up being this complicated. I came down here thinking I would see some things, have a laugh and leave. Now, I'm questioning everything. I—I—' She sighed in frustration. 'I had a difficult life before, when we lived as mortals. You know this. Being married to the Pandavas' – she looked up at Kunti quickly, not wanting to offend her – 'I mean, they were good men.'

'But they were difficult to be with. I know, my dear, I was their mother, and as much as I love them, they could drive one crazy,' Kunti admitted with a smile.

Draupadi acknowledged her smile with a momentary one of her own before continuing, 'I never had anything of my own. My life revolved around theirs. My education and my intelligence were wasted, as far as I'm concerned. Krishna's last words to me when I asked him to let us visit were "this is your second chance" and that meant nothing to me before but now—now, I can't help but think maybe he knew this was going to happen. I have the chance to really live the way I wanted to in the first place. I have the opportunity to change the world if I should but take it.' Her eyes blazed.

Kunti nodded sadly. 'Yes, but at what cost?' She paused for a moment before saying, 'I'm in the same situation, Draupadi.'

Draupadi replied, 'I know. That's partly why I'm confiding in you. What are you going to do?'

Kunti looked at her carefully, in a measuring way, before saying: 'My decision should not have any influence over yours, Draupadi. Our lives and souls will have journeys of their own, and we must make our choices independently.'

Draupadi was a little confused by Kunti's unwillingness to give her an answer but was too preoccupied to dwell on it. Karan and Goalie walked into the room at that moment and Kunti was immediately distracted, fussing over Karan's arm and beaming at him. Draupadi's mood lifted a bit when she saw the warm smile and hug that Karan gave Kunti in return and even went up to him and asked him how he was feeling.

Karan thought for a moment and then replied, with a cheeky look, 'Hungry.'

That made Draupadi laugh and she quickly walked the two boys and Kunti to the closest eating house and plied them with food. Once their bellies were filled, Karan brought to Draupadi's notice the fact that the other children at the orphanage had probably not eaten anything either. That statement led to Draupadi asking the manager of the eatery to pack a large quantity of food for them to carry back to the orphanage while a thrilled Karan and Goalie looked on.

As they walked back to the orphanage, their arms laden with bags full of lentils and rice, Karan looked over at Draupadi and said matter-of-factly, 'You look like you're rich. Can you help the orphanage?'

Draupadi considered that and said, 'I have a little money, which I would gladly give to help, but it won't last for long. Still, it'll buy a few more meals like this at least.' She smiled at him.

That seemed to satisfy him and he remarked, 'You're a good lady. Thanks.'

The children at the orphanage cheered when the food was brought in, and even the sour look on Shashiben's face, brought on by a discussion with the social worker, vanished as she saw them tucking into the meal. Kunti stood back after serving everyone and surveyed the scene with a smile. Rows of ravenous children shovelled the food into their mouths, some delicately mixing the lentils in the rice and scooping it up in bite-sized balls, some grabbing unmixed handfuls and almost scrubbing their faces with it and some even licking their steel plates unabashedly while stealing glances at other unfinished meals.

Kunti murmured to Draupadi, 'They deserve to eat like this at least twice, if not three times a day. Even if we could arrange a free education for them as Sonalji has suggested, it's difficult to learn things when you've got an empty belly.' She sighed. 'So much that needs to be done.'

Without waiting for a reply, she stalked off to help the children who had finished eating to drink water and wash up. Draupadi watched her as she worked, watched the children – who called her Kuntiben – responding to her familiar warmth. She noticed how Kunti spoke to everyone; how she gave the cook as well Karan and the other older children instructions in a soft, but firm voice. Shashiben appeared to be standing back, letting Kunti take over, watching her constantly with a casual, but careful expression.

Just like that, in a fleeting but pivotal moment, Draupadi realized what Kunti's choice was probably going to be. This didn't look like a woman who was preparing to leave.

That made her own decision all the more difficult. She wished Amba was here. Well, the old Amba anyway, the one who was her steadfast friend and confidante, not the sullen, distracted Amba that had replaced her. Draupadi wondered where she had stormed off this morning. Probably into Zafar's arms.

She sighed and looked up at the sky again, from where she felt sure Krishna was watching, his eyes dancing with even more mischief than usual. Much as I appreciate your sense of humour, she thought at him irritatedly, I don't find this situation with all of us very funny.

A drab grey sky stared disinterestedly back at her.

Chapter 35

'He's *what*?'

Sania's voice sounded agitated. 'He's gone. Zafar didn't come home last night. He messaged me, saying that he's travelling for a few days, but he didn't have any luggage when he left the flat yesterday and he never said anything about travelling before. He's not even picking up our calls. I thought, since he left with Amba, that he might be with you.'

Draupadi frowned. 'He left with Amba?'

'Yes, she came to our house yesterday morning. She was really upset, and Zafar took her away before we could invite her inside. Is he there?'

Draupadi shook her head as if Sania could see her. 'No. Amba didn't come back last night either.' They thought she'd be back at some point during the night but began to get worried when they woke up and her bed had not been slept in. Draupadi had tried to call Zafar but to no avail. This was so unlike Amba. Who would think that a woman with thousands of years of age and experience could behave with such immaturity!

Suppressing her anger, she said calmly to Sania, 'Don't worry. I'm sure they're all right. She had an argument with Gandhari before she left.'

'About her relationship with Zafar?' Sania's voice interrupted. 'Zafar had a fight with Ammee about Amba too. Ammee, you know how she is, she wants him to marry a Muslim girl. Not that she doesn't like Amba,' she added quickly. 'She does. But she said some things to Zafar, and he got angry. When it comes to me, he thinks it's funny, but now that *he's* at the receiving end … never mind, what should we do?'

'I don't know. What do people around here do when someone goes missing?'

Sania thought for a moment. 'Well, we could go to the police, I guess.'

Draupadi looked around at Kunti and Gandhari, who were listening to the conversation. After what had happened with Vaishali, not to mention Karan, the police weren't exactly on their 'most preferred people to deal with' list. Her mind racing, she said, 'I know someone who would be perfect for speaking to the police. She's the warden at the orphanage that we are helping. Can you meet us there in a little while?'

Sania agreed and said she would bring Ammee, who was worried sick, with her.

Draupadi put down the phone, saying to Kunti and Gandhari: 'No point waiting for her over here. I think it's clear she's not coming back any time soon. We'll have to find her instead.'

They soon reached the orphanage and tracked down Shashiben. Karan and Goalie, now living permanently at the orphanage and staying – relatively – out of trouble, sat in on the conversation as Draupadi explained the situation to a highly amused Shashiben.

'Run away with him, has she?' she cackled loudly. 'I doubt the police will help, but I'll do my best.'

Draupadi was less than amused. She was responsible for Amba and hardly thought that an irrational, lusty suitor could be trusted to keep her safe. But she kept her composure long enough for Sania to arrive with a rambling and extremely upset Mrs Kapoor, who burst into the room and launched herself towards Kunti, exclaiming, 'Who could have thought, Kuntiji? Such a nice, polite girl. And my Zafar! He's such a sensible boy, I don't know *how* he can do this to me. If I had known he felt so strongly, I would never have stopped him. What kind of a mother would I be if I drove my children to run away? I just don't understand how he could do this to me—' And then she burst into what was obviously the latest in many rounds of tears.

Kunti put a consoling arm around her and said, 'Don't worry, Nazliji, I'm sure he doesn't blame you for anything. It was our fault as well.'

Mrs Kapoor avoided Kunti's eye and said through incessant weeping, 'I didn't *not* like her, you know. But you understand that I went through such a bad time because I married a Hindu—'

Sania exclaimed in frustration, 'Ammee, that was thirty years ago! Let it go, things are different now.'

Mrs Kapoor looked down and cried quietly, subdued for the moment. Karan and Goalie gaped at Sania, who was dressed in a tight, skin-baring top and even tighter jeans. Kunti and Gandhari looked at Mrs Kapoor uncomfortably as Draupadi tapped her foot on the floor.

Shashiben grinned. 'As much fun as it is to watch you all, maybe we should proceed to make a police report. You two boys wait here. The rest of you, follow me.'

She then walked them, at a snail's pace, down a few busy roads until they came to the police station. She hobbled up to a uniform-clad moustached man who was seated behind a desk, with a belly that made him look heavily pregnant. With a weak, distressed expression on her face, Shashiben spoke in a quivering, old-lady voice that none of them had heard before. 'Beta, we need to report two missing people. Please help us.'

The policeman behind the desk, his valiant efforts at doing as little as possible so rudely interrupted, did not look encouraging as he asked: 'Name of missing person?'

Shashiben gave him the names. He didn't bother writing them down, choosing instead to pick the dirt out of his ears, roll the bits up between his fingers and flick them on to the floor.

'Age? Male or female? Last seen?' His tone was sullen.

Shashiben patiently explained the entire situation and then, when he looked away with a bored expression, inquired, 'Aren't you going to file a missing person report?'

The policeman looked irritated and said, 'I have filed it already. Now go away, and if they are still missing after two days, you can come back.'

Shashiben turned and gave the others an I-told-you-so glance, which spurred Draupadi on to ask the man in a cutting tone, 'So, you're not even going to bother to look for them?'

The policeman ran his gaze up and down Draupadi's body with withering, and slightly lecherous, eyes. He clearly didn't think she deserved a reply, instead turning to Shashiben and saying, as if she were the scum of the earth, 'If they've run away together then what can we do? I don't have time to waste. Now go away.'

Before Draupadi could make any sharp comebacks about what he was actually doing with his time, Shashiben ushered them all out muttering, 'This is how it always is, impossible to get a policeman to write anything down. Only two things get these lazy bastards moving money and a call from their supervising officer.'

Mrs Kapoor's eyes widened a bit when she heard 'bastards', but she kept silent while they left the station and walked back to the orphanage. Upon entering the common room, she finally wailed, 'What do we do now?'

Shashiben shrugged. 'We wait.'

Draupadi was troubled. 'No. Amba's only been down in Delhi for a few weeks. She can't take care of herself. We have to find them.'

Sania said, 'Zafar is with her. He'll take care of her.'

Draupadi's reply was caustic. 'If he had such good judgement and was genuinely interested in her welfare, he wouldn't have made her run away from her family.'

This was too much for Mrs Kapoor. 'My son would never have thought about doing this himself.' She looked defensively at Kunti's feet. 'I'm sure he was influenced ...'

Sania rolled her eyes. 'Does it matter? It's obvious they love each other. Ammee, you have to be sensible about this or you'll lose him.'

Mrs Kapoor looked quite struck by the thought and went silent.

Meanwhile, Karan piped in and asked Sania, 'So the police refused to help?'

She nodded absently.

Karan cast a meaningful glance at Goalie, his eyes twinkling, and then back at her. 'We could help find them.'

Sania frowned. 'How?'

Karan shrugged and said, 'Kids on the street see everything and everyone. Goalie and I can ask Billu to help us.'

Sania was confused. 'Who is Billu?'

He smiled importantly and stood a little taller as all the women in the room turned to look at him. 'Street kids work all over the city. We have different beats and groups but we sort of know each other through Billu. He knows all the kids working in the city, and if he asks you to do something, you do it, you know what I mean?'

Kunti interjected, 'No, no, Karan. You just got out of Ustaad's company, now don't go tying yourself up to another gang.'

Karan shook his head vigorously. 'No, no, he's not a gang leader. I mean, he is, but it's not that kind of gang. Mostly begging and harmless stuff like pickpocketing, nothing serious. And he looks out for other kids like us, so we all respect him like a big brother. Anyway, if these two have been on the city streets, chances are Billu knows someone who's seen them.'

Sania brightened up. 'Okay then, let's get him on the job.'

Kunti exchanged a worried look with Draupadi but said, 'All right, Karan, but only if you promise me that you're not going to start getting involved—'

Karan patted her shoulder and grinned. 'Don't worry, Kuntiben. I promise. No trouble from now on.'

Kunti stared at him for a moment and smiled. 'That was the first time you said my name.'

Karan shrugged, a little embarrassed.

After much discussion and argument from everyone except Gandhari, who sat meditatively in a corner, it was decided that only Draupadi and Shashiben would accompany the boys to meet Billu. The rest agreed rather grudgingly to wait at the orphanage.

The auto rickshaw ride to Billu's neighbourhood was spent in silence until at last they pulled into the car park of a crowded marketplace. Draupadi was surprised to see quite a few white-skinned people, many of them with yellow and even red hair, milling around in between shops and in small lanes filled with vendors. Karan explained that this place was called Khan Market, one of the most lucrative beats for street kids because of all the foreigners that shopped here. Foreigners were known to be a lot more generous than the Indians, completely unable to resist a pitiful face in ragged clothing. Billu and his group guarded this beat jealously. It was one of the reasons why he was so influential in their circles – he was by far the richest of them all.

One certainly wouldn't have guessed that by looking at Billu, however. Dressed in filthy, tattered, blood-stained clothes and hobbling around one-legged on a single battered crutch, Billu turned out to be a young man who could have been anywhere between eleven and fifteen years old. He was short and skinny, his hairless face covered in grime and scabs. They saw him from a distance as he was 'working', according to Karan, who sat them down under a nearby tree to watch. Billu limped up to a tall, white-skinned lady and looked pathetically into her eyes, one bandaged hand outstretched. He spoke softly to her the whole time as she initially cringed, then looked guiltily at his missing leg and scabbed face and eventually reached into her bag for some money.

'See?' said Karan, admiration in his eyes. 'It's so easy in this part of town.'

'What happened to his leg?' asked Draupadi.

Karan's eyes clouded over as he replied matter-of-factly, 'They cut it off when he was little. He can earn more money if he's crippled.'

Draupadi saw that he was serious and she shuddered. 'Does that happen to a lot of kids?'

Shashiben sighed and said, 'Too many.'

Karan nodded. 'If I hadn't been at the orphanage when I was younger, who knows? Anyway, he has a fake leg, which he wears when he's not working.'

Billu glanced briefly at them before continuing to solicit a few more ladies who walked past him. Then, after a few minutes, he hobbled over towards them and sat down on the ground with difficulty.

Karan and Goalie looked eager and greeted him respectfully. Billu nodded at them, his childish, pathetic eyes now alert and intelligent, his manner confident and authoritative, making him look older than Draupadi had initially thought. He glanced at Draupadi and Shashiben watchfully, with an enquiring raise of his eyebrows at Karan and Goalie. He didn't say anything.

Karan started with, 'Bhai, these people saved our lives. In the shoot-out with Ustaad's men.'

Billu nodded. 'You were lucky,' he said and then, 'What do they want?'

Karan replied, 'Their relatives are missing. A man and woman, they've run away together. They need to find them.'

Billu nodded and gave Shashiben a searching look. 'I've seen you before. You're the lady from the children's home.'

Shashiben nodded back, regarding him with amusement.

Billu slowly smiled at her. 'You're a good lady. Everyone thinks you're a witch from hell, but I know you don't get paid for it.'

Shashiben snorted. 'You need to be a witch to live in hell.'

Billu laughed. 'Good one! I know all about hell. I've been outrunning demons my whole life. Anyway' – he sighed and adopted a business-like tone – 'I normally charge for my services. Except street people, who I help for free, and the police, who I have to pay instead. You' – he cocked his head at Shashiben – 'I'll help for free. Write down their full names, age, description, their mobile phone numbers, where they were last seen and what they were wearing and if they're in a car, then model and licence plate number. And your mobile number also.' He fished out an expensive-looking, black leather-bound diary from his raggedy bag and handed it to them with a pen.

While Shashiben painfully wrote down all the details, he talked to Karan and Goalie, asking questions about the children in their area and at the orphanage, inquiring about their future plans and offering to give them a loan in case they needed one. Shashiben firmly declined the loan on their behalf without looking up.

Amused, Billu took the diary back from her and told them to go back and wait for him to get in touch.

On the auto rickshaw ride back to the orphanage, a thought occurred to Draupadi. She asked, 'If he's so well off, why is he still begging?'

Shashiben shrugged. 'It's a profession, like any other. It's difficult enough for educated people to get jobs, let alone an illiterate boy without a leg.'

Draupadi considered Karan and Goalie. 'So, if these two are not going to be in a gang any more, then what are their prospects?'

'Depends.'

'On what?'

Shashiben gazed out on to the road. 'On whether your *mother* decides to stick around or not.'

Draupadi could see Karan listening carefully to the conversation.

Chapter 36

'What the *hell* do you mean, you're still thinking about it? Didn't you *hear* what I just said?' Angela was almost screeching into the phone. 'Vaishali's case has been taken up by an advocacy group that is fighting to change the law so that women get treated better by the police and rapists get arrested and tried in court faster and get a more severe punishment. So that men who rape women, irrespective of whether those women are their wives or not, get charged for their crime. We have a chance to partner with groups like this, Draupadi, *dammit*—'

Draupadi interrupted softly, 'Angela, listen to me—'

'No, *you* listen to *me*. I like you, I really do, Draupadi, but I need a decision. You're either with me on this or you're not. It's going to be an awesome ride. We're going to get shit done for millions of women, we're going to be the change this country deserves. You think about that, think about whether you want your life to stand for something or you want to go lock yourself up – all your talent, your intelligence, all your drive and passion – in that fucking prison you call an ashram. You ask yourself whether you'll ever be happy after refusing what could be the biggest opportunity you'll ever get in your life. Think about that before you act pricey with me.' She took a breath and continued, 'I'm *done* chasing you. You have until tomorrow to call me back, and if you don't, I'm auditioning other people. Got it?'

'Yes.' Draupadi's voice cracked and she cleared her throat. Angela hung up the phone.

Draupadi let out a long, tortured breath, alone in the common room. Sania had long since taken Mrs Kapoor back home, Gandhari had returned to the zoo and Kunti, Shashiben and the kids were going about their business.

Tears started pouring uncontrollably down her cheeks, and she covered her face in her hands and wept. The last time she had cried like this was when she was told she would be marrying five men. That day, she had cried for everything she would be. Today, she cried for everything she couldn't be.

Chapter 37

'Kuntiben?'

Kunti, in the middle of scrubbing down a previously filthy kitchen at the back of the orphanage, turned to find Karan standing at the door looking awkward and unsure of himself.

She immediately wiped the sweat off her brow and put down her cleaning implements. If there was one thing she had learned by being a mother to so many boys, it was that they rarely chattered. So if they wanted to talk, it was almost always about something important.

She beckoned him inside to a few steps leading out into the yard area, where a group of young children were playing with sticks and a worn out ball. They sat on a step and Karan, after a moment, said, 'Shashiben said you have to decide whether to stay here or not.'

Kunti didn't know what to say. In her own mind, she had already decided that she would try her best to stay. She had made an unforgivable mistake in her old life by abandoning Karan and she would not make that same mistake again. Yes, she knew that meant re-entering the cycle of rebirth but she was prepared for it. If she went back now, she would be tortured for eternity by thoughts of what would happen to Karan. No, she would rather spend an eternity in the Kalyug for one lifetime with him than an eternity in heaven without him. She didn't, however, know if that was even an option. Shashiben seemed to think it was. But Narad Muni wasn't the most easy-going of heavenly beings and it would mean nothing to him to just snatch her up and cart her back up to heaven against her will.

In fact, he'd probably enjoy that, she thought bitterly. She immediately regretted her thought. If she had any chance of reasoning with him, there must be no hostility from her side. She clutched her head in her hands, worriedly pushing her hair back from her forehead. She had stayed up nights wondering what to say to him, wondering what would happen eventually.

Karan broke the silence. 'Is it true?'

Kunti sighed. 'Yes, beta. I can't tell you the details, but it's true.'

Karan asked, his voice cautious, his eyes becoming a little hard, 'Do you want to stay?'

'I want to stay more than anything, but I may have to go. The choice may not be in my hands.'

Karan looked upset for a moment and then, as if he had put on a mask, suddenly his face was set in the bitter sneer she knew so well. 'Great, what a fucking fool I've been. You're no better than the crack whore.'

Kunti slapped him across the face, shocking him into silence for an instant.

Taking advantage of his stunned state, Kunti quickly took the opportunity to get through to him. 'Don't do that. Don't become that boy again. You don't need to be. You're a good boy, I know you are. You're kind and brave and smart, and you have the potential to achieve anything you want if you put your mind to it. I know you've been hurt by people—'

He had recovered by then and angrily retorted, standing up and backing away as he did, 'I'm not hurt, I'm angry. Angry that everyone keeps doing this to me. Everyone I've ever cared about has left me. First her and now ...' He looked away, almost as if he wanted to storm off but still he stood there.

Kunti stood up and replied softly, 'Your anger comes from hurt, Karan. You have every right to be hurt, but don't be angry. Anger will hold you back, will make you into somebody you're not.'

Karan laughed bitterly. 'Easy for you to say. You haven't had the life I have. You haven't had to fight for each bite of food or starve. You haven't had to fight off grown men who want to rape you or cut off your fucking limbs. You haven't been awake all night because you're scared that someone will slit your throat if you sleep. *She* gave me this life. It's *her* fault that I've become like this.'

'Your mother loved you, Karan.'

That produced the biggest laugh of all. 'Sure! She loved me. That's why she dumped me on the orphanage steps and pushed off, right? Because she loved me.' All the bravado and sarcasm in the world couldn't hide the raw pain in his eyes.

Kunti was firm. 'Yes, because she loved you. Your mother had her limitations, beta, but she did. Do you know how I know that? Because she left you with Shashiben. She knew that had she kept you with her, you would have probably become like her. She let you go so you could have a chance for a better life. That is also love.' Tears began to drip down her cheeks. 'It is the most difficult thing in the world for a mother to let go of her child. But sometimes, mothers do it because they don't see any other way out. Your mother did what she thought would be the best for you, and it must have been hell for her.'

Karan was shaking, on the verge of tears too. 'Good. I'm glad. She deserved it. She had a choice. We could have made it work, together. I would have taken care of her. I would have been strong if only she had given me a chance.'

Kunti whispered through her tears, 'I'm so sorry.' She began to walk towards him, but he backed off so she stood where she was and said louder, 'I'm so very, very sorry ...'

She looked down at the ground and tried to compose herself. Indulging her own emotions wouldn't get them anywhere right now. She had to focus on him, so she looked up and said in a stronger voice, 'Letting you go was a weak thing to do. But that was then and this is now. I am not weak now, Karan, and I promise you I will fight God himself to stay with you. You have to trust me when I say that.'

He looked away, not saying anything.

Kunti took a step closer, and when he didn't move, another step and another until she stood in front of him. She moved his chin gently so he could meet her eyes. 'I love you, my child. I need you to be strong now, for the future. Will you fight with me for us to be together? So we can make it work this time?'

Karan stared at her and then down at the ground. But he stayed where he was. Kunti took that as a yes.

Chapter 38

It was a written message which appeared in Shashiben's phone from an undisclosed number that jolted them all into action the next morning. The message read: 'Zafar Kapoor and Amba Kuru getting married at the Sri Krishna temple on Mandir Marg at 11 a.m. today.'

After a few frantic phone calls, Sania and Mrs Kapoor picked up Draupadi, Kunti, Gandhari, Shashiben and Karan from the orphanage to make their way to the temple in Sania's car – a small, old, bright purple monstrosity with pink stars painted on the doors. The drive was extremely uncomfortable for the five of them squeezed in at the back, with Kunti sitting on Draupadi's lap, Shashiben sitting on Gandhari's and Karan wedged into the middle.

In the front seat, Mrs Kapoor was in full lament mode while Sania drove with admirable restraint.

They drove down a road which seemed filled with enormous, colourful temples that were interspersed with minarets and carvings and large grounds. Finally, they arrived at the Sri Krishna temple, a small, beige structure under a big banyan tree that was discreetly tucked away in a quiet lane. A wide, arched gateway with a few carvings and inexpertly painted murals led to a paved courtyard, into which the six women and one reluctant boy stormed only to be greeted by the most astonishing sight.

Amba, looking radiant and calm, was dressed in a simple red sari, her only embellishment the delicate, gold border of the sari that framed her face as it covered her head. She sat on a low stool next to Zafar, who was dressed in a shirt and jeans, and held his hand as they faced a small sacred fire. Two men sat around the fire, one obviously a priest, with a shaven head, sacred thread around his chest and only a voluminous dhoti as clothing. The other was a thin, bespectacled man, dressed also in a shirt and pants, who carried a small stack of papers and looked on impatiently.

Mrs Kapoor exclaimed, 'Allah!'

That made all four people sitting around the fire look up in surprise. Amba gasped as she saw her companions and Zafar muttered, 'Ammee?' and got up immediately and walked over to Sania and Mrs Kapoor in anger.

'How did you find us?' he asked Sania, frowning.

Sania glared at him. 'What the hell do you mean by disappearing like that? And now you're getting *married?* Without even telling us?'

Mrs Kapoor wailed, 'In a *Hindu* ceremony! Oh, Zafar beta, how *could* you do this to me? When I have *dreamed* about your nikaah!'

The priest frowned at Zafar. 'You're not a Hindu?'

Zafar pointed at Mrs Kapoor and exclaimed at Sania, 'This is why!'

Shashiben laughed.

Meanwhile, Draupadi had reached Amba, who kept sitting on her stool. 'What are you doing?'

Amba replied calmly, 'Getting married.'

'Can we talk?'

'There is nothing to talk about.'

The bespectacled man shifted uncomfortably. 'Look, I can only stay for the allotted time.'

Zafar turned to him. 'Please stay, sir. We are getting married.'

Draupadi asked, 'Who's he?'

Zafar was irritated. 'He's registering the marriage.'

Sania piped in, 'I don't see what the tearing hurry is.'

'Sania, please, you don't understand.'

Shashiben cackled, 'Trying to do it before he shows up, are you?'

Gandhari asked Amba, 'You think this will change anything?'

Amba glared at her. 'Yes.'

Kunti raised her palms, gesturing placatingly. 'Please, let's all be calm.'

The priest scratched his head. 'I don't have all day, you know.'

Zafar snapped at him, 'Just hang on, I'm coming.'

Mrs Kapoor caught his arm. 'Beta, *listen* to me—'

'Ammee, look—'

BOOM!

Draupadi heard someone scream in fright as she, and everyone else, jumped and whirled around at the explosion.

It was a cloud of smoke. Dear god, it can't be ... thought Draupadi in panic. But before she had time to complete the thought, she saw Narad Muni's bony hand waving away the smoke and her heart fell. It was time.

Chapter 39

'Oof! You would think, after all these years, they would make moving through the worlds a more pleasant experience for me, but no! It's all about the dramatic entrance, never mind that I have to breathe in this stuff on a daily—' Narad Muni turned towards them and stopped short at the sight of Zafar and the others.

'Oh dear, mortals. I thought you'd be at your lodgings. Well, never mind. It's a small job of erasing this memory from their minds. Done it countless times before.'

He saw Shashiben, who was smiling at him in amusement. 'You?' He cast her a look of dislike, but since she did, technically, outrank him in the heavenly scheme of things, he reluctantly folded his hands and bowed, muttering 'Salutations, O Goddess Saraswati' quickly, before getting back to business.

'And now' – he looked over Draupadi, Kunti, Amba and Gandhari – 'shall we be on our way?'

No one answered him. The mortals gaped at him, their jaws hanging open. The priest began to loudly chant prayers as if to ward off demons, which made Draupadi snap, 'He's a god, you idiot.'

Narad Muni cast his gaze over the four women, the sacred fire, the temple altar behind them, the priest and the mortals and his eyes narrowed. 'Am I interrupting something?'

Well, since I'm the leader of this expedition, thought Draupadi ...

'I'm not going back,' said Amba in a calm voice, her hands folded over her lap. Draupadi gazed at her friend with new eyes. Amba looked every inch a princess as she sat, her back straight, her chin high and spoke to Narad Muni with composed authority. She was going to fight this. Never had Draupadi seen her so resolute, determination screaming from every inch of her. Her normally sedate friend, so easy-going and acquiescent previously, had been transformed.

'Neither am I.' Kunti walked over to Karan and put her arm around his shoulders.

Gandhari sighed and shook her head. Draupadi, very unlike herself, couldn't think of anything to say. It wasn't as if either Amba's or Kunti's declarations should have come as a surprise to her, but they had. She had never thought they would actually go through with it. It cast her own dilemma into a new light. Her mind ran over everything that had happened to her in the last thirty days – the time she crossed the road and nearly killed herself, the time she tasted biryani and felt the flavours bursting upon her tongue, when she was in the lift soaring into the sky. She thought about how she had felt in the studio, with Vaishali. The fire that had burned within her to right the wrongs that the unfortunate girl had suffered. That feeling of sheer exhilaration as it had ended and everyone had clapped. The way she had danced with abandon at the party, the hours spent watching the aeroplanes fly, everything ran through her mind. Just as if it were on TV.

Draupadi smiled. These thirty days had been the happiest of her existence. She had known a freedom here that she couldn't even have dreamt of when she had lived as a princess.

And then Angela's words rang through her mind. She thought of Vaishali and of how her life had been changed and how justice had been served. *She* had made that change possible. Her own life had been a series of acceptances while others had made decisions for her. This world was different. She didn't have to accept anything she didn't want to. This was a world where she could fight for the things she believed in, make right the injustices done to her through other women.

One lifetime to be everything she could be. To be free. To make all the dreams she hadn't even dreamt yet come true. Only one. Was it worth it?

Yes.

'I'm staying too.' She braced herself for a fight and stared at Narad Muni, her eyes alight.

Narad Muni, who had been momentarily stunned into silence, recovered quickly. 'What do you mean you're not going? You don't have a choice. If you want extra time, ladies—'

'We don't want extra time,' interrupted Amba. 'We've decided to stay permanently. And re-enter the cycle of rebirth upon our natural death.'

Narad Muni's eyes widened, as they did any time a mortal who entered heaven chose to return to this world. He couldn't imagine how anyone could prefer it to heaven.

'Well, I've never heard anything so ungrateful in my life! What about you?' he asked Gandhari. 'Don't tell me. Let me guess. You want to stay too, right?'

Gandhari, her expression resigned, said, 'No, I don't. I will return to heaven.' She turned to Kunti. 'Sister, you will not rethink your decision?'

Kunti smiled at her. 'No,' she said and came over to give her a hug. 'I wish you much happiness, sister.'

Gandhari, never one to break a promise, hugged her back sadly and said, 'And I you.'

'Very touching,' sneered Narad Muni almost villainously, 'but no point saying your goodbyes, ladies, because you're all coming with me. You want to be born again, you speak to Krishna about that. My job is to take you back to heaven and nothing more.'

Kunti shook her head. 'We don't want to be born again. We each have made commitments here, O great Narad Muni. I know that was not the initial plan, but we have the opportunity to really help mortals now and ease their suffering in this terrible Kalyug. Surely, Krishna would only see the good in that.'

The priest's eyes widened once he heard the words 'Narad Muni' and 'Krishna' and his face broke out in an ecstatic smile. He quickly picked up his prayer tray and began to transfer the sacred offerings, meant for the marriage ceremony, into it. Then he started, softly this time, singing a song in praise of the heavenly being that had graced his lowly temple with his presence and performing a prayer ceremony while circling the tray in tune with the song.

The bespectacled man who had come to register the marriage, however, quickly whipped out his phone and pointed it towards the apparition in front of him.

Narad Muni, after an irritated glance at the singing priest, proceeded to glare at Kunti but before he could say anything, a now-recovered-and-confused Zafar asked Amba, 'What's going on? I thought they were going to take you back to the ashram?' He nodded towards Gandhari, Kunti and Draupadi.

Amba sighed and finally got up, walking up to Zafar and taking his hands in her own. 'Do you love me?'

Zafar didn't blink. 'Yes.'

'Are you willing to marry me and keep me for the rest of our lives?'

'Of course. Why else would I be here today?'

Amba nodded. 'Then you deserve the truth.' She looked at Mrs Kapoor and Sania. 'All of you do.'

She took a deep breath and started, 'The four of us used to be mortals, like you. We lived here many thousands of years ago, and after our natural deaths as old women, we had our youth restored and have been living in the heavenly world. You don't need to know details about that.' She shook her head as Zafar opened his mouth. 'All you need to know is that we were allowed to visit your world for thirty days, and speaking for myself, I was entirely prepared to go back after my visit was over. Until I met you. You—you have made me feel, in thirty short days, how I have desperately yearned to feel for thousands of years. And now, now I want to be with you and be your wife and bear your children and' – her eyes welled up – 'finally feel ... loved.' She burst into tears as Zafar gathered her into his arms.

'I don't entirely understand but I don't need to,' Zafar said resolutely as he held her. 'All I know is that I love you and I'm not letting you go.' He looked over at his mother, who stared back a little doubtfully but dared not argue. Then, he looked at Narad Muni and remarked, 'I guess I believe in God too now.'

Draupadi spoke spitefully, 'Well, technically he's more of a pseudo-god. Although, there are real ones too. Take my word for it.'

Narad Muni gave Draupadi a withering glance, looked at Zafar as if he were a weed that required trimming and said sarcastically, 'I admire your conviction, boy. Tragic love and all that. Breaks my heart, really. Never gets old.' He sighed dramatically. 'So, if we're done with the clichés, can we please make a move? I have other engagements, you know.'

'Just a minute O' – Shashiben cleared her throat – 'Great Narad Muni.' Her lips quivered as she addressed him. Once his unfriendly gaze was upon her, she continued, 'As you know, I've been down here for the last eighty-five years and am now the warden of the orphanage where this boy' – she pointed at Karan – 'lives. Kunti has been helping me with my duties, and since I am to leave my mortal avatar soon, I would like to appoint her as my successor. I'm sure you can't argue with that, considering who I am.' She raised her eyebrows pointedly.

Narad Muni's tone was stiffly respectful, but hostile all the same. 'I cannot dare argue with you O' – he cleared his throat – 'Great Goddess Saraswati, despite your frequent quarrels with the Majestic Brahma, the Merciful Vishnu and the Magnificent Shiva.' He looked pointedly back at her. He waved his hands over the four women. 'But bringing them here was not my decision in the first place, it was Krishna's. And so only Krishna can allow them to stay. I'm afraid not even *you*' – there was a glint of triumph in his eye – 'can argue with that.'

Shashiben glared at him. Suddenly, a child's voice rang out from inside the altar room.

'He's right you know, Saraswati.'

There was a collective gasp as everyone turned to stare at the altar room. The priest, stopping his ministrations to Narad Muni, ran to the altar with a shocked face, only to find that it was empty. Except for the vermilion-stained statue of the boy Krishna, whose normally flat, blue, serene face had come to life and was grinning back at him. The priest swooned and fell on to the floor in a dead faint.

The rest of the mortals, upon seeing Krishna, had become frozen in shock and stood with slack jaws, with Mrs Kapoor sputtering and the marriage registrar looking as if his eyes were about to leap out of his head. Zafar stared in wonder and said to Draupadi with wide eyes, 'I guess I don't need to take your word for it now.'

Shashiben laughed and went closer to the statue. 'Trust you to make a grand entrance, Krishna.'

The statue examined the tiny flute in its hand and smiled at her. 'I come when I am needed.' It then turned its gaze on Draupadi, who was standing back with a sheepish expression on her face.

'Come here, child.'

Draupadi walked up to the altar like a truant expecting punishment. She stood before him and hung her head.

'No need to look so sorry, my dear. I fully expected this.'

'You did?'

'Of course.' He grinned. 'You were always the one to stir up the pot. It's one of the things I love about you.'

Draupadi fidgeted. 'Then ... we can stay?'

The statue looked at her and then at Kunti and Amba. 'You must all remember that heavenly re-entry and rebirth have clear rules to which every mortal is subject. Mortal life may end at any time. Your loved ones in this life may or may not be with you in the next. Are you prepared for this?'

All three women nodded.

'In that case, you have my permission to stay.'

Amba resumed crying on to Zafar's shoulder, this time in relief. Zafar, for his part, held her tightly with an awestruck expression on his face.

Kunti let out a long breath and beamed at Karan, who was still staring, mouth open, at the statue. Shashiben grinned at the two of them.

Draupadi smiled a wry smile at Krishna and said, 'Thank you, my god. Although do try not to pop us off too soon, will you?'

The statue laughed and she heard its voice in her ear, unheard by the others, 'I pity poor Yamraj whenever he comes for you.'

Draupadi thought hard towards the statue, 'Will I ever see you again?'

'I hope you will see me in everything every day.'

She bit her lip. 'No, not that. You know what I mean. Will we ever meet again?'

'I hope so.'

She knew that was all the answer she was going to get, so she smiled at him and thought, 'I love you.'

The statue smiled, its eyes twinkling with the same mischief she had always seen in Krishna's. 'I love you too, my dear. Enjoy your second chance. I shall be watching with pleasure.'

And then, the life left them and they became flat, painted on. The statue was once again just a statue.

For a moment, everyone stood where they were, no one really knowing what was to be done next. Then the marriage registrar, who had been pointing his phone at the whole scene, started backing away towards the gate, about to make a run for it.

'Oh, for heaven's sake,' Narad Muni exclaimed irritably and waved a hand, freezing the man in mid-step, along with Zafar, Mrs Kapoor, Sania and Karan.

'What are you doing?' squealed Amba, looking worriedly at Zafar, who stood frozen, with his arms outstretched towards her, seemingly turned to stone.

'Calm down, woman,' Narad Muni dismissed her. 'I've just detained them for a moment while I erase their memories. And delete the videos off this idiot's phone.' He looked at the marriage registrar with disgust.

'Will he remember who I am? That he loves me?' Amba asked, worried.

Narad Muni rolled his eyes. 'Yes, yes. Their memory will be intact up until I appeared.'

He looked at Draupadi, Amba and Kunti and sighed, as if washing his hands of this whole affair. 'I suppose there is no need to tell you that you will, from the moment I leave, lose your lodgings and everything in them. You'd better give me back my phone too.' He held out his hand, into which Draupadi dropped the phone he had given her.

He said to Gandhari, 'I suppose *now* would be a good time for goodbyes.'

Gandhari looked at Draupadi. 'I want to thank you for agreeing to let me come with you. I didn't like what I saw, but at least I saw it. There are no questions left in me.'

Draupadi nodded.

To Amba she said, 'I wish you happiness and I'm sorry for my words. I hope you'll forgive me.'

Amba smiled and replied, 'I do forgive you. And I wish you eternal peace.'

Gandhari smiled a little in return and turned to Kunti, whom she hugged again. 'Goodbye, sister. I will cherish our friendship forever.'

Kunti hugged her back and said, 'As will I. Goodbye, my sister, and may you be happy.'

Gandhari nodded, her face sad, and then turned to Narad Muni, who cast one glance around impatiently and declared, 'May god's grace be with you. You'll need it.'

He put a hand on Gandhari's head, and they disappeared in a dramatic puff of smoke with a loud boom.

The next moment, the frozen mortals burst back into life. The marriage registrar, who had been in mid-step, fell over and Zafar frowned in confusion at his empty, outstretched arms.

Mrs Kapoor wailed, 'Zafar, beta, how could you *do* this to me?'

Sania looked from Zafar to Amba. 'I don't see what the tearing hurry is?'

Zafar clutched his head. 'Please, Sania. You don't know all the details.'

Karan looked at the priest, still lying unconscious on the floor. 'What happened to him?'

Shashiben, thoroughly amused, assessed the priest with a hand on her chin and said, 'You'd better go get some water to throw on him.' Karan eyed her expression with some confusion but did as he was bid.

Draupadi, Amba and Kunti looked at each other for a stunned moment. Then they burst out laughing, much to the chagrin of everybody else except Shashiben.

Mrs Kapoor huffed, 'I don't see what there is to laugh about.'

Amba quickly put on a more serious face and walked up to her, taking one hand in hers. 'I'm sorry you had to find out like this. I truly am. I know you don't like the idea of Zafar marrying me, but I promise you I will love him and keep him happy. I will take care of him and cherish him, and you and Sania, for the rest of my life. If you accept me as your daughter-in-law, you can do any kind of ceremony you wish. We won't even get married today if you don't wish it. Please let us be together.'

Zafar frowned. 'But, Amba, you said you had to go back to the ashram—'

'No, she doesn't.' Kunti stepped forward and spoke to Zafar. 'I will give my blessings to this marriage.' She turned to Mrs Kapoor. 'I hope you will too.'

Mrs Kapoor looked a bit put off. Zafar went up to her and Amba and said softly, 'Ammee, I love her. This is what I want. I'm going to marry her today, and it would mean the world to me if you were happy for us and gave us your blessing.'

Sania put an arm on Mrs Kapoor's shoulder from the back and pleaded, 'Come on, Ammee. Say yes and put these two out of their misery. And since Zafar wants to elope Hindi-movie-style, I say let them do this right now. I actually think it's quite romantic.' She winked at Amba over Mrs Kapoor's head.

Mrs Kapoor looked at the determination in Zafar's eyes and, thankfully, better sense prevailed and she sighed in resignation. She asked a little sulkily, 'Will you do a nikaah also?'

Zafar rolled his eyes but Amba nodded vigorously. 'Yes, yes. Anything you like!' She saw Mrs Kapoor give her a reluctant smile and she laughed, hugging her future mother-in-law impulsively. 'Oh, thank you!'

Sania grinned at the priest who, after having a pot of water splashed over his head by Karan, had regained consciousness and was sitting up and frowning in disorientation. 'So, should we get this show on the road?'

Zafar laughed, gave his mother a quick hug and turned to the priest and the marriage registrar. 'Yes. Panditji, get me married!'

Draupadi watched Amba, who was glowing with happiness, walk towards the sacred fire with her new family as the priest fumbled with his mysteriously mixed-up props and implements for the marriage ceremony. She watched her gaze into Zafar's eyes soulfully and felt reasonably sure that like Arjuna and Subadhra's, theirs was the kind of love that would survive whatever life threw at them. She hoped it was anyway.

She saw Kunti whisper something in Karan's ear and saw him beam back at her as they sat down with Shashiben to watch the ceremony. Kunti seemed distracted and Draupadi knew her mind was already occupied with the mountain of new challenges that awaited her back at the orphanage. Hers would be the most difficult journey of all, but at least she would have her son by her side.

She looked up at the scorching almost-afternoon sky, with its sun blazing ferociously into her eyes. Whatever lay in store for her, she didn't regret her decision. As Krishna said, she belonged in this world. Later today she would call up Angela, take that job and hope for the best. There was so much to be done. In fact ...

She went and sat down next to Shashiben. 'I just had an idea that might help with the funding situation at the orphanage. Have you ever been on TV?'

Acknowledgements

I've got so many people to thank for this book …

My grandfather, H.P. Varma, who told me stories from Indian mythology when I was a kid. My grandfather, B.S. Das, for being the first author in the family. My grandmother, Kamala Varma, in whose house I devoured women's literature while growing up.

Jane Austen, who is my personal god. Every writer that ever wrote anything about the Mahabharata.

Jayapriya Vasudevan, who took me on with three chapters and who tells me it's all good when I most need to hear it.

My editors Ajitha G.S., for totally getting it and for loving female characters who are unapologetic and kick-ass, and Karthika V.K., for being kick-ass.

Mr Rajiv Mehrotra, who makes it look easy.

Mom, Pops, Vir and Shivani, for standing behind me. And pushing.

Deeps, who makes it all happen.

R & J, for whom I'd stay in hell too.